Dear [?],

Rejoice
Christ is born
and Risen

with love
[signature]
21/8/14

Dear Sass

Rejoice

Christ is risen

with love
dede Bruno

21/9/19

# A Kingdom to Buy

BRANKO VINCIC

BALBOA
PRESS
A DIVISION OF HAY HOUSE

Copyright © 2014 Branko Vincic.

All rights reserved. No part of this book may be used or reproduced by any means, graphic, electronic, or mechanical, including photocopying, recording, taping or by any information storage retrieval system without the written permission of the publisher except in the case of brief quotations embodied in critical articles and reviews.

Balboa Press books may be ordered through booksellers or by contacting:

Balboa Press
A Division of Hay House
1663 Liberty Drive
Bloomington, IN 47403
www.balboapress.com
1 (877) 407-4847

Because of the dynamic nature of the Internet, any web addresses or links contained in this book may have changed since publication and may no longer be valid. The views expressed in this work are solely those of the author and do not necessarily reflect the views of the publisher, and the publisher hereby disclaims any responsibility for them.

The author of this book does not dispense medical advice or prescribe the use of any technique as a form of treatment for physical, emotional, or medical problems without the advice of a physician, either directly or indirectly. The intent of the author is only to offer information of a general nature to help you in your quest for emotional and spiritual well-being. In the event you use any of the information in this book for yourself, which is your constitutional right, the author and the publisher assume no responsibility for your actions.

The Orthodox Study Bible New Testament and Psalms, New King James Version, Thomas Nelson Publishers, Nashville, Tennessee.

Any people depicted in stock imagery provided by Thinkstock are models, and such images are being used for illustrative purposes only. Certain stock imagery © Thinkstock.

ISBN: 978-1-4525-1822-0 (sc)
ISBN: 978-1-4525-1824-4 (hc)
ISBN: 978-1-4525-1823-7 (e)

Library of Congress Control Number: 2014912096

Printed in the United States of America.
Balboa Press rev. date: 07/03/14

# Contents

Acknowledgment ..................................................................... vii
Foreward ...................................................................................ix
Preface ....................................................................................xi

1. A Surprise Visit ............................................................... 1
2. Negligent Protector ......................................................... 7
3. Dangers of Schooling .................................................... 15
4. First Love ...................................................................... 20
5. Going Into the World .................................................... 25
6. Teenager ........................................................................ 33
7. Romantic Adriatic ......................................................... 43
8. Exciting Train Ride ....................................................... 49
9. Betrayal ......................................................................... 57
10. The Real Big City ......................................................... 63
11. Things are hard to Grasp .............................................. 72
12. High Learning ............................................................... 84
13. Trouble with Nuts and Bolts ........................................ 97
14. Getting Up .................................................................. 118
15. America, the Blessed ................................................... 127
16. Tying the Knot ............................................................ 145
17. The Enemy`s Plotting ................................................. 154
18. The Family .................................................................. 159
19. Visiting "The old country" ......................................... 170
20. The American Dream Hobbling .................................. 181
21. A busy, Busy Life ........................................................ 189
22. Word Sowing Business ................................................ 201
23. The Frustrations ......................................................... 211
24. The Future Has Arrived ............................................. 220

25. The Golden Years ................................................................ 238
26. Buying Time........................................................................ 241
27. The Undressing .................................................................. 248
28. The Second Wind ............................................................... 252
29. More Word Sowing ............................................................ 256
30. The Word Sowing Finale.................................................... 260
31. Closing the Curtain ............................................................ 264

# *Acknowledgment*

It would be very hard for me to complete this book without help from my family and friends. I am expressing my gratitude for their help, advice, and support:

My daughter Sava Vincic, who read my manuscript, gave me valuable comments, edited and corrected the manuscript and helped me to put the book together.

My son Milan Vincic, my sister Mirjana Katic and her friend Ms. Julia Frankel, who read the manuscript and gave me excellent ideas to improve the content of the book and gave me helpful comments and encouragement.

My friend George Budimir, who read the manuscript, gave me wise, valuable comments and advice and wrote wonderful foreword.

My daughter Djurdja Prostran and her husband Igor Prostran, my daughter Sava`s fiancée Nikola Pijanovic, my daughter in law Dawn Vincic, who all helped and encouraged me to write this book.

My grandsons: Milan and Luka Vincic, Pavle and Vukasin Prostran for being my inspiration to write this book.

My wife Bosiljka Vincic for tolerating me during my long hours spent at the computer writing, erasing and rewriting.

# *Foreward*

This thought provoking book is deeply moving and spiritual. It is a tremendous story in two quite separate dimensions: moral integrity and extraordinary courage of imagination. Above all it stands the figure of a little boy, growing up in uncertain times in communist Yugoslavia.

'A Kingdom to Buy' is such an interesting creation by Branko Vincic, a brilliantly crafted story of 'Boro' and 'Stefan', an earthling and his guardian angel, whose words were a divine source of motivational instructions. That theme threads throughout the book, by turns joyful and sad but always haunting. It tells of Boro, little Serbian boy born and raised by his loving parents and his beloved baba (grandma) in a place called Pridraga, Dalmatia.

Boro's journey takes him from the warmth of his home to boarding school where he faces new challenges of a "morally complex world." He had cut loose from the past, he was eager for the future. Normal bonds of society gave way to mindless pursuit of the 'dolce vita', often crossing into irresponsible behaviour. All of these events, the author points out, have shaped the fellow named Boro. Yet, the possibility of redemption is the authors message, cleverly brought home in the wordplay of Boro and Stefan. Boro was often refreshingly honest and quick to confess his failures. "What would my parents think?" And "I wonder what my guardian angel would tell me?" he would ask. "Best way to honor your parents is by making lives they would be proud of," Stefan would tell him.

Boro's life trail stretched ahead like an invitation to the future. That future led him to America and a new life. And new hardships. And, unfortunately, to new transgressions. But, this was something he must conquer if he was to have any peace within himself. For it all happened before, and now he had fallen from grace again. What followed was an extraordinary tale of stratagems and reversal and sudden twists of fortune as Boro tried to come to grips with his life. But, soon Boro discovers that he possesses a rare talent, a gift for preaching, which leads to his 'word sowing mission.'

'A Kingdom to Buy' is a fictionalized story by Branko Vincic and much of it draws from his experience. Here, he lists numerous cases of events that cannot be understood or explained scientifically, but they do bring the esoteric contents closer to our comprehension and belief.

'A Kingdom to Buy' is a riveting religious story of considerable importance, well thought out and well written. It deserves a large and appreciative readership.

Written by: George Djuro Budimir, author and long-time editor of newspaper 'Serbia.'

# *Preface*

As a young man I had dreams of a good life with success and achievements. When I reached my mature years, I looked back at my life, and said to myself: "Look man, you are getting towards the end of your life journey. You had a lot of big, exciting dreams when you were younger: none of them have been achieved. You are a failure buddy!"

Since I did not like to look like a failure, I had to find a good excuse for losing my dreams. I became an expert in "excusitis." My favourite excuse was simple, but powerful. The reason for my lost dreams and failures was God; for allowing three demons to stick to me from my younger days: Mr. Coward, Mrs. Lazy and their child, the eternally young demon, Manana boy.

This unholy trio, had me in their grip. My "favourite" was Manana boy. Going along with him seemed to solve everything. His advice was: "Don`t do it today, leave it for tomorrow." When I was able to slip from the grip of this demon, his mom, Mrs. Lazy, would hug and embrace me saying: "Rush, work….what for; it is much nicer to relax, do nothing. Try it, you are going to love it."

When I was able to escape from the grip of son and mother, father of the family, the head demon, Mr. Coward, was waiting for me. He was determined to defend his family`s honour. "My wife and son allowed you to slip from their grip, but I am very strong, beaten only when Mary`s Son helps humans."

This unholy family stuck to me like scales on a fish. I got used to them. Sometimes, when they were bit late to do their job on me, I wondered: "Where the heck were they? Hello Manana, Mrs. Lazy, Mr. Coward, show up, where are you hiding?"

And they obliged, responding to my call, and doing their job with an additional zeal. Mr. Coward would convincingly assure me: "You are nobody, non-achiever, stay in your hole boy, don`t try to get out; you might get hurt." Madame Lazy would show me some beautiful images of relaxation in enchanting places, doing nothing and just goofing around; "See how beautiful it is to relax, enjoy, do nothing." As last, the demon kid would shout with a victorious laugh: "Don`t do it today, leave it for tomorrow: manana, manana, mananaaa!"

What helped me to begin to shake off this unholy trio, was getting older, and wiser. The real eye opener was reading the Gospel Parable of the Talents. I saw myself as that lazy, ungrateful servant that took his masters talent and instead of investing it and earning the profit for his master, he buried it in the ground, and returned to his master without any earned interest. It took me a while to understand the message of the Parable. I got scared and panicky.

What kind of 'interest' am I going to return to my "Master," my Creator when He calls me to "settle the account?"

My humble attempt, to earn at least "a talent of the interest," is this book. "The interest" will be realized if this book helps at least one person, to invest his or her talent, to return it with "an earned interest," to our "Master" and Creator.

This is the life story of Boro, "My best good friend" as the famous American Forrest Gump said.

Enjoy reading!

## Chapter 1

## *A Surprise Visit*

Assuredly, I say to you, unless you are converted and become as little children, you will by no means enter the kingdom of heaven *(Matt. 18-3.)*

That year spring came early in its extravagant colours and beauty to the hamlet of Pridraga. The hill above the house was covered with a brand new green coat. The acacia trees beside the house were full of white, succulent, sweet smelling flowers. The meadows in the river valley were buzzing with bees alternating between the trees and a rainbow of meadow flowers.

Little Boro lived with his family in a small stone house that was built at the foot of a big, steep hill, just above the source of the Pridraga creek. The house had no electricity, or indoor plumbing. A wood fired stove was used for cooking and heating the house.

This was Boro's favourite time of year. He loved to listen to the birds singing and chirping in the bush and in the meadows. He knew they were busy building their nests, and laying colorful little eggs. His favourite birds were swallows. He was told by grownups never to harm them, or destroy their nests. Swallows were the first messengers of spring. Fed up with cold and snow; everybody eagerly awaited their return from the south, announcing, "Rejoice, spring is here." They got busy repairing their nests and raising more families of little swallows. He was sad seeing them flying south in the fall to the mysterious lands of eternal summer-- Egypt and India.

Boro was an unusual child, a day dreamer. In the warm summer nights, he used to lie on the soft meadow grass beside his sister. Lying on their backs, they would look straight up at the immense, heavenly canopy above them, decorated by twinkling stars and a silvery moon. They would gaze at this majestic cover, enchanted by its beauty, dreaming and imagining. "Wouldn't it be wonderful to have the wings like birds or angels and fly to heaven, the moon, and maybe even farther among the stars and the Milky Way?"

Tired from their adventure, they would land again on their meadow, and an unpleasant thought would strike them. "Adults say that we are all going to die and that we will never, ever again see the sky, moon and stars nor our valley, the river, our house, or anybody else. Why is that? That is not fair!" There was no answer to this mystery.

Luckily, their attention would turn quickly to the simpler, more pleasant things in life. That was the blessing of childhood; forgetting, unpleasant and complicated things, and a resurrected feeling that there would be no end to this wonderful life under the blue canopy of heaven, a silvery moon and twinkling stars.

Boro's biggest pleasure was to run barefoot through the meadows, as he enjoyed the grass and flowers kissing his legs. One day, he ran and ran and ran through the meadows until he was almost out of breath. To cool off, he stepped into the icy cold water of Pridraga creek. Afterwards he was very tired and barely able to stay awake during dinner with his family. After dinner, a small petroleum lamp was extinguished and the whole family went to bed.

Their small house had just three rooms. Boro and his older sister, Dana, had to sleep in the same bed. They both hated this arrangement, often quarrelling, fighting, and pinching each other, and hoarding heavy wool blankets in the icy cold room in the dead of winter. That night, his sister was surprised that Boro did not fight her at all. He was just too tired. Soon after his head touched the pillow, he sunk quickly into a deep sleep.

Shortly after falling asleep, Boro felt somebody standing beside his bed. Terrified, he pulled the covers over his head, expecting the apparition to go away. To his surprise, he felt his fear melt away, as if the mysterious visitor was giving him the message: "Don't be afraid. I am your friend. Uncover yourself. Look at me."

Still a bit scared, Boro slowly pulled the cover off his head. His sister was sound asleep and turned away from him.

Looking at his side of the bed, Boro saw a tall, beautiful young man bathed in golden light standing beside his bed. He was no longer afraid of the stranger. Rather the opposite; he felt as if he knew him all his young life. He was sure, without any doubt, this was a friend.

Boro felt his visitor's warm, soft hand on his cheek. He started to talk to Boro. His voice gently entered Boro's head even deeper, right into the center of his being, echoing in his heart: "Hello Boro, my friend, how are you?" greeted the visitor while caressing his cheek and giving him a warm, gentle smile.

Excited and still shy, Boro replied, "Good, and how are you?"

The visitor instantly replied, almost as if he knew what Boro's answer would be, "I am glad you are well, my friend. You are probably wondering who am I, and why am I visiting you tonight?"

"Oh yes, I am wondering," said Boro shyly.

The stranger stopped caressing Boro's cheek. He sat on Boro's bed. Now, Boro felt his presence even stronger. He felt a strange power flowing from his visitor right into the depth of his being, making him feel happy, relaxed, and light as air.

The visitor continued: "Boro, I am an angel, sent by God. I am your guardian angel."

Boro's mouth opened wide in amazement. "Wow! An angel! But where are your wings?"

The visitor smiled. "Wings, why do you think I have wings?"

"Because my mom and grandma (baba) told me angels have wings. I have seen angels on the icons and in our monastery on the walls inside the church. They all had wings. If you are really an angel, you must have wings. How else could you fly from heaven to my house?"

The angel said smiling, "Boro, you are a very special, very sharp boy. I think we are going to have fun with each other. I have wings, just as those angels on the monastery walls, and on the icons, as your mom and baba told you. You did not notice my wings right away because they were folded. Would you like to see my wings?

"Oh, yes, yes," the little boy shouted with excitement. The visitor immediately spread his huge wings, which reached to the walls and ceiling of Boro`s bedroom.

Boro was absolutely thrilled. "Wow, how big and beautiful your wings are. Can I touch them?"

"Sure, go ahead," said the angel.

Boro stretched his hand to touch angel's wing. He felt strange warmth as he touched the beautiful, white, angelic wings. They seemed as if they were made out of the finest, softest silk, sprinkled by golden dust.

"Happy? Convinced?" the angel asked, smiling.

"Yes, yes, I am happy. I am convinced," said Boro. "Could I get wings like yours?"

"Wings like mine? Why do you want that?"

"It was always my dream to fly, to get off the ground and soar with the birds. That would be wonderful. I dreamt many, many times that I had wings and was flying above my house, the meadows, river, even above mountains and clouds."

"Were you scared of falling and hurting yourself while flying in your dreams?"

"No never. Because I knew that I was given a special gift, like no other boy; to fly."

"And then you woke up, with no wings."

"Yes, waking up from my dream was the worst thing that happened to me. I begged God; 'Oh please, God let this be for real. Let me be free like a bird. Don`t break my dream. Let me fly."

"You woke up every time without the wings?"

"I did. Could you arrange for me to get the wings?"

"Sorry Boro, I have to disappoint you. You are seven years old. You won't get wings for a long, long time."

"So, I will get some wings someday. When is that going to be? Could you please shorten that time, so I could get my wings sooner?"

"Sorry Boro," replied the angel with a hint of sadness. "You must wait for the right time."

"I will wait, but I am very disappointed," complained Boro.

"I understand that," said the visitor retracting his wings, making them again invisible to Boro. "I will leave soon, but before I leave, I am going to explain a few things. These meetings between us will be our secret. Tomorrow, when you wake up, you are going to have just a vague memory, as if you dreamt. You will not be able to tell anybody about our meetings. If you need my help, just think about me, or say what you want. I will watch over you and protect you, though you won't see me, hear me, or touch me. Do you understand what I am saying?"

"Yes, I think I understand," said Boro. "You will protect me against my teacher if she tries to slap me for not doing my homework. You will protect me from my older brother or mother if they want to beat me up for being bad. You will protect me against my sister if she pinches me and tries to push me out of bed. You will protect me from bigger boys."

Angel smiled, amused. "That was quite a list Boro. It won't be exactly that way, because guardian angels have rules when and how we are allowed to help people we guard."

"Rules?" exclaimed Boro, "Don`t you set your own rules?"

"No, our Lord sets the rules," said the angel reverently.

"Who is that?"

"God," said the angel with awe. "I must go now. We will continue our talk soon and then I will explain about the rules I must obey."

"You are leaving, but you did not tell me your name?"

Angel smiled: "How would you like to call me?"

Boro thought for a few seconds. Proudly, he said to his visitor: "I will call you Stefan."

"Stefan," repeated the angel. "What a beautiful name. I am your protector and guardian angel Stefan. Bye for now my friend."

Stefan gently kissed Boro on the forehead, and disappeared through the roof of Boro's house.

A new day was being announced by a pink dawn behind the mountains on the East. Boro's mom came to wake up his sister to take the sheep to the pasture. Little boy was left to sleep bit longer. He had a happy smile on his face, as if remembering some pleasant dream.

Boro had a very vague recollection of his encounter with Stefan. Sometimes, it seemed that it was more than a dream, as if he stepped into a strange world, very much different from the world he lived in.

One thing surely happened; Boro changed after meeting his guardian angel. The boy became a wide eyed dreamer, almost living in the imagination world of his own creation.

## Chapter 2

## *Negligent Protector*

Since Boro was to go to school that year his father bought him new rubber shoes. These were his first shoes. He was excited and proud that he probably would be the only kid in school with new rubber shoes.

He could do wonderful things in his new rubber shoes. He ran over thorns and rocks without getting hurt. He could kick any piece of wood, or rock on the road. It didn`t hurt him. Boro thought that he could even fly in his new rubber shoes. He tried few leaps from rock to rock. It seemed that he almost fooled gravity.

In all this excitement Boro got a bit careless. He tried a big flying leap at the edge of the road. He misjudged and landed flat on his stomach two meters lower in their garden. He was dazed and remained lying on his stomach, crying and sobbing. His mom ran to help. She lifted him, cleaned off the dirt, and worriedly asked him if he was hurt. Clinging to his mom and still sobbing Boro showed her his stomach. Mother took him inside the house and placed him on his bed. She gave him a big slice of her home baked bread with butter and honey. Judging how eagerly he ate it, she figured out that her little boy was bit shaken and dirtied, but luckily unhurt.

While enjoying his treat, a thought flashed in Boro`s mind: "What about my guardian angel Stefan? Didn`t he promise to always protect me? Why didn`t Stefan catch me when I was falling down from the road into the garden? He had those huge wings, he could have easily caught me in the air. True, when I was falling down, I didn`t call him, nor thought of him. No time, I was scared stiff. Maybe, Stefan shows up tonight. Boy, oh boy, am I ever going to scold him for being a negligent guardian angel. If I knew how, I would complain to his boss, God, about this."

Thinking these heavy thoughts, little boy fell asleep, not finishing his snack. Mom took off his new rubber shoes, covered him with a blanket, kissed him on the forehead and left.

That night, Stefan appeared early. Boro sensed his presence. This time, he saw him more clearly, but he looked somehow different. He was not as brilliant as the first time he appeared.

Stefan broke the uncomfortable silence first: "Hi, how are you Boro?"

"I fell down from the road into our garden. It was very, very high. I fell on my stomach. I got hurt. My tummy still hurts," saying this, little boy was crying.

Stefan touched his cheeks and wiped off his tears, kissing him on the eyes. His hands were softer, than Boro`s mom`s hands when she caressed him.

Boro felt better instantly. Joy and peace returned to his heart. Nothing hurt him anymore. He was no longer mad at Stefan, but still wanted to find out why Stefan didn`t help him.

All of a sudden, Stefan was again looking like a bright, beautiful angel.

"I knew that you fell down today, and got hurt a little bit," said Stefan.

"How did you know that? Who told you?"

Stefan smiled: "Nobody told me. I know everything about you, every moment, because, I am your guardian angel."

"Did you see me falling down?"

"Yes, of course. I am on guard all the time. I see whatever happens to you."

"Well, if you saw me falling, why didn`t you catch me in the air, so that I don't get hurt. Isn`t that what guardian angels suppose to do?"

Stefan smiled with the expression of a patient teacher: "Boro I have instructions as to how to do my job. I must always follow these instructions."

"Could you explain these instructions? I need to know."

"Remember Boro what I told you the first time I appeared to you?"

"You said lots of things, I don't remember everything. Please tell me again."

"I told you when I help you, you won't see me, nor hear me. I may be helping you without you knowing it. I told you I must always follow my instructions of when and how to help you. The most important is that Our Lord sets those instructions."

"What are the instructions?"

"Instructions are God`s rules of what I do as your guardian angel."

"God`s rules, eh? Must you always obey these rules?"

"I must obey them always."

"If I get into a problem, how do I know if you are going to help me? I am not sure if I can count on you?"

Stefan shook his head, almost in frustration. "Boro, it is hard for me to explain how us guardian angels work, so that you, a seven year old boy, would understand it. Since Lord God kicked man out of the Garden of Eden, the communication between angels and man has been obscure."

Boro was listening with his mouth open: "I didn`t understand a word you said. You used some big words I never heard before. I am just seven years old, first grade in Public school. My mom and baba are very good at explaining things to me in simple words. I believe them because they are adults and they know everything, especially my mom."

"Boro, this is wonderful that your mom and baba are so good at explaining things to you, especially your mom. Is your father as good in explaining things to you?"

"Oh yes, he is very good, but he does it different than my mom and baba."

"How is his way different?"

"He has a way of convincing me to obey him, and I do."

"That's very nice of you," complimented Stefan.

"Yeah, I have to obey, or else. My father told me, not to pull our cat Mica's tail. It was fun for me pull her tail, to hear her noisy 'meow', and watch her jump like crazy and run away. Once, I pulled her tail real hard. Mica turned around and scratched me on the hand. It hurt a lot. I was bleeding. My father saw me doing it. He grabbed my left ear, pulled it up and twisted real hard. It hurt badly. Tears came to my eyes. 'Now,' said my father, 'Why did I tell you not to pull Mica's tail'? Through tears, I murmured angrily; 'I don't know.' 'Well,' said my father 'I told you several times: Mica is our cat. We need her to catch the mice. She does not like her tail to be pulled, because it hurts her, just as it hurts you when I pull your ear. I told you also, that both me, and Mica would punish you one of these days, when you pull her tail. Mica scratched you and I pulled your ear. Tell me, what you learnt today?' asked my dad looking me straight in the eyes.

"Nothing," I said angrily.

"Well, looks like I have to pull your other ear, so that you hear, what you are supposed to learn today."

My left ear still hurt. I sure didn't want more pain, so I swallowed my anger and pride, and asked my dad: "What was I supposed to learn today?"

"When your parents tell you something, you must believe them, because they know what is good for you. See what happens if you disobey your parents. Mica scratched you, I pulled you ear. When you disobey, you will be punished, but that is for your good, to protect you and others. Do you understand this?"

I didn't understand, but I didn't want my ears to be pulled again. No sir, I was not that stupid. I said; 'Yes, I understand."

That 'explanation', stuck in my mind. I never pulled Mica's tail, at least not when anybody was around. But even then, it wasn't very hard, just to get a bit of a revenge on her for scratching me and for my left ear."

Stefan was listening very carefully with approving smile. "Boro, that was a nice explanation. Lord has big a job for you."

"What Lord? What job? What are you talking about?"

"Nothing, nothing, I was just speaking with myself. Forget it," said Stefan as if caught doing something improper. Listen Boro, I will give you explanation now, keeping in mind that you are a seven years old boy."

"I forgot, what you suppose to explain?"

"Our relationship."

"Relationship? What's that?"

"It's how we behave with each other."

"That's easy, you just do what I ask you. I want that kind of relationship."

"Adam's child," whispered Stefan.

"My dad's name is not Adam. His name is Jovan."

"I know that," said Stefan a bit frustrated. "We will talk about Adam when you get older."

"No problem," agreed Boro.

"I think your dad, mom and baba did well explaining how you should behave. You believe them, because you know they love you. They are responsible for you. They provide your food, clothing, place to sleep, toys."

Boro interrupted him: "Toys? What toys? I never had any toys."

"I will see if I could arrange, for you to get you some toys."

"Wow, toys! What kind of toys are you going to get me, gun, ball, truck? Could you get them all? Please, please, please."

Stefan smiled at such sincere enthusiasm of the boy. "I will not give you toys personally, but I will make sure that somebody sends you these toys. It is important for you, to get the toys. How I arrange it, should not concern you."

"It is important I get the toys. When my baba was telling me that God made everything, including people, she didn't explain how she knew that. She just told me that a monk in our monastery told her that. My baba believed because this monk was close to God, and also because her baba told her the same thing. I believed my baba, because she really believed in God."

"Boro, you amaze me," exclaimed Stefan.

"Whatever, Just get me the toys!"

"I won't bother you any more with the explanation of our relationship. As you grow, we are going to discuss more details. Your baba told you that God created everything; the earth, moon, stars, animals, plants, men, sky, angels."

"That is big, adult stuff. But, even if I believed it, I have no idea how God could do that. It is such a big, real big job," said Boro.

"Don't worry because you don't understand. God knows how He did it. Not even us, angels, know."

"I thought you angels knew everything as God?"

"No, Boro. Angels were created by God like everything else. We are just God's helpers. We do what God instructs us to."

"Really?" exclaimed Boro.

"Yes. You told me that you had to obey your parents because they are responsible for you and they love you."

"I don't see how pulling my ear was for my own good, but I believe that my mom and dad do things for my good."

"Do you believe that God created everything, including you?"

"I was told that by my mom and baba. I am confused about that stuff."

"What are you confused about?"

"How could I have two creators; my parents and God?"

"You said you never had any toys. Did you make your own toys?"

"Yes, I did."

"Please tell me, how you made that toy?"

"I found a piece of wood, got a small knife and I carved out my buddy Mico."

"You made a little wooden boy?"

"Yes."

"Since you made Mico, aren't you his creator, his maker?"

"I am," said Boro proudly.

"You made Mico, but who created you?"

"What do you mean who created me? I don't know what are you talking about Stefan. I am not a wooden doll. I was born like other kids."

"Sorry Boro. I did not ask the question clearly. What I meant was: how were you born?"

"My mom told me that she found me in the cabbage patch, while our teacher told us the story how the storks carry babies on their beaks and drop them to the parents through the chimney."

"What do you think? Were you found in the cabbage patch, or dropped through the chimney by the stork?"

"Adults know these things. Ask me when I grow up."

Stefan laughed heartily. "You are truly a special kid Boro. We will have lots of fun in the future."

"Fun? What kind of fun are we going to have? Are we going to play 'hide and seek,' soccer, games?"

"I meant our meetings would be enjoyable to both of us."

"Oh, that`s what you call fun. I like that."

"Who took care of you? Fed you, washed you, tucked you in bed, clothed you?"

"My mom and baba?"

"Your parents did not 'create' you, like you carved Mico out of a piece of wood?"

"Well, how did they create me?"

"We won't go into details of that right now. You are going to learn about that when you are lot older."

"Are you saying that my mom did not find me in the cabbage patch, nor did some stork drop me down the chimney of our house?"

"You did not come from the cabbage patch, nor were you dropped by a stork down the chimney."

"But, where did my parents find me?"

"Let`s say Boro that God gave you as a gift to your mom and dad. And please do not ask me to explain how God did it. Let this be a secret for a while. For now, we will say that your parents created you in partnership with God."

"That is even harder to understand. Partnership, what`s that?"

"All I am saying, Boro, is that without your parents and God, you would not be a seven year old boy now."

"Aaaaah, I see what you mean."

"Wouldn`t you agree that you have 'two creators,' your parents and God?"

Boro's mouth opened in amazement: "Well, it is kind of confusing, but if you say so Stefan, I will agree that I had two creators; God, and my parents. I don't understand how can that be, but I trust you, because you are my guardian angel. I believe you would not lie to me."

"I cannot lie. I can speak only the truth, nothing but the truth. Lying is used by fallen angels, Lucifer and his crew. You know that your parents and God want the best for you?"

"Yes, but it hurts sometimes. I don't understand how letting me fall from the road was good for me. I just don't get it."

"For now, it is important that you realize that your parents and God care for you. Do you realize that?"

"I do, but sometimes that caring hurts."

"I am God's helper. I work for your good. Sometimes, it might look like I neglected you, that I am a bad guardian angel. Never believe that. I cushioned your fall from the road, thus preventing bad injury? With time, you will understand why I did not prevent you from falling. I did as instructed by God."

Boro was scratching his head in dilemma. "I am confused. How do I know if you are going to help me?"

Calmly, with gentle love in his beautiful angelic voice, Stefan said: "Since I have no visible body, you cannot see me, nor hear me. You need to trust me, just like you trust your parents."

All of a sudden, Boro changed the tune: "Stefan, my head is full. Please, don't forget, you promised to arrange to get me some toys. I want a red fire truck, black gun and a big pink ball. Soon please!"

Stefan laughed heartily: "Okay Boro, we will see about that. Remember what we talked about: trust and believe."

"Truuuust," murmured little boy.

Stefan kissed him on the forehead, and in a second was gone.

# Chapter 3

## *Dangers of Schooling*

At age seven, Boro started attending first grade of public school in his village. He had to walk alone three kilometres from his house to the school. The road led through a dense bush. Boro feared that any time a huge, blood thirsty wolf would jump out and attack him. He had nothing to defend himself. No gun, no knife, no guard dog. He never saw any wolves while going to school. Few times, something rattled in the bush, causing some stones to roll down the hill. That was all, but his fear persisted.

After school, Boro had to watch his family's sheep. It was December, a bitter cold day. Light snow covered the ground. Boro took his flock up on the plateau. While sheep scattered amongst bushes, searching for grass, he sat on a big stone, enveloping himself within a heavy woolen coat.

All of a sudden, he saw his sheep bunched together. He was told sheep do that when attacked by wolves. His parents told him: "If wolves attack, shout as loud as you can to scare them off." Boro thought that he saw a wolf It looked huge. He tried to shout, his mouth was wide open, but no sound came from his throat. Fear had him paralyzed.

It all lasted just few minutes, then sheep continued grazing. Boro was pretty sure that the wolves attacked the flock. Scared and shivering from cold and fear, he just wanted to go home. He collected his scattered sheep and rushed down the hill, terrified that at any moment a blood thirsty beast would jump on him and slaughter him.

Crying, and sobbing all the way home, he brought sheep to the barn and went into the house.

His mom sensed something bad happened. While wiping off his tears with her apron, she asked, "What happened honey?"

Still shocked, Boro replied barely audibly: "wolves."

"Did they kill any sheep?" asked mom.

"I don`t know," replied Boro crying.

Mom went with Boro`s brother in the barn to count the sheep. Two sheep were missing. Since it was already dark, they decided to search for the missing sheep the next morning.

Early the next morning, Boro, his mom and brother went up the hill to search for the missing sheep. Boro was supposed to show them where the attack took place. The ground was slippery, covered by light snow. Going slowly up, Boro saw on the ground droppings different than sheep`s.

Immediately, a terrifying thought, flashed in his mind: "The wolves are here, watching us. They might attack and kill us any moment." Boro slipped on a snow covered stone and fell hitting his forehead on a sharp stone. It made a deep bleeding wound above his right eye. He panicked, crying in pain. His mom was ahead about twenty paces. She came back, cleaned his wound and tied her kerchief around his head to stop the bleeding.

She told Boro to go back home. Her and Rade would continue the search for the missing sheep. He walked very slowly and carefully down the hill. In an hour his mom and brother came back. They found only the remnants of two sheep scattered close to where the wolves attacked.

That night Boro slept tight, recovering from the stress, fright and pain of the last two days. Some time passed and he sensed a visitor beside his bed. It was Stefan. This time Boro was angrier at Stefan, than when he fell from the road. He was upset, mad, and disappointed.

Stefan broke the silence smiling: "Boro, you had a few tough days. How do you feel?"

"What do you think how I feel? I was attacked by wolves. I was scared to death and lost my favourite sheep, Mrka and Gala. My head is broken but otherwise, I am 'great.' Where were you when I needed you?" said Boro sarcastically through tears.

Without a word, Stefan wiped off Boro's tears, and gently, just like his mom, kissed him on the forehead. The angelic 'magic' worked. Boro felt immediately better, his anger and disappointment waning, but not disappearing entirely.

"I bet you are upset with me and have few questions, and complaints" said Stefan.

"Wouldn't you be upset if something like that happened to you?"

"I sympathize with you Boro, but why don't we find out exactly what happened last few days,"

"I just don't know where to start," replied Boro, still with the trace of anger in his voice.

"Why don't you tell me what happened after you took your sheep to pasture yesterday?"

"You told me last time when I fell from the road that you work under strict instructions of God. These rules tell you what to do."

"You said it perfectly," agreed Stefan.

"What bugs me is; why were wolves allowed to slaughter my two innocent sheep; Mrka and Gala. They just grazed the grass. Never harmed anybody?"

"You really liked these two sheep?"

"I liked them like my brother and sister. I liked them since they were born. We played together on the meadows and on the plateau. I often shared my bread with them. They even licked my hands."

"Hmmmm, Interesting" mused Stefan, continuing. "What other animals your family keeps?"

"Stefan, you know that. You said you know everything about me."

"Yes, I do Boro, but I like you to tell me. You do it so nicely."

"Oh, no problem" said Boro. "We keep: sheep, cows, pigs, chicken and a cat."

"No donkeys or horses?"

"No, we never had horses. We had a donkey, Revan. Last year wolves ate him."

"Why did your family keep all these animals?"

"We kept them for meat, wool, eggs, feathers, and to catch mice."

"Did you have any other use of the animals?"

"What do you mean 'any other use?'"

"Did your father ever sell any of your animals?"

"Yes, he sold them on the market, when we needed the money."

"Did your father ever slaughter lambs or pigs?"

"He did, I helped him," declared Boro proudly.

"Your family owned all these animals and used them for whatever was necessary. Right?"

"Yes, we used them for whatever we wanted."

"You said that your baba told you that God created everything; earth, moon, stars, heaven, men, plants, animals."

"Yes, that`s right, so what?"

"I am coming to that. Would you agree with me that God created wolf?"

"He didn`t really need to. I don`t see what is wolf good for?"

"You don`t know why God created wolf, but God does. If wolves knew how to talk they might ask: 'Why God created such a bad, cruel, useless being as man?'"

"Are you joking Stefan? I don`t understand what are you trying to tell me. I am seven years old."

"I know how old you are. When God created wolf, He created food necessary for his survival."

"What do you mean created food?"

"Wolf eats meat. He hunts any animal he is able to overpower and kill. That animal becomes his food. Your favourite sheep became wolf's meal."

Boro shook his head: "I just don't see why God had to create some animals like wolf, mouse, or snake. What good are they for? They are useless, just give us problems, it isn`t fair. I think God made a few mistakes."

"God created every animal, with a purpose and a role in the creation. Not even angels know why and how God does things," replied Stefan reverently.

"But, Stefan why didn't God provide for those wolves some rabbits, or somebody else's sheep. Why my favourite sheep? What did I do to God to sentence my best friends Mrka and Gala to become wolves' meal?" complained Boro.

"But if wolves killed sheep of your neighbour, wouldn't he complain to God; 'Why me? Why my sheep? If wolves killed some rabbits, somebody might complain: 'How could God allow poor little, innocent rabbits to be eaten by wolves."

Boro's head was getting full. "I still don't like why God allows things, that are not fair. But you said that He is the Master. He can do whatever He likes."

Stefan was pleased with Boro's comment: "Thank you Boro. You already understand more than some adults."

"Stefan, I want to know; did you protect me when wolves attacked my sheep?"

"Well, wolves did you no harm, did they?"

"You protected me?"

Stefan smiled secretively: "I was there when wolves attacked your sheep. No harm was done to you."

"But, why did you not prevent me from falling down and hurting my head real bad?"

Stefan shook his head with slight teasing smile: "As I told you Boro, I strictly follow God's instructions. God allows some bad and painful things to happen. Eventually, Lord may reveal to you why He allowed this to happen."

"I am confused. This is all so complicated," sighed Boro.

"I think we discussed a lot today," said Stefan, kissed Boro's cheek, and in a second was gone.

Boro and his sister continued sleeping in the cold room, with frost on the windows.

## Chapter 4

## *First Love*

Boro loved to go to school. He was friendly with all kids, but his special friend was Vesna, a girl who wore beautiful flowery dress, real shoes and a red silk tie in her golden hair. Vesna was born in the city. When Boro saw her for the first time, he fell crazily in love with that golden hair and red silk tie. He would blush profusely every time their eyes met.

He remembered that 'fatal' day in the early spring. When he came to school, to his horror, Vesna was not in her usual seat. Crazy thoughts rushed through Boro`s mind: "Why isn`t she in the school? Did she get sick? Did wolf attack her? Did …?" Poor Boro was frantically running through various scenarios to explain Vesna`s absenteeism. His guessing was cut short by the teacher:

"Children, Vesna will not be in our class anymore. Her father got a job in the city. They left the village yesterday."

Boro felt dizzy. He fought, to hide his feelings from the classmates to avoid merciless teasing, if they noticed how much he was saddened by Vesna`s departure. Boro was impatient for the class to end, so that he could go home and cry his heart out.

He was mad at Vesna`s parents for taking her from him. A terrifying thought struck him. "Maybe, I will never, ever see my love again. Oh God how unfair you are?" This huge emotional shock tired him. Right after supper, he went to bed and fell asleep quickly. His sister was still doing her homework at the light of a small lantern.

*A Kingdom to Buy*

And there came Stefan in his angelic majesty. Seeing him, Boro started to cry: "Why do all these bad things happen to me Stefan? It is not fair."

Stefan kissed his young protégé on the forehead and caressed him with his angelic hands. "You really loved that girl Boro?"

"I did. Why God allows such things that hurt people very much?" sobbed Boro.

"Did you ever talk to Vesna?"

"No."

"Why not?"

"Because if boys saw me talking to her, they would tease me. I would look a sissy."

"You didn't know if Vesna liked to live in the village?"

"I never thought about it. I thought they would stay in the village forever."

"Was Vesna born in the city?"

"Yes, she spent only a short time in the village."

"Did she seem happy? Did she play with other kids?"

"She spent most of time with her cousin Masa, talking about life in the city and swimming in the sea."

"Your heard them talking?"

"Yes, I did. She seemed excited when she spoke about the city, her friends, and the good times they had swimming in the Adriatic."

"Hmmmm, It seems to me that Vesna was eager to go back to the city."

Sadly, Boro admitted; "I think you are right. Maybe, she even didn't like me. She probably liked city boys who had real shoes and nice pants and shirts, not like us poor villagers."

"She liked you, because you are such a nice boy and the best student in your class."

Boro was very pleased with Stefan's compliment. "You really think she liked me?"

"Absolutely, she just was not used to life in the village. She liked city living. I am sure if you were in her school in the city, you would be her favourite boy."

Boro was beaming. "Really Stefan, you believe she would like me better than city boys?"

"Sure she would. So don't be disappointed Boro. God's plan was for you and Vesna to be in contact only a short time. It does not seem that your path and Vesna's will be crossing again."

"Thank you Stefan. I don't understand God's plans, but after your explanation I feel better."

"I am glad that you feel better. Anything else I could do for you to make you happy?"

"Yes Stefan, there is something I always wanted to do; fly. I know I cannot do it except in my dreams, but I thought you could perhaps give me a ride. I could hold on to your wing."

"I will be glad to give you a ride Boro. Here is a nice chair, strapped under my wing. Sit there and enjoy. Where do you want me to take you?"

"Please take me to the beach where Vesna used to swim with her friends?"

"Hop in Boro," said Stefan.

Boro climbed up and sat in the soft, comfortable chair. It felt as if he was sitting in the finest feathers.

"How fast do you want me to fly," asked Stefan.

"Can you fly faster than birds?"

"I can fly at any speed. How about if I fly slowly like an airplane, so that you can see down under?"

Stefan took off, nice and smooth. In a moment they were flying high above mountains enveloped in the clouds. They were going through a thunderstorm. Stefan climbed above clouds. The scene was absolutely majestic. The sky was full of bright, twinkling stars. The moon, like a huge silvery ball lit the clouds full of rain, thunder and lightning. It was scary and wonderful for Boro to watch the heavenly fireworks. Every few minutes lightning was tearing through the clouds, followed by booms of thunder.

"I am scared Stefan. I could fall down to the ground and hurt myself?"

Stefan smiled, touching Boro's head gently: "Nothing to worry about Boro. You cannot fall down. Even rain does not make you wet. You are with me now. Relax and enjoy."

Boro felt happy and safe after Stefan's assurances.

He clapped gently on Stefan's gold dust wings. "This is wonderful Stefan. I wish I never grow up, but be always with you and fly like this all over the world, even to the moon and stars. Could we fly to the moon?"

"You are asking lot of questions Boro."

"Well Stefan, I thought you can do anything I ask you. After all, aren't you my guardian angel?"

"I am afraid I am going to disappoint you Boro. I cannot do everything you might ask me to."

"I am sad to hear that. Are there guardian angels who know everything and can do whatever asked?"

"No such angels Boro. Only God knows everything, and can do anything He wants."

"I understand that, but how about flying to the moon. Could you fly that far?"

"I can fly anywhere if I have approval of Our Lord."

"Why do you need approval?"

"I need the approval because I am God's servant and I obey God always."

"What harm would be done if we quietly fly to the moon? I am curious to see what's up there."

"Sorry Boro, Lord says, not well for you to fly there. It is not the right time yet."

Soon they were over Vesna's town. The little town was asleep. They flew over Vesna's beach. It was a beautiful sandy beach, with pine trees in the background.

Boro sighed: "Oh Stefan this is where she swims. I am sad again. Let's go home please."

Stefan put on 'angelic speed.' In a twinkle of an eye they were back in Boro's room. Boro got out of feathery seat and lay in his bed.

The dawn was peeking through pale pinkish light behind the Eastern hills. Stefan caressed Boro`s head, kissed him on both cheeks and said like caring, loving mother: "Boro, Vesna will be a nice, pleasant memory in your life. Be glad you met her. She helped you to experience wonderful emotion of love. This was God`s gift to you."

"Oh Stefan, I got the toys."

"That`s wonderful Boro. What did you get?"

"I am so excited: I got a big yellow rubber ball, red fire truck and a chemical writing pen. I am the richest kid in school. Nobody else has these things, except maybe our teacher."

"Who got you the toys Boro?"

"My brother from America. He escaped to America after the big war. I don't remember him at all."

"Remember Boro I promised you some toys, and look, you got some toys."

"Did you buy these toys for me Stefan?"

"No Boro, but I arranged that you get them."

"Did you tell my brother to send me the toys?"

"I won't go in details. You just enjoy your toys."

"I will, believe me, I will. Thank you Stefan."

"Glad to do it my friend," said Stefan, kissed little boy on the cheek, and the next second was gone.

# Chapter 5

## *Going Into the World*

Boro progressed very well in school. His teacher concluded that he was wasting time in grade two. She promoted him to grade four. He excelled in grade four having all marks excellent. The family council headed by his brother Marko concluded that Boro, being a bit clumsy and a day dreamer, was not fit to be a good farmer, or miller. It was decided Boro would continue his education in the nearby town.

Leaving his home and village was both a sad and joyous occasion. His mom was in tears, because her little boy was going into the world. Only eleven years old, he still was just a skinny, insecure little boy.

Mom gave Boro all kinds of advices. To dress well and not to catch cold and it always ended with; "Study well honey, so when you become an educated gentleman you can buy your mom nice shoes and skirt." Boro promised that he would take care of himself, study diligently, and when he becomes an educated gentleman, he would buy his mom really nice shoes and a skirt.

His brother Marko found them a small flat on the outskirts of the town. Marko`s job required him to travel all over the county. Sometimes he was absent for several days. Boro was alone in their flat. He was not scared, because his landlords lived on the same floor and they had a cute girl of Boro`s age.

Life in the city was very much different than in his lonely house in the village. The first thing that struck Boro was the huge, tall buildings. Some of them taller than three of his houses stacked on top of each other. Then, people; so many people on the streets.

Boro thought all girls in his class were beautiful. If he could, he would be in love with all of them. They were all so smartly dressed; skirts, blouses, long hair, some in braids, some with colourful ribbons in their hair.

The princess of his heart was Dunja. She was the smartest girl in the class. Only Boro had better marks than her. The peculiar things about Dunja were her eyes, her smiling eyes. A few times him and Dunja touched accidentally. That was a day of Boro`s joy and excitement.

Things were going good. His marks were all excellent except in free hand drawing and music, where he barely made passing marks. Boro just couldn't draw any difference between a cow and a donkey, nor did he care for those sissy signs of musical notes, even less for singing.

He discovered new passions: movies and reading books. He registered at the local library. When he first came into the library, he was astounded by the number of books on the shelves. He started with fairy tales, reading all the books on fairy tales he could get. He enjoyed reading fantasies. His imagination went into full gear. It was pleasurable to escape into that other world through the window of his imagination. He could do there what he could not do in normal, 'regular' life, a brave knight riding a winged horse across the sky, fighting giants and dragons, saving beautiful princesses who would all fall in love with him, their saviour and benefactor.

Going to the movies was even more exciting. He could see drama developing right there on his eyes. He loved movies on adventures, science fiction and Westerns. He could hardly scrounge the money to buy the cheapest ticket for movies in first five rows closest to the screen. It was so close to the screen that his head and neck hurt after.

A good Western was showing in the city`s cinema, "The Best of the Worst." It had a lot of fist fights, shooting, and chasing Indians. Boro had to see it. He could not miss such a jewel of the movie.

The problem was; he could not go to the movies when Marko was in town. Lady luck seemed to smile at him.

One evening Marko told him that early the next morning he would leave town. He might be back in two days. Marko told him to behave in his absence, be a good boy, study, and --no movies. Marko indeed left early the next morning. That evening Boro was in huge dilemma. What to do? Since Marko was away he decided to see "The Best of the Worst." His buddies were right. It was a great, action packed movie, just to his liking. Still excited, he came back to their apartment.

To his terrible surprise Marko opened the door and let him in. He was unnaturally polite, addressing him as 'young gentleman." Boro froze; "Oh my God this is going to be real bad. Too much sweetness and politeness--something stinks here."

Marko politely asked him how the movie was. His excitement evaporated, Boro murmured 'good.'

Then, Marko gave him a lecture. "Our parents and I sent you to school to become an educated man. This is very expensive for us. We would not mind sacrificing if you studied diligently and obeyed us. It seems to me that you want to do whatever you like, ignoring my orders. I have no choice but to take you out of the school. Tomorrow morning get your junk, buy one way bus ticket and go home. Maybe you will be a good farmer or miller."

Boro couldn't believe what he heard. He was stunned. Him, be a farmer or miller? No more library, no more movies? No more watching smartly dressed girls? His world was coming to an end.

The next day, he collected his books and some dirty laundry in a wooden suitcase, went to the bus station, bought a ticket, and was on the way back to his village.

As the bus was going through the city, with teary eyes he contemplated his misfortune: "Oh what a shame. I am being kicked out of the school, even being the best in my class. What am I going to say to my mother, father, sister? What would my friends in the village say? For sure they will joke and tease me, being jealous that I was going to be an educated gentleman. What am I going to answer when somebody asks; 'how is the school?'"

With these unpleasant thoughts, Boro got off the bus. He still had to walk couple kilometres across the valley and cross the river. He came to the bank of the river and started waving his arms, hoping that his sister or father would notice him and come to take him across the river. Nobody was coming. Boro felt alone and abandoned in this cruel world. He started calling his dad and mom. Nobody answered.

Just when he started to despair, he saw his sister getting out of the house and walking in his direction. She did not say a word while they were crossing the river. When they came to their side of the river, Dana tied the boat to a big wooden post, took Boro`s suitcase and they started walking across the valley to their house. Boro was walking with his head down awaiting dreadful questions; "Why aren`t you in the school." She asked him just that question.

"Marko kicked me out of school, because I went to see a movie. He told me to go home and be farmer and miller. He said that school was over for me." Saying this, Boro had to hold tears not to run down his cheeks. After all, he was twelve, on good way to become an educated gentleman. It was not proper for a future educated gentleman to cry like a girl.

His sister was upset and felt sorry for Boro. She consoled him telling him that life in the village could be nice. He could make good business in the mill. In few years, parents would find him a nice village girl and marry him off. Dana`s consolation totally missed the point. Boro imagined himself getting married to some rough village girl and working in the dusty cold mill among the clouds of fine flour dust, coughing, like his father, his lungs full of flour dust. No books, no movies, never again to see Dunja. Oh what a pitiful, horrible, cruel fate!

To his surprise, his parents were not overly upset. They told him that help was always welcome on the farm : tending cows and sheep, working in the mill, fields or vineyard. He was tired of it all and emotionally exhausted. He ate big plate of bean soup and a good piece of mom`s homemade bread, and went to bed. He fell asleep almost immediately. Soon, he felt a gentle touch on his cheek. He knew Stefan was there. He was overjoyed to see his guardian angel.

"Stefan, I really need your help. I am in a bad, trouble. My life is being ruined. What am I going to do?"

"Tell me what happened."

"Where do I begin?"

"At the beginning. How did this crisis began?"

"Well," hesitated Boro, "It started with 'The Best of the Worst.'"

"The movie you went to see?"

"Yes."

"You liked it that much, to break your brother's order?"

"My buddies who saw the movie were praising it as the best they had ever seen. Also, advertising for it was so tempting and inviting. It showed a big handsome cowboy, blasting ugly, evil guys with a big silver gun, while a beautiful, long haired blonde looked lovingly at him. I had to see it."

"Was it good? Did you enjoy it?"

"Oh yes, it was great. I wished I could fight, shoot and ride like that cowboy. No fear, strong, brave man."

"You liked main character that much?"

"Yes, he is my idol."

"Boro, the movie is just fiction, a show, an invented story. It is not real life."

"Who cares? For these two hours, it was reality to me. I enjoyed myself tremendously and forgot everything else. I escaped into the world of brave, strong, fearless heroes. That's life."

"Your brother does not like these kinds of movies?"

"No, my brother is old fashioned. He just works and attends some stupid communist party meetings."

"He doesn't think these movies are good to watch for a young boy like you?"

"His idea of a good student is one that stays home and just studies. That would be a pretty boring life."

"You knew you were going to displease him very much if you went to see that movie."

"Yes, I knew, but I was sure that he would be away at least one more day."

"Did you expect Marko would kick you out of school and send you back to the village?"

"Never. I thought I might end up getting a bad beating."

"Marko surprised you?"

"Big time. Because I went to movie my life is totally ruined. It is not fair Stefan. Not fair at all."

"I know, I know Boro. Life on earth does not seem fair occasionally even to devoted, God fearing people."

"What am I going to do Stefan? I am desperate. Please help me."

"You don't want to live in the village and be a farmer?"

"No, I hate it. It is stupid, dirty, hard work."

"You think life in the city is much better, easier and enjoyable?"

"For sure."

"Why?"

"In the village we have to go to bed early like chicken, because we have only a little petroleum lamp. In the city, I flick the switch and I have the light. I can read books all night. In the village we don't have toilet. Got to go in the bush, or wherever. In the city, you go to a nice room, sit, read paper, or book, then pull the lever and flush down everything. In the city you can have a bath whenever you want. In the village, people get a bath when they are babies, perhaps when they get married, and for sure when they die. People in the city have soup for lunch every Sunday. In the village, they only have it for Christmas and Slava. If you want anything you can buy it in the store; candies, chocolate, salami, toys…"

Boro was going on and on with his tirade against village life and glorification of the city life.

Stefan interrupted him: "I got the message Boro. You don't want to be farmer. You want to be an educated gentleman, live in the city and enjoy all of its conveniences. Am I right?"

"You are right, but it looks like I have been sentenced to be a farmer. Help me please."

Stefan smiled: "Remember; nothing happens without the purpose and Lord`s permission. Just a hint: God did not bless you with the talent to be good farmer, or miller."

Boro jumped in excitement: "Do I go back to school? Did God say that to you? Please say, yes, yes."

"I see that you are very anxious to continue your education, but it is important that you learn something from this incident, which will help you in your life."

"What do you mean that I have to learn something from this incident? I didn`t do anything bad. I just went to see a movie for two hours. It is Marko, who did the bad thing. He ruined my life."

"Are you upset and angry at your brother?"

"I am upset. I will never forget this."

"Boro, did you learn anything from this incident?"

"I guess I did," admitted Boro reluctantly.

"Could you please share that with me?"

"I learned that I could screw up my life with just one little innocent looking mistake I made."

"And what mistake was that?"

"It was mistake to ignore Marko`s order not to go to movies."

"What made that mistake so bad?"

"Marko is my oldest brother. He helps to pay for my education. My parents would do whatever he told them. My future was in his hands."

"You are going to be thankful for this incident, for getting an invaluable lesson. Be thankful to your brother and forgive him. In his own way, he loves you and really wants you to become an educate gentleman."

"I don't like this kind of lesson," interjected Boro. "It was big shock and caused me lot of anxiety. Why couldn`t Marko ask me nicely not to go to movies? Wouldn`t that be better than this horrible, nerve wrecking kicking me out of school? I am too upset with Marko. I will never, ever forgive him this," finished Boro angrily.

Stefan shook his beautiful angelic head. "Do you think it would have the same effect if your brother told you politely; 'Please Boro, don't go to movies again without my permission. It is not nice?"

"If he asked me politely not to go to movies, without threat of the punishment, I wouldn't take that very seriously. I would go again, because there is nothing to fear, no punishment."

"You would quickly forget that 'nice' plea and would have kept ignoring your brother's orders. No lesson learned. Do you see it like that?"

"Yes I do," said Boro.

"Now, if by some miracle, Marko decides to allow you to continue your education, would you again disobey his orders, knowing that he has power to stop your education and send you back to the village?"

"No, I wouldn't be that stupid. I wouldn't do anything to give him an excuse to kick me out of the school. I would be very good boy and an obedient, respectful brother."

"Boro," said Stefan lovingly. "Things that are painful and bad turn out to be a blessing. You will appreciate this more as you grow older. God does not appreciate people having grudges, and not forgiving other people. It would please God if you don't harbor bad feelings against your brother. God rewards people that forgive others."

"If you fix things up that I am back in school on Monday, I will forgive the whole world, including Marko."

Stefan chuckled. "You like bargaining Boro! As for me fixing this, leave it to me. I am always working for your good. And remember, you won't know when and how I helped you. Just believe that I would."

"That bugs me. Why can't you at least give me a hint of when and how you help me?"

"My instructions spell out exactly what I can do with my protégés. With time, you will be able to grasp more things and see the signs of heavenly intervention. Time for me to go," said Stefan. "See you soon."

The pale light of the coming day fell on the young boy smiling in his sleep.

# Chapter 6

## *Teenager*

On Sunday, Marko told Boro that he spoke with their parents and they all agreed to give him one more chance to continue his education. Marko made it clear that he would pull him out of the school for good, if he did not study well and behaved properly. Boro solemnly promised that he would be good student and obey Marko's orders. He kept his promise.

Monday, Boro was back in school. He was happy to see his classmates, particularly Dunja, who in few days, seemed to grow up into a beautiful young lady.

Boro was fascinated by the complexity and intricacies of the world he learnt in Biology, Physics and Chemistry. The secrets of mother nature, a self regulating machine that regulated itself, and kept improving itself all the time. He was slowly abandoning the belief and the faith inspired into him by his mom and baba. He thought; "My baba and mom had no clue of the secrets of the nature discovered by the scientists. How stupid was I to believe in the fantasies of God, angels, saints. Who ever saw any of these? If anything like this existed, scientists would for sure have discovered it. This was just an illusion for uneducated people."

Boro forgot Stefan. Actually, he was quite ashamed, that he, a future educated gentleman believed in such a fairy tale of a guardian angel coming to his room and talking to him. How naive and stupid was he?

He sensed the change in his body, as he was going into puberty. But, the most amazing change was on girls. Their bodies got more rounded. Breast, hips, legs, were being sculpted by mother nature as if teasing boys; "Here we are, look at us, look how beautiful we are." Boro was too timid to ask any of the girls for a date. Most of the other boys talked with girls and flirted with them.

He was dreaming how he would approach Dunja, and ask her to go to park with him, to walk around, sit on a bench as real lovers do, hold hands and try a first kiss. Boro wondered years later, what would happen if he asked Dunja to have a date with him? Would she agree? His life might have gone entirely different way.

At the end of grade eight, on a beautiful May day, Boro and Dunja looked at each other at exactly the same time. Their looks 'struck' each other as they met halfway in the air. Dunja flashed him such a seductive, sweet, tender smile of a budding girl, aware of her beauty and charm. Boro`s reaction was-- profuse blushing. He pretended not to care for her seductive smile, but his eyes and face betrayed him, showing how much he loved and enjoyed that exchange. All this lasted few seconds, but the magic of this romantic exchange was unforgettable, touch less, wordless Eros.

After Boro graduated grade eight, Marko and parents decided to move him to much bigger town at the Adriatic, to attend grade nine. When they told Boro, he was disappointed and unhappy. He was puzzled why these unpleasant things happen to him. Why move him now from his friends, from Dunja?

A thought flashed in his mind. "Few years ago, when I was young and ignorant I would contact Stefan, so called guardian angel, to talk to me and help me to understand things. Who am I going to talk to now? My parents wouldn`t know anything. I don't dare to ask Marko."

He felt like an orphan. No friendly support and advice from anyone. To his surprise Stefan showed up that night. Boro sensed strongly his presence. He had mixed feelings. Why would he, a graduate of grade eight, almost an educated young man, talk to 'the air,' to a non-material being; to an angel? But, he sensed positive energy, love and care radiating from his visitor.

*A Kingdom to Buy*

Stefan broke the silence first. His voice resonated with loving care and tenderness: "Wow, you changed Boro. You are a tall, good looking young man. Glad to see you again. How are you?"

Boro tried to show that he was bored by this 'hallucination' but he just couldn't help it. He was glad his guardian angel was back with him. "I am fine, and how are you Stefan. It has been a long time since we spoke."

Smiling, Stefan replied; "I am always well Boro, thanks for asking. Just to let you know, I was watching you all these years and helping you, whenever I had permission from Our Lord."

Boro felt himself warming to his trusted protector and advisor, but budding scientist and future educated gentleman in him, did not want to give up that easily. "Stefan I am not going to hide it from you, but I think I was having hallucinations of seeing an angel and having him as my guardian and protector."

Stefan kissed him gently on the forehead. "I understand what you learnt in school. Such is your educational system, your society. I am not surprised by your words of doubt regarding the existence of God and angels. Your teachers were obliged to teach you that."

Boro was astounded at Stefan's reaction. He expected Stefan to argue with him, attempting to convince him of the existence of God, angels and heaven. He was ready to give him 'irrefutable scientific and logical' arguments to defend modern science . "Are you saying Stefan that you understand that I don't believe in existence of God and angels and that it is proper to believe that?"

Stefan smiled patiently. "No Boro, I was saying that I understood you were compelled to believe what was the official belief of the state, and education system. I have not said that this was right belief. It is actually the wrong belief, propagated by the Enemy."

"The Enemy?"

"He is known under different names; Lucifer, Satan, Devil. Have you heard these names before?"

"I did many times from my mom and baba, in the books, movies, jokes. Everybody has heard of these names. But what is the connection between these three guys and science?"

"This is an evil angel known under these names."

"Are you kidding me? Devil is an angel?"

"Devil, known also as Lucifer was created by God as a good, angel. He had high rank among the angels."

"And what happened to him? Why isn't he still an angel, since God created him as a good angel?"

"He rebelled against God, wanting himself to be in God's place."

"And then, what happened?"

"God kicked him out of the heaven."

"Why didn't God destroy him?"

"God has His plans. He will destroy Devil in due time."

"And when is that?"

"God only knows that time."

"Stefan what is connection between Devil and modern sciences that deny the existence of God?"

"The Devil has nothing to do with the true science, but everything to do with the false science."

"I don't understand what you call true and what false science."

"The true science is one that strives by experiments and logic, to explain natural order. Like chemistry, physics, biology. The false science is the one that presents itself as true, but is based but on some false assumptions."

"How do you call this false science?"

"Men call it, the theory of evolution."

"Oh yes, I remember now. We learnt about it in biology."

"What did you learn about evolution in your biology class?"

"We learnt that man became from monkey."

Stefan shook his head disapprovingly. "How did that happen?"

"Are you joking with me? You know all these things. I am just telling you what was taught by our teacher."

"I never joke with you Boro. Could you please explain what you learnt in this theory of evolution?"

"The teacher said that everything had its beginning in something like a huge ocean of soup. The soup was gurgling and boiling for a long, long time, then, by accident, some simple cells formed on their own in that soup."

Stefan was trying hard not to laugh. "And then?"

"Over a very, very long period of time, these primitive cells, again on their own initiative, became more complex organisms, something like an ugly fish."

Stefan couldn't suppress his laughter. "And, what happened with the ugly fish?"

"Teacher explained that over long, very long period of time, some of these fishes did not like to live in the water any longer. On their own, they went out of the water and decided to live on the dry land developing, blood, nerves, and legs."

"What did these creatures look like when they came to live on the dry land?"

"To my recollection teacher said that they looked something between a mouse and a dog."

"And then?"

"Some of these ugly land creatures over long, very long period of time, developed again on their own, bigger legs, bigger brains. Some of them decided to live on the trees, and these were our monkey ancestors. Naturally, it all happened over long time period and on creature's personal decision."

"So what happened with your monkey forefathers?"

"Some of these monkeys on their own, and over long, very long period of time, decided they had enough of the life on the trees. They came down to firm ground, started to walk upright and perfected front legs into hands. These were our human ancestors."

"Boro, thank you very much. You explained the theory of evolution in a very interesting and easy to understand way."

"My biology teacher would give me failing mark. He would criticize it as very unscientific."

"But I, your guardian angel, am giving you excellent mark for a theory simply and brilliantly explained."

"Thank you Stefan. You are just being nice. I know I don't deserve excellent mark for this explanation."

"Boro, don't underestimate the talent God gave you. I can see flashes of your talent in every encounter I have with you."

"Talent, what talent God gave me? I am not aware of any talent I have. You are kidding me, aren't you?"

"No Boro," said Stefan seriously. "Remember, I told you that us, guardian angels are not allowed to joke with our protégés. As for your talent, it is premature to talk about it now. In due time, we will discuss it."

"Am I some kind of genius, who will save our planet?" asked Boro sarcastically.

"Every man was given talent by God. Some get more, some less. A good farmer has talent of farming, a good tailor has talent for making suits, a good artist has the talent of painting."

"Why can't you tell me what my talent is? It could help me to make money, and become famous?"

"Sorry Boro, you are not ready for it yet."

"When am I going to be ready to discover what my talent is? Do I need to wait; five, ten, fifty years?"

"You had to crawl, before you learned to walk. You need to acquire some basic skills, and go through trials and experiences, before you become aware of your talent."

"I have no clue how to make myself ready to become aware of my talent."

"The most precious inheritance you got from your mom and baba is genuine faith. They have sown good seed in your soul. It may lie dormant long time, but when right conditions occur, it will grow into a living faith."

"Faith sown by my mom and baba into my soul? What are you talking about Stefan?"

Stefan smiled like a, patient teacher. "When you were little boy, who taught you how to cross yourself?"

"My baba."

"How she taught you to cross yourself?"

"Every time I made sign of cross properly, baba gave me a walnut, complimented me and kissed me."

"And who taught you first prayers?"

"My mom."

"How did you learn your prayers?"

"I loved my mom, and the best treat in the world for me was when she allowed me to sleep with her. It was the best during cold winter nights. Our house had just a small wood stove in the kitchen. No heating in the bedrooms. All windows were covered by ice. Rooms were freezing cold. We had to cover well with several heavy rough domestic wool blankets, made by my mom and baba. I would cover even my head to avoid breathing in that icy cold air, and snuggle to my mom, feeling the warmth of her body.

My mom prayed same prayers every night. She prayed mostly in Church-Slavonic, the language used in the Church. The first prayer was: 'Lord`s Prayer." I did not understand most of the words of the prayer, but it sounded so holy as if my mom was talking to that Divine Person, she addressed, 'Our Father.' She would continue with prayer to God`s Mother; 'Hail Mary. 'It sounded as if my mom talked to some important, wonderful lady.

Then she continued with 'The Creed of Faith.' It seemed that my mom was in contact with some wonderful world, very much different than the world we were living in. 'Vjeruju vo Jedinoga Boga Oca...' (I believe in One God The Father...). My mother completed her prayers, with two prayers in Serbian. First was the prayer for her departed children and other members of our family. She prayed for the souls of her three children, her brother, father, grandfather, and relatives. It was a wonderful prayer. "My dear departed, may God grant you eternal peace, paradise of heaven. May the soil be light upon your bones. May your souls be in the Lords realm?"

She completed her praying with the prayer for all living members of our family for their blessing and health. It was pleasant to fall asleep, listening to my mom`s voice bringing us in contact with an unknown, wonderful, mysterious world. I imagined how wonderful it would be to meet that God my mom prayed to every night. Would He be kind to me? Maybe He would be like a jovial, good natured grandfather sitting up, up high in the heaven on a special cloud, being served by beautiful, winged young men? I would usually be sound asleep by the end of my mom`s praying. It was so relaxing and calming."

"What about your baba? Were you close to her?"

"Being the youngest grandchild, I was her favourite. My baba was illiterate. She just had very simple childlike faith crowned by, 'Fear of God and shame of people.' She hated nobody, gave peace of bread to wandering beggars, helped her neighbours, and had kind word for people in distress. Baba's life was ruled by prayers, fasting and work.

I was in school away from my village, when that freezing January, baba got quite sick. She sensed that her life journey was coming to the end. She had no fear of death. She told us: 'Why would I be afraid? I know more people on the other side, than here. My husband is waiting for me there, my son, daughters, grandchildren, brothers, sister, mom, dad.' Sighing deeply baba used to say: 'It is time for me to depart. I have eaten the bread allocated to me by God. I have lived my given days.'

My sister Dana was named baba's 'nurse', a job she hated. It was freezing in the little stone walled house. Family had dinner and everybody rushed to the only place they could warm up; in their beds under coarse woollen blankets. Baba did not eat anything. She just drank a glass of wine. Seeing that his mom was not feeling well, dad told Dana; 'Watch baba tonight.'

In the morning Dana woke up. She touched baba's face. It was cold. Terrified, she called baba few times and got no reply. She hurriedly dressed and went to the kitchen, where mom was starting fire in the wood stove. Dana screamed: 'Baba is not answering, come quickly.' Father quickly got out of bed, dressed and went to see his mom. She was dead. He covered her, went to the kitchen, took a beeswax candle, prepared for this occasion, crossed himself, lit the candle and put it beside the head of his dead mother. They started to cry inconsolably, except the father. It was not fit for him to shed tears like women and children.

The sun did not show up that day. Terrible blizzard piled huge snow banks, keeping people in the safety of their houses.

Dana was sent to the village to notify their cousin Luka to organize grave diggers and pall bearers, and baba Milica to ask women to come and prepare baba for burial. Women came, washed baba and dressed her into folk costume, she prepared for her burial. Baba was put on a stretcher, and covered by a white burial shroud. There was no coffin.

Four strong young men, carried baba's stretcher struggling against wind and snow to a cemetery, five kilometres away. Family and few villagers followed behind them. When small funeral procession came to the cemetery, grave diggers had already completed their job, the grave was dug. Monk from the monastery came wrapped up in several coats, his long silvery beard and moustache full of icy crystals. Baba was taken off the stretcher and put on the ground besides her grave. The monk hurriedly said the prayers, poured the wine and put some soil in the shape of cross on baba's burial shroud and left in hurry to the warmth of his monastic kelia.

After baba was buried, everybody visited the graves of their loved ones in the cemetery. Women started crying and lamenting. It was heart breaking hearing them hitting their chests and calling their departed sons, daughters, husbands, brothers, parents. The end chapter of baba's quiet, hard life, was a memorial meal in Boro's house. His father slaughtered a sheep. The meat was boiled and served to the people. The biggest treat was soup with rice in the broth of boiled mutton, because rice was expensive and was food of rich, city folks. Huge pot of boiled sauerkraut with bacon, sausages and ham warmed up all. There was plenty of grapa and wine. Everybody talked how good and God fearing woman baba was and how she was good to them."

Stefan was listening attentively. When Boro finished story about baba's life and death, he said to Boro: "That was a truly wonderful story about life, faith and death. This is the seed of faith I am talking about. It is buried in your soul. Perhaps, you won't be aware of it for years, but it will germinate and grow at the proper time."

"What is the proper time Stefan? I doubt it will ever come."

"God knows the proper time. It depends on your life and behaviour and on God's providence."

"Are you saying Stefan that you actually don't know when my talent is going to be revealed to me? I am surprised to hear that. Aren't you my guardian angel that knows everything about me?"

"Boro, do you recall what I told you how us, guardian angels work?"

"You told me many things. What particularly did you have in mind?"

"I told you that I work always under instructions of Our Lord. You need to trust me that I am going to help you and intervene when God allows."

"You are saying. Believe, and hope for the best."

"That is part of what I am saying. You need to have right faith and live according to that faith. Don't let that seed of faith, sown in your heart, shrivel and die. This is the foundation of your salvation."

Boro interrupted. "Stefan, you mentioned few times the word 'salvation.' You said; 'your salvation.' What do I need to be saved from? Is somebody threatening me, to beat me up, kill me, and steal my stuff?"

"Boro, this is again a flash of your God given talent," said Stefan with admiration.

Boro laughed. "What are you talking about Stefan. What kind of 'God given talent,' you saw in my question?"

"You had in your question a hint of the answer that is essential for every human being."

"What is 'the salvation,' and why is it so important, 'essential' as you said, to every human being?"

"Boro, do you understand the meaning and importance of salvation of your soul?"

"Salvation of my soul? That is heavy stuff for me to understand Stefan. My head is full."

"Thank you for being honest Boro. Let's talk about it some other time," said Stefan and vanished.

# Chapter 7

## *Romantic Adriatic*

Since it was decided that Boro would go to school in town on the Adriatic, father took him to town and bought him a suit, couple of shirts, and a pair of real leather shoes. Boro started to look like an educated gentleman.

Shortly after moving to the town on the Adriatic, Boro went to zoo. He was stricken with awe seeing tigers, lions, bears, giraffe, but wanted to see his old nemesis, the wolf. When he came to the wolves' cage, he saw couple of the older skinny malnourished wolves, pacing nervously up and down the cage. 'Why was I afraid of this thing,' wondered Boro. He felt almost sorry for the poor king of the bush, sentenced to life imprisonment.

Grade nine was easy. The only subject he did not have excellent mark was Mathematics. His strongest subject was; 'the mother tongue.'

Most of girls and boys were dating. He still loved only at a distance, being all the time in love, but never having enough guts to approach his 'princess' and talk to her. His longing for girls was growing stronger and stronger, dominating his thoughts.

He forgot Stefan and his message about the salvation. "Salvation is making love to every girl you want."

The only thing resembling a date was with a school friend of his cousin. The girl was from an island. She was Boro`s age and shy like him. Quite an average girl, except her eyes. It was something wonderful, and seductive about them. They were just as Adriatic

Sea looked at from the hill above the port; bluish --greenish, deep and warm. They had a date in the pine forest on the sea shore, just after dark, when stars and moon came out on the clear warm sky. They spent couple of hours, sitting on the bench, talking, looking at the sea, listening to the waves crushing on the stony shore and a slight breeze playing music within the pine trees.

The night was made for lovers; clear sky full of shiny stars, blinking to two shy lovers on the bench. At the end of the date, there was no kissing, no embraces, no hand holding, just a shy, 'good bye' handshake. The first date remained deeply ingrained in Boro's memory. It did not matter that the date was hundred percent Platonic. All the elements of a romance were there. Boro thought in later years, that it was best that this date was innocent, and just old fashioned first meeting of a growing young man and girl. If he and Mare were engaged in a passionate love, it would spoil the sweet, innocent memory of his first date.

At the end of tenth grade, Marko told Boro that he would change schools again. This time, he was to go to the real big city. He would reside in a village twenty kilometres from the real big city with their cousin and her family, and travel to the school by train.

Boro was very disappointed for leaving town on the Adriatic. He loved the sea, the sunshine, beaches, pine forests and beautiful Dalmatian girls.

Stefan appeared one night. Boro sensed him, but was not very eager to talk to him. He did not look as bright, young and beautiful as before. "Wonder what happened," thought Boro. "Angels don't age, or do they?"

"No, we don't age" said Stefan smiling.

Boro was taken aback. "You read my thoughts?"

"I did."

"Does that mean that you always know what I am thinking?"

"I have that power, but I don't use it very often."

"Why not?"

"My instructions tell me when I am allowed to use my power. The Lord has power to do miracles any time, but He is very selective about that."

"Why wouldn't God make one grand miracle to come and appear to everybody to see Him, making some fantastic miracle like bringing the Sun down from heaven and holding it in His hand, or raising from the dead all people that ever lived, or making a mountain disappear. If God would do that, everybody would believe in Him instantly. Don't you agree with me Stefan?"

Stefan shook his head. "Boro, Neither man nor angel understands how Our Lord operates His creation. One big misconception of men is that they try to understand God by logical speculation, by their reason. You cannot understand immaterial spirit by your reasoning mind."

Boro scratched his head. "Stefan, this is too religious, too complicated for me. You know that I need simpler explanation."

"It would make it much easier for you to understand all this, if you read the Bible."

"What benefit would I get from reading the Bible? It is not a subject in school, so that I could get good mark. What could I learn from the Bible that I cant learn in biology, physics, chemistry? Nobody reads Bible in our age. This is for old men and women who have nothing better to do. Young people, have many more interesting and enjoyable things to do other than reading the Bible. Another important reason why we don't read the Bible is that it is frowned upon by our teachers and our society."

Stefan smiled," Boro, you gave very good and apparently convincing reasons why you and other young people should not read the Bible. All the reasons you gave are very practical and seem reasonable, but there is another side of the coin."

Boro chuckled sarcastically. "Are you going to tear down my arguments and convince me that I was wrong in refusing to read the Bible?"

Stefan shook his head. "No Boro. My job is to help you to realize that it would be good for you to read the Bible. It is essential that by your own free will, you convince yourself of the benefit of reading the Bible."

"I just see no reason to read the Bible."

"As you grow and mature your attitude will change. You need to be patient, and keep your mind open."

"My mind is always open."

"Where were we?" joked Stefan.

"Stefan, you did not answer my question why God does not produce one huge, spectacular miracle, so that everybody on earth, once and for all time would have no choice but believe there is God and that He is all powerful."

"This is an interesting concept of God. A lot of people share your concept, which is quite different than teaching of our Lord Jesus Christ, as He explained it in the Bible".

"What is the difference?"

"Even though, you did not read the Bible, you are probably aware that Lord Jesus Christ performed many miracles during His three years ministry on earth. He healed the sick, made dumb people speak, the deaf hear, the paralyzed walk. He raised dead people. He walked on water. At the end, as the miracle of miracles, He rose from the dead after being buried in the tomb for three days. He has risen in incorruptible, eternal body.

After spending forty days on earth in His resurrected body, and meeting with His Disciples, He ascended to Heaven. People were amazed witnessing miracles performed by Jesus, but they quickly forgot them. Even though they witnessed those great miracles, lot of people still did not believe that Jesus was truly Messiah, Son of God, and Redeemer of mankind, fully God and fully man. Jesus was aware that people had; "ears, but did not hear, had eyes, but did not see." He was aware that some people would disbelieve, even after witnessing numerous miracles. This is my answer to your question on "One time big miracle."

"Your explanation makes sense Stefan. But I am surprised that people who witnessed, miracles performed by Jesus, healing people, raising them from dead, His resurrection; still did not believe, that He was, who He claimed He was."

"Are you sad Boro for leaving Dalmatia, blue Adriatic, and sun soaked beaches?"

"Of course I am. Can you use your power to persuade Marko and my parents, not to move me to the real big city? I love it here. This is my land."

"Sorry Boro, I cannot do what you ask me. It is not in my instructions to interfere the way you are asking me. Your moving to the real big city is not an accidental thing. This is a part of your growing and maturing. Lord uses people around you and situations you get into, to form your character and prepare you for your calling."

"Instructions, instructions," complained Boro. "Stefan you seem to me like a slave. You have no free will, but must always do whatever these famous instructions order you. Can you bend them a bit sometimes?"

Stefan smiled shaking his head: "Boro, I have free will, as a gift of our Creator. I choose to be in perfect obedience to God. Lucifer and his followers also had free will, but decided to rebel against God. Instructions, you are complaining about are the covenant between us angels and God."

"Wow Stefan, you went way too deep, too religious. Most of that stuff is over my head. I read somewhere that the angels are immortal and out of our space and time. How could that that be?"

"The angels are immortal because, not having mortal bodies, they cannot die bodily death. No body, no death."

"Since you have no mortal body, there is nothing within you to die. Am I close?"

"You are right on. This concept of time is harder for you to grasp. Since you have mortal bodies, born out of the seed, with limited duration, you are within the time since your life clock starts ticking when you were conceived, and stops when you die. Your life is marked by different segments of the time. First, you are a baby, then a teenager, adolescent, grown up man, and finally an old man. Everything within your material, visible world is within the framework of time. It was created, it will exist for a period of time, and then it will change, or as you say on earth 'die.' Do you now have a better understanding of you being locked in time?"

"I understand it better now after you explained it, but I am still unable to understand in my mind how you can be outside of the time. It is just hard for me to grasp this. It frustrates me."

"Since angels have incorruptible bodies that lasts forever, they do not go through the cycle of birth, life, death and resurrection, as men do. That is why angels are out of the earthly time frame. Just to help you ease your frustration; no man while in his mortal body has the ability to understand this concept of time."

"Thank you very much Stefan. It was very interesting and educational discussion for me."

"I am glad Boro that you found it beneficial and interesting. You are going to enjoy the real big city. Time of bodily and spiritual growth is ahead of you. I will be invisibly with you all the time. Time for me to go now, good-bye my friend."

Boro continued sleeping mumbling something with a faint smile on his face

# Chapter 8

# *Exciting Train Ride*

Finally, the day of Boro`s departure to the real big city came. His mom was wiping tears from her eyes. Her boy was going far away into the world. There was no food on the train, so mom roasted a chicken for her growing boy, and added half a loaf of her home-made bread and a chunk of cheese pita. Boro had everything packed into a wooden suitcase. After much hugging and tears mixed with his mom`s advice; to be good and study diligently, Boro went to catch the bus to the train station. As usual, there were more passengers than seats in the train coaches, so everybody pushed and scrambled to get a seat. Boro had to sit in the corridor on his wooden suitcase. After three hours, he was lucky to get a seat in the coach, when a passenger disembarked.

In the coach was a very homey atmosphere. People that never met before were talking to each other like old friends. Two elderly women were telling their life stories to each other. Right across Boro, sat a girl, a plump blonde. She looked few years his senior. She was reading a small book. Boro wanted to talk to her, but was too shy. "What do I say? What kind of opening would be good here?"

Feeling hungry, Boro opened his wooden suitcase and pulled out goodies his mom prepared. He took out the roasted chicken, pita and bread and began to eat. He offered his neighbours sitting beside him to his food. One neighbour declined saying he just ate. The other neighbour, an elderly peasant, took a piece of bread and a chicken drumstick. He offered Boro ham, cheese and wine. Boro tried the ham and cheese and took few sips of wine. The wine was good and strong; it warmed him up and emboldened him to offer the plump blonde: "Please join us, help yourself."

She closed her book and put it aside. "Thank you young man I will try your food." She took a chicken wing and a small piece of mom`s home-made bread. She ate like real lady, taking small bites, chewing slowly with her mouth closed.

The elderly peasant offered her wine. She took out plastic cup from her purse and poured half a cup of the wine from the bottle. She raised the cup to Boro and the elderly peasant; "To your health, long life." The elderly peasant touched her cup with half full bottle saying; "and to your health young lady." He gave bottle to Boro who gladly toasted with blonde and enthusiastically greeted her: "to your health beauty." They were all warmed up by good, strong Dalmatian wine. Plump blonde got rosy cheeks, which made her even sexier. Boro was hot and excited by good food and wine, but mostly by plump blonde. He suggested: "Let's get some fresh air." The blonde, who introduced herself as Nada, gladly accepted his invitation.

They went into the coach corridor and opened the window. They talked about their villages, parents, school, movies, and sports. As they were talking and leaning on the window, Boro collected the courage and put his hand around Nada`s shoulders. To his surprise, she did not remove his hand- she seemed to like it there. Encouraged, Boro came close against Nada, feeling her hip pressing on his hip. No rejection again. He was astounded by his success. Emboldened, he put his hand on her long blond hair and very gently slid it from the top of her head almost down to her waist. No rejection again! It seemed that she enjoyed it as much as Boro.

There were other people walking through the corridor and some standing by the window, talking.

"Why the heck these people don`t go to their seats, shut the light off and sleep. Oh my God wouldn't that be fantastic for me and Nada." Then, a great opportunity came; the train was to enter a tunnel. Boro smiled, Nada smiled back. As soon as they got into the tunnel it was almost pitch dark, because most lights in the coach were off.

Boro put his hands around Nada`s waist. That was the most exciting moment in his life. He squeezed Nada tight against him and his mouth found her eager mouth. He was nervous, because this was first time he kissed girl. Luckily, that inexperience was well covered by Nada`s experience and passion. Feeling Nada`s body tight against his, Boro was in seventh heaven. The darn tunnel was way too short. They stopped kissing, straightened their clothing, leaning again at the window, cooling their burning faces. "This is life, nothing compares to this; desire, passion, and pleasure. Everything pales beside it. How much more wonderful would be 'the real thing'? That must be something divine, that makes man feel like being in heaven," thought Boro.

They continued their conversation, getting to the point where they both had one thing in mind; to make love. They wished there was a dark corner right there on the train, where they could forget the school, parents, the world, and engage full speed in their awakened passion.

Then another much longer tunnel came. This time Boro went even further, squeezing Nada tight against his body and passionately caressing her. At the end of the tunnel she gave Boro big, deep kiss, saying; "Young boy, you are some hot man." Boro was very happy and proud of himself. He kissed the girl first time in his life, was intimate with her almost to the end. She allowed him everything, enjoying it just like he did.

"I am a man, not any more a shy, clumsy teenager. Probably, Stefan would criticize me as doing an immoral thing. Hey, who cares? We both enjoyed it, we didn`t hurt anybody. God wouldn`t object to that," reasoned Boro.

The dawn was almost breaking over the plains. They were approaching the real big city. Getting ready to disembark, Boro asked: "Are we going to see each other again?"

Nada gave him a seductive smile . "My boy, you like 'older' women, don't you?"

"Older," Boro protested, "You are just few years older than me. That isn't important to me."

"Actually, I am more than few years older than you, doesn't that bother you?"

"Not at all, unless it bothers you."

Nada smiled; "Noooo, what's a few years. It's actually good. I am going to teach my young boy how to be warm and gentle lover. Interested to learn young man?"

"Am I ever? When is the next lesson my beautiful red rose?"

"You need to be patient. We will be very busy studying, and also you live far away from me."

"Patience! I hate patience. I would want you now, or yesterday," said Boro squeezing her warm hand.

"Aren't you a very hot and aggressive young man? You just met me and you want to take me to bed. We have only known each other only a few hours. We got to know each other little better, don't you think so?"

"I feel as if I met you not seven hours ago, but seven years ago."

"Oh that is very nice. I must admit I feel similar to you. Maybe that strong red wine made me feel like this."

"Where can I find you?" asked Boro.

"That is good question," said Nada. "I have no phone. I bet, you won't have a phone either?"

"No, my cousin has no phone in her house."

"Well, we can meet at my faculty, or at your school, but we don't know each other's schedule."

"Why don't we meet this coming Sunday right here at the railway station. By that time we will know our schedules. Let's meet, at noon," proposed Boro.

"Let's meet at four in the afternoon, because I have to visit my cousin during day. Is that okay with you?"

"Yes, it is. I will be counting days, and hours until I see you again."

"Okay, romantic boy, don't forget; Sunday at four, here at the railway station. Bye until Sunday."

"Bye my beauty," sighed Boro.

*A Kingdom to Buy*

It took Boro another train and another hour to get to his cousin's home. Everybody greeted him excitedly, his cousin, her husband and their two children. After very rich dinner, Boro felt very tired. Long trip and passionate adventure with Nada did their job. He hardly kept his eyes open. His cousin saw this and told him to go to bed. He gladly obeyed.

He hoped that Stefan wouldn't come, but he appeared. Boro felt guilty for his behaviour on the train. No matter how much he tried to justify it to himself, that guilt was there, it stuck to him. It was impossible to shake it off.

Boro broke the silence: "Oh Stefan, you again, what a pleasant surprise."

Stefan smiled. "Is it really a pleasant surprise?"

"Well, it is always pleasant to talk to you."

"It seems to me that you would feel better if I didn't show up tonight."

"Since you are able to read my thoughts, there is no sense in pretending. Yes, I feel uneasy to talk to you tonight. I hoped that you were busy elsewhere, and would not come tonight."

"Thank you Boro for being honest with me. Why do you feel uneasy talking to me today?"

Boro felt quite uncomfortable. "You know what happened on the train. Do I need to tell you all the story again?"

"You have free will. It is your choice. Aren't you aware that I am invisibly present with you all the time?"

"Yes, I am aware of that, but since you already know what I did why don't you just go ahead and criticize me. That would be much easier for me. Short and sweet."

"I could do that, but I am not judging you. I would like to hear from you what happened."

"I see I have no choice but to give you my story. Where do you want me to begin?"

"How about start from the moment you took the seat across Nada."

"Well, it was the wine that made me do it. I just couldn't control myself. I took too many sips."

Stefan smiled, "Boro, you are not the first man with this kind of excuse. Man started giving excuses for his actions, since the first man and women, Adam and Eve. They sinned, and began making excuses for sinning in the Garden of Eden.

Their descendants just continued, infected by the disease of the 'excusitis,' and every generation has gotten more and more crafty and skilful in it. They were proud; 'Wow, we tricked God with this excuse.' God cannot be tricked, because He is the all-knowing God. Nobody can hide anything from Him, not even the most secret thoughts."

"Wait, wait Stefan, you lost me with your lecture and your lengthy elaboration. Could you please be bit simpler?"

"Sorry Boro, even angels sometimes talk more than necessary. Could I ask you a few questions?"

"My goose is already cooked," cried Boro. "There is nothing for me to tell you, you already don't know. Please cut it short and tell me what my punishment is."

"Don't worry Boro you are not in men's court. You are not accused of anything. Do not be scared. My job is to help you to become aware when your behaviour violates Gods Commandments. When you had that passionate encounter with Nada, on the train, did you at any time feel guilty?"

"Yes, I did," admitted Boro reluctantly.

"Did that feeling of guilt change in the intensity during your passionate foreplay?"

"The more intimate we were getting, feeling of guilt was getting weaker."

"Your God given conscience was telling you that your behaviour with Nada was not within a God intended relationship between boy and girl meeting for the first time."

"You are saying Stefan that my behaviour was inappropriate. Why didn't you, my guardian angel prevent me from getting involved with that girl? Wasn't that within your instructions?"

"No Boro. Rule number on in our instructions; do not violate your protégé`s free will."

"If I decide to commit suicide and jump from the tenth floor of a building, your instructions would not allow you to help me? You would let me go ahead and kill myself?"

"If God permits, I wouldn't interfere and you would kill yourself. Lord might instruct me to arrange another human to rescue you, or a situation which would prevent you from killing yourself."

"You observed what I was doing, but did not get involved?"

"I am always involved. You are just unaware of that. I am not going to disclose the manner of my involvement."

"What is going to happen to me now? How am I going to be punished?"

"Our Lord is loving and forgiving God. He knows that your flesh was fighting against your conscience. Your flesh wanted passionately to engage in the foreplay with that girl. Your conscience was giving you the message: 'Don't do this, it is wrong.' That time your flesh won, as it will many more times in your life. This is the fight every man has within himself, between his flesh and his soul. My job is to help you to achieve a happy balance between your flesh and your soul."

"Does that mean that I am forgiven?"

"God forgives man who repents and asks God to forgive him his sins."

Boro smiled. "I thought that God noted down my transgression in His Book. One day He opens that book, and reads: 'Boro had inappropriate foreplay with Nada. Boro to be punished, Nada to be punished.'"

"It is not quite like that Boro. Do not despair if your flesh wins. This happens many times during younger years, when young men and women have very strong sexual desire. Be brave and fight the flesh."

"My flesh is my body. How do I fight myself?"

"You are not just your body, what you can see, touch. There is an invisible part of you, your mind, your will, feelings, emotions, soul. Your soul and your body are in a mysterious way interconnected."

Boro interrupted him; "Stefan, my head is full. I know now that there is nonstop struggle within myself, and that I need to help my soul, to rule over my body. Am I right?"

"You are. Let's say 'bye,' to each other now." With these words the angel spread his huge golden dust wings and flew like a supersonic rocket through the roof of Boro`s cousin`s house.

# Chapter 9

## *Betrayal*

Boro waited eagerly to see Nada again. On Sunday, he took the early afternoon train. The date was at four, he was at the station by three. He walked around the railway station observing people. When the station clock was showing four, he started to wonder; "Where the heck is she, how could she not be on time?" Ten minutes passed. No sign of Nada. He started getting angry and decided; "I will wait twenty more minutes."

As he was pacing nervously up and down in front of the station`s main door, a short, skinny girl approached him. "Excuse me young man, are you Boro, waiting for Nada?"

Surprised, Boro mumbled "Yes, I am. Is she all right?"

"She is all right, "said the girl. "She asked me to give you this letter."

The girl took out a letter from her purse, handed it to Boro, said "Good bye," and left.

Boro felt all blood rushing to his head. He tore open the envelope and took out a handwritten letter on half a page. His hands trembling, he read Nada`s letter:

Boro, you will probably wonder why I did not come to meet as we agreed. I hope you wont get mad at me. Let me assure you that I enjoyed meeting you and having fun with you on the train. I will never forget it. This will be always my very pleasant memory.

I told you that I was three and a half years older than you. I lied. I am almost five years older than you. Next year I will be graduating. I was already promised a job in a big company, right here in the real big city. The director of that company is a war colleague of my uncle. He has son finishing medicine this year. He is three years older than me. We met here at a blind date. He liked me right away .I like him too. We decided to get married next year. He is going to be good husband for me.

I hope you understand why I did not come to meet you today. Believe me it is not because I didn`t like you, but because it is the best for me and for you to discontinue this short romance. You are a, charming young man, and I am sure that you wont be lacking girls interested in you. Good buy my train lover boy. Kiss and hug. Nada.

Boro`s eyes filled with tears. He couldn`t understand Nada`s letter. She liked him, but she stood him up. "Liar, liar, liar," shouted Boro angrily. Confused and upset, he took the train back to his cousin`s house.

Depressed, he sat in the corner of a half empty coach and analyzed his first love debacle .

That night, his guardian and protector arrived in all his glory and magnificence. Boro felt his angelic hand caressing his cheeks.

"Stefan, I am glad to see you. How are you?"

"Thanks for asking Boro, I am great as usual. How are you?"

"I could be better. Do I need to tell you about my predicament, since you know it already, better than me?"

"You are flattering me Boro. Yes I know everything, but I don't know it better then yourself. That power is not given me."

"I am surprised to hear that. I believed that since you can read my mind, you know all that is to be known about me."

"Well, not quite. The big difference between you and me is the body. You have it, I don`t."

"I don't get it. Why would lack of body prevent you to know me?"

"Because, having body gives you the ability to experience bodily passions?"

"How can you exist without body? Are you like air, fog, or without any kind of body?"

"Only God is an absolutely bodiless spirit. No other created being is like God. I have body, but it is very light, very thin. It is so light; it seems as if it does not exist. Consider the difference between earthly materials. On one side a thick, coarse material made out of sheep wool. On the other side the finest, the thinnest silk. That is a rough comparison between your and my body. Is this clear to you now?"

"Yes, it is Stefan. You explained it perfectly. Why do all these unpleasant things happen to me? I met a girl, I fell in love with her, she seemed to like me and then-- boom. She drops me for some doctor. Are all girls cruel like Nada?"

Stefan chuckled. "Boro, you are judging this as your failure, but I think this was your admirable 'success.' Think about it. You met a girl older than you, more experienced than you. You charmed her so much that she engaged with you in a passionate foreplay. She would not do it if she did not like you."

"It seemed that she liked me from the moment we shared food and that strong Dalmatian wine. Do you think she was drunk, and just played with me as with a little boy?"

"The most important the attraction between you and Nada. Wine, good food and a star studded heavens encouraged you, with ample hormones in young healthy bodies, to engage in a passionate foreplay."

"You don't think she was drunk?"

"No, as I said, the wine, food and ambiance relaxed her, lowering her inhibitions."

"Do you think, she just teased and toyed with me?"

"It does not look like that. Not having a perishable body, I cannot feel like humans feel, but sexual impulse is very strong in young, healthy people. When sexual desire fights mind and conscience, lot of times Eros wins hands down."

"Eros?"

"Eros is the god of sexual love as old Greeks believed. When I say that Eros wins, I mean that the desire for sexual intercourse overcomes all inhibitions of the person."

"Did Eros lose this time?"

"Yes, he lost the struggle with Nada`s mind and consciousness."

"You said that Eros wins easily lot of times. Why did he lose this time?"

"He did not lose the fight against your conscience and mind. Actually, he would be easy winner. He lost the struggle against Nada`s mind and conscience. He fought bravely, but was at the end overpowered."

"Are you saying that my mind and conscience would lose struggle against Eros?"

"You have very strong sexual drive. You are healthy. You just want to do it: again and again, with this girl and with that girl."

"Wow Stefan, you are describing me almost as a sex maniac. Am I that bad?"

Stefan shook his beautiful angelic head smiling: "No Boro, you are not a sex maniac, but you have strong sexual drive, characteristic of artistic and creative people."

"Are you saying that I am artistic and creative person? You are joking with me, aren`t you?"

"I told you Boro that I never joke with my protégés, because this is against my instructions. When I say something, I mean it."

"My apologies Stefan. I keep forgetting your instructions. The reason I asked you if you were joking when you said that I was creative and artistic person, is because I just don't see that in me."

Like a very patient teacher Stefan explained: "Boro, your concept of being creative and artistic is too narrow. Creativity and artistic talent are displayed in the way a person thinks, sees things and people, adding to this his personal stamp. Your creative ability is in the process of being developed. Sometimes that process goes very slowly. One cannot even notice it, as you did not notice your bodily growth. Most people do not realize their potential and abilities, down playing their capabilities and talents. My job, as your guardian angel is to guide you and help you to develop talent God gave you."

"Stefan, my head is full. You threw lot of things at me. I am not interested in making, or fixing things. How can I then be creative? As for the artistic ability, this is even worse. I struggled to get passing marks in music and in the free hand drawing. Where is that 'shy' creativity and artistic ability hiding within me? I do not see it, I do not feel it."

"God gave you gift of creativity and artistic ability. It is not fully developed yet. You and I will be working on it. I did not say; 'You must,' because you have free will. You can dismiss me and refuse to do anything with me, or you can cooperate with me in developing your God given talent. The choice is yours."

"My head is swelling; I am going to become 'Somebody.' I just have no clue what. Please tell me, what kind of 'somebody,' am I going to become?"

"Boro, I am not going to disclose any more about your talent. In proper time we will talk about that."

"In 'proper time'. When is that 'proper time?' I am very curious to know what is my talent, so that I could use it right away. Maybe, I could make some big money. Why wait? Please tell me, or at least, give me a hint."

"I won't go into details. I will give you a hint; it is something you love to do."

"I love many things: soccer, movies, and girls. Are one of those my talent?"

Stefan smiled: "Sorry Boro, I can't give you any more information. This encounter with Nada on the train and cancellation of Sunday date, and of all the future contacts was part of your growing process. I played a role in this. You can keep guessing, but I won't tell you what my role was. Nada's guardian angel was very pleased with her integrity and the fact that her conscience and mind won over Eros."

"But why didn't Nada come on Sunday and explain all this to me? Wouldn't that be fair and honest?"

"If she came, she would be under strong attack by Eros. He surely would use this opportunity to do his thing, to set both of you ablaze with the passion. Who knows, he might have overcome her conscience. This could lead to a relationship unstable and bad for both of you. She is a mature girl, ready to get married and start a family. I bet, when you dream that you got married, you treat it as a worst nightmare, don't you?"

"Yes Stefan, you are right. I love my freedom. If I ever get married, it will be after I had lot of girls and fully enjoyed myself. I agree with you that not coming on Sunday was a wise decision by Nada, because I would be very aggressive. I am still upset for missing the opportunity to love her fully and passionately. Did you spoil our Sunday meeting? Please tell me."

"I am always honest with you. I told you that I played a role in preventing yours and Nada`s meeting on Sunday, but I cannot disclose to you what my role was."

"Instructions, instructions, always instructions. Can't you bend them a little bit?"

"Are you trying to bring me into trouble? Bending instructions given to me by God? Can`t be done. We discussed lot of things this time. I am leaving. Bye for now."

Stefan kissed the sleeping teenager on the forehead, and in the next second was gone.

# Chapter 10

## *The Real Big City*

Boro fell in love with the real big city. It was a friendly city, welcoming everybody.

The same year Boro came to the real big city, government decided to build a dam on the river about twenty kilometres downstream from Boro's house in Pridraga. A huge accumulation lake would be created. Many villages, vineyards, meadows, fields, several cemeteries and churches, would be submerged in the lake.

His father never believed that the engineers would be able to do that. He was sure that water would find its way and leak out somewhere in the river valley through some caves and crevices. He was so sure, that even when the accumulation was filling and water rising right to the steps of his house, he still expected that miraculous, 'saving' leak.

It didn't leak. It held water like a steel pot. The villagers had to come to rescue Boro's mom and dad and grab the most essential things, while water was flooding their house.

Few months before the lake began filling, people had to move bones of their deceased family members from the cemetery that was to be flooded, to the new cemetery on the higher ground. Moving their dead was a sad and emotional event for people. Boro was told that when bones of his departed brothers and sister were taken out of the grave, his mom, lamented long and sadly, washing their skulls in her tears.

Boro was sad to see his birthplace murdered and buried in the watery grave. Thou he knew it would happen; he was like his father, waiting for a miracle so the darn thing would leak. His brother sent him few pictures of the rising lake waters, submerging their mill, vineyards, and house. Seeing the pictures, Boro felt sad. A rainy and foggy day just intensified his low feelings. He wondered; "Why bad things like this happen to me all the time?"

He needed somebody to talk to and spill out his complaints against the cruel faith. He did not consciously think about Stefan, but he came that night.

Boro loved to hear Stefan`s, melodious, warm and loving voice: "Hello Boro, how are you my friend?"

"Just like this rainy and foggy day," said Boro melancholically.

"You don't like fog and rain?"

"I don't know anybody that does. Farmers like good rain for their fields, but this drizzling, bone chilling rain and fog, no, nobody likes it."

"You wouldn`t get bored with the eternal sunshine and warm weather?"

"Are you kidding me Stefan? How could anybody be bored with a clear, sun soaked, warm day."

"The sunshine and warmth are cherished by most men. Rain, fog and snow are also necessary. God has created everything in perfect balance: some sunshine, some clouds, some warmth, some cold, little bit of rain, occasional thunderstorm, clearing wind, cleansing snow, moisturizing fog. All this is in balance to promote and sustain life. So is in the life of man. Good, pleasant, joyous events, take turns with sadness, anger, depression. Life is like mosaic, with squares of many different colours."

"Stefan, you said that our Creator is loving God. If He really is loving God, why didn`t He set up for man to be always happy, healthy, living in the sunshine bathed beautiful land, without working, without any stress?"

"Boro, that is a great question. You may not at this time be able to understand my answer."

"Why not?"

"The first reason is that you did not read God's Manual, nor any books of God's saints. The second reason is that you don't attend church, nor do you pray. And the last reason is that you don't live as per God's Manual."

"Wow, I did not realize I was that bad. You mentioned God's Manual, isn't that the Bible?"

"Yes, it is."

"Interesting that you call it God's Manual. Are you saying that The Bible contains all the knowledge and instructions how to be healthy, happy, rich, good looking?"

"I am saying that the Bible is a God inspired Manual for life. It instructs man how to live this short earthly episode as a training and preparation for the eternal life."

"You talk about this life as a training session, a preparation for something you called; 'eternal life."

"You heard that term 'the eternal life' before?"

"Oh yes, many times, but I never gave much attention to it."

"Why not?"

"I thought it was just a meaningless word to persuade people to go to church and give money."

"What does 'eternal life' mean to you?"

"It means: the life that never ends. I believe this is impossible, because everything in the nature has limited life. Every life ends with death. How can dead bones and a handful of dust have 'eternal life'?

"Thank you Boro for explaining your understanding of the eternal life."

"Stefan, I am afraid that even if I did everything that I am not doing now, that is; read God's Manual and other books of God's saints, lived a good, clean life, prayed to God daily and obeyed His commandments; I would not understand the meaning of the eternal life, even if I sincerely believed in it. Is that possible?"

"No mortal man can understand what eternal life is. It is important that people believe, that in some form, they will continue their life as personalities after bodily death. I am sure that your mom and baba firmly believed in the eternal life, having no clues of the details. It was sufficient for them just to trust God, believe in Him, striving to live a life of the faith and virtues, and God would grant them this big reward. Just like a small child believes his mom and dad, they had a childlike faith in God. That kind of faith is very dear to God. Indeed, very few men are blessed with a childlike faith."

"This is heavy stuff for me to understand Stefan. I have no childlike faith. I doubt anything that I can't hear, see, touch, or smell. That is the only life I know, care for and believe in. Why spoil my life by thinking about death? What good is thinking about it? It is the same for one who believes in the eternal life, and the one who does not believe in it. Both of them will have the same end; being buried six feet under. Only old people think about death and eternal life, because death is close to them, 'just around the corner'. Why me? I am young. I need to enjoy my life, not to spoil it with morbid thoughts."

"You are talking like most of people of your generation, who see themselves as only the flesh. They see nothing beyond that, relying exclusively on their senses to guide them through the life. I am sure that you will be changing your attitude, and your spiritual eyes (to your great joy) will begin to open. The seed your mom and baba have sown into your soul will start growing and bringing forth the fruit. The talent given to you by God will start more and more to manifest itself. I am not going to attempt to convince you what you should believe and how to live. You are going to convince yourself. I am just going to help you with that."

"I am surprised Stefan that you did not criticize me and threatened me with strict punishment unless I correct my belief and my living. You are a very permissive and liberal guardian angel. Are you sure this agrees with your instructions?"

Stefan smiled contently. "Oh yes, it agrees perfectly with my instructions. I told you several times that I always follow my instructions. We went a bit off the question you asked me."

"Question, what question? I forgot."

"You asked a very reasonable and sensible question: "If God is a loving God, why didn`t He create man to always be happy, healthy, without any stress and worry, living always in the warm sunshine?"

"Oh yes, yes, I remember now. Why didn`t God do that? Instead, man has to toil and to struggle just to survive."

"I told you that no angel or man is to question Gods providence. He decided to create man with free will, not a robot. God created Adam, the very first man, to live a perfect, happy life in the beautiful Garden of Eden. He was to be forever young, without stress, without pain, living in perfect surrounding."

"What happened with Adam? Is he still in the Garden of Eden?"

"No Boro, he is not there anymore."

"Why not?"

"Because God created him with free will, he chose to disobey God, who kicked him out of the Garden of Eden. Adam became subject to aging, sickness and pain. He had to work the land to feed himself and his family. Eventually, he died. Men are his descendants and they are subjected to the same fate as their forefather Adam; sickness, pain, old age, and at the end, death."

"Wow, Adam must have screwed up badly, for God to kick him out of that garden."

"God told Adam that he 'would surely die,' if he disobeyed God`s warning. Exercising his free will Adam did just that."

"This story about the Garden of Eden and Adam, seems to me like a fairy tale; too fantastic to be true."

"I appreciate that it is hard for you to believe in this. With time your spiritual eyes will begin to open and you will be amazed of the change in your faith and the attitude. Perhaps, we need to leave this topic for later. Let's see what bothers you now."

"Oh Stefan, I will miss my Pridraga so much: the meadows, swimming in the river, crayfish in the creek, playing soccer on the field near the river. I would like to see it once more."

"Would you like to see Pridraga and your village right now?"

"I have no money for a train ticket. I cannot afford to get the time off from the school."

"Do not worry about money and time. Make yourself comfortable under my wing, and we will leave immediately for Pridraga. No money needed. No time off from the school."

"I flew with you before, but I am still scared that I could fall off, and hurt myself."

Stefan laughed; "Here is this glass gondola and strong ropes holding it to my wing. Are you convinced now that you are safe and secured there."

"Well, it looks good, but are you still a good and reliable flyer?"

"Rest assured Boro that I am an excellent flyer. How else could I fly all the way from heaven down to your room? As for the experience, I have a lot of it, thousands of years of flying time. Trust me and just hop in."

Boro got up from his bed and, walked into a beautiful glass gondola under Stefan's right wing. A pleasant surprise awaited him there. There was a chair lined with the material like silk, but even finer and softer. It had soft rich cushions on both ends for reclining. There was also a table made out of the earth colour wood. In the middle of the table stood a beautiful glass vase full of the sweet smelling flowers. Besides the vase was a large glass bowl full of fruit: figs, bananas, persimmon, apples, and pears. It looked like all the fruits that grow on earth were there. Boro was impressed with all this richness and decor.

"Thank you Stefan. I am surprised and pleased with this abundance and beauty. How did you arrange all of this instantly?"

"Boro, you are now in my world. We are not chained by the time and space like you are. Anything is possible here, providing it is within our instructions."

"Where did you get such a beautiful fruit? I have never seen anything like this before. So perfect looking and such a pleasant aroma."

"We have lot of rich gardens in the heaven, with any kind of the fruit the heart desires. Shall we go? Do you want me to fly man's speed or angelic speed?"

"Fly man's speed please. I would like to take a look down on the land, and I will taste these fruits. They look so tempting and appetizing."

Jokingly, Stefan said: "Mister Boro, here is your captain Stefan. We are ready to take off for flight to Pridraga. We expect the flight to last, 'a blink of an eye.' The weather is always perfect on our flights. The temperature is always perfect, whatever you like. Please enjoy your flight and your snack. No, you do not need to fasten your seat belts. There are none. Not necessary in heavenly flights."

Boro decided to taste the fruit from the heavenly gardens. First, he tried persimmons. It was delicious, juicy, emanating some pleasant heavenly aroma. He tried grapes, figs, apples, pears, plums. He was afraid that he would spoil his stomach thinking; "Am I ever going to get huge diarrhea." But, it looked as if heavenly fruit was quite different then earthly. No matter how much he ate, he did not feel his stomach full. Encouraged by that discovery, he tried almost all the fruits from the glass bowl.

Soon, they were over Pridraga, which did not exist anymore. Boro's beautiful Pridraga, his stone house, the mill, meadows, Pridraga Creek, river, vineyards, fields, orchards; everything was buried in the dark, deep watery grave.

"Would you like to go into your house?" Asked Stefan.

"What is the matter with you Stefan. It is dark, cold, and deep water. We would drown in this darn lake."

Stefan shook his head: "I have no body, so I can't drown. As for you, do not worry, you are not in your time and space. You are now as safe as me." Saying this, Stefan landed softly on the water and the next moment they were on the entrance to Boro's house.

Boro did not feel any cold, wetness, or fear of the depth, but had a strong feeling of discomfort. They stepped into the house. All stone walls were still standing, except the gable on the east side, it was half torn down. Inside walls were still standing; plaster from the walls was gone, bare bricks stood. Boro first went into the room where he slept. There, in that corner stood baba's bed. She died there. In the other corner was the bed where Boro and

Dana slept. That is where Stefan came to him for the first time. There was the kitchen, and then mom and dad`s bedroom. In the left corner stood the bed where Boro was born. That is where he slept with his mom, and listened to her prayers. Boro cried in the depth of the accumulation lake, faced with a huge amount of death, darkness and abandonment. He had enough of it. He wanted to get out of this watery tomb.

"Let's go Stefan. I have enough of this darkness and death."

Without a word, Stefan instantly got out of the house and in a blink of an eye they were again above the water. "Where to now?"

"I want to see my school and village."

"I suppose, you want me to go slow."

"Please go slowly. I want to see the road I went to school, the bush I took my cows and sheep to pasture, and my school."

"No problem," replied Stefan, gliding slowly above the dark waters of the lake.

Boro saw the road which was already hard to recognize, being destroyed by the water.This is the spot where the road was squeezed between two hills. This is the place he feared the most, because if wolves were to attack him, he couldn`t escape. Shortly, they abandoned the lake, following the road leading up to the village. The road above the lake was not in much better shape. Leading into the lake, it was not travelled nor maintained any more. "It was a dead road," said Boro to himself. Soon, they were over Boro `s old school.

"Do you want to go in?" Asked Stefan.

"No, will just see it from above," said Boro.

The school was in rough shape. Junk was scattered all over the school yard; rocks, plastic bottles, rags. The fence around the school was half torn, with several steel posts missing. "This is a dying school in a dying village. Lets go see the village," said boro sadly. Lot of houses were in disrepair and abandoned. Many villagers left after the lake flooded the river valley, vineyards, meadows and the best fields.

"This is a dying village," conclude Boro sadly.

At the end of the village, Stefan asked; "Where to now?"

"I saw enough of this dying village. Please let's go back, go angel speed."

"Yes sir," nodded Stefan, and in the next moment Boro was out of the glass gondola and in his bed.

"This is amazing. How could you arrive instantly from such a distance? Are your wings that powerful?"

"First time I visited you Boro, you asked me about my wings. Do you recall what I told you?"

"I forgot. Please tell me."

"I told you that I really don't use the wings to fly, but that if you insisted to see my wings, I would gladly show them to you. In our time and space moving from one place to another, is not constrained by the earth laws. It would be useless to go now into 'how' I move so quickly from place 'A' to place 'B'. Later on, you may be able to understand more about this."

"I am just curious Stefan. Are you able to travel as fast as light?"

"Speed of light is irrelevant for me. I can travel at any speed my instructions allow."

"Wow, that is amazing. Please give me a hint; can you travel twice the speed of light?"

"I will give you more than a hint: In heaven, we don't have the concept of the speed."

"I just cannot understand that. It is beyond my brain."

"Boro, you are not alone. No man can understand this by his mind. I think we talked enough this time."

"Stefan, thank you very much for treating me to the heavenly feast, and for taking me to see my Pridraga. You are a great guardian angel."

"It is a part of my job Boro. I am touched by your gratitude and compliments. Together, we will achieve great things to God's glory. Bye now my friend."

Stefan bent down and kissed Boro gently on the forehead. The next second, he was gone.

# CHAPTER 11

## *Things are hard to Grasp*

During summer break, Boro went to his parents' new house built in the small town near Pridraga.

That year he got his first girlfriend. She was student from the big city coming to spend the summer with her aunt in the little town. They saw each other almost every evening. Though the same age as Boro, Rada had significantly more experience in love matters than Boro.

The summer ended and Boro went back to school in the real big city. He wrote Rada a love letter full of tenderness and emotions. In a few weeks, she replied: "This past summer you were not enough of a man to make me happy."

Boro was dumbfounded. "I thought she was happy with all the kissing, hugging and poetry I recited her. Looks like she expected 'the real thing.' Why didn`t I do it? I was a real chicken, and she told me that."

He suffered for a while from a bruised ego and self-esteem that went dangerously low. Luckily, young healthy body helped him to heal that wound, forgetting Rada and paying attention to other girls.

One day Boro was coming home from the school on the afternoon train, used mostly by students commuting to school in the real big city and workers going to their jobs. When he came onto the train, he was not keen to talk with his buddies. He found a place in the corner of the coach, sat down and snoozed. When he got up to exit at his station he noticed a big red book on the luggage rack opposite his seat. Curiously, he reached for the book. It was nice hard cover book, evidently well used, but still in good shape. He read the name of the book: "Holy Scripture of the Old and New Testament."

"Who might have forgotten this book? Not any students, they don't bother with the Bible. Not any workers, they either play cards, or sleep. Priest? I have not seen one on this train in years. Should I take it? What for? I have more interesting books to read, lot of better ways to spend my time."

The train was stopping, Boro had to get out. He put the book back on the luggage shelf and went to exit. All of a sudden, just before reaching the door, he turned around, went to the compartment, grabbed the big red book, and jumped out of the train. While walking home, he opened his unusually obtained book. He felt a certain respect towards it, remembering prayers of his baba and mom and reverence they had hearing or saying the words: "Holy Scripture" and "Holy Gospel."

Curiously, he opened on the first page. In big, bold letters it said: "The First book of Moses, Genesis." Walking on the street, he read; "In the beginning God created the heavens and the earth. The earth was without form and void." He had to stop reading because he was close to his cousin`s house. He put the book behind his school books, knowing that his cousin and her husband would not be pleased seeing him reading that "priestly propaganda." They would tell him: "Don't waste your time reading that stuff. It won't bring bread to your table. Study your school books and become a gentleman, an educated man."

To Boro`s surprise, Stefan appeared that night in all his angelic glory and majesty. "Oh Stefan, pleasure to see you again. How are you?"

"Always good, and how are you Boro?"

"I am well, but today I was very much absent minded. I was just day dreaming."

"Anything else unusual happened to you recently."

"I found this thick, red hard cover book on the train, the Bible. Somebody must have forgotten it. I didn't intend to take it because I had no use for it. If my friends knew I read the Bible, they would ridicule me."

"And despite that, you took the book?"

"When I read the title, it reminded me of my baba and mom teaching me prayers. I recalled how reverently they pronounced the words 'The Holy Gospel,' and 'The Holy Scripture." It was as if somebody told me: "This is not an ordinary book, it is a special book. Take it.""

"This is a great sign that the seed sown will not wither, but in right time will germinate, and grow."

"What do you mean by that seed and germinating? You speak like my Biology teacher."

"Remember Boro what I was telling you about the seed of faith that your baba and mom sowed into your soul when you were little boy?"

"Sowed the seed of faith into my soul? As if my soul was a field, and my baba and mom were the sowers, walked on it, after it has been ploughed, and sowed 'the seed of the faith,' into the furrows of my soul."

"Boro, you have described it beautifully, poetically, and similarly to the way our Lord Jesus Christ told it in the Parable of the Sower."

"Is that story in this big red book?"

"Yes, it is."

"I don't think this is very exciting book."

"You will be surprised when you read Holy Book and see how exciting it is."

"Really? I doubt it, but when I have nothing better to do I might open it for few minutes."

"It is important that you begin opening it and reading it. Eventually, you will want to read it, because it will give you great pleasure. Just give it a time."

"You really think Stefan that I would fall in love with this big red book and read it as eagerly as I read fairy tales, when I was in public school. How can you compare wonderful stories about giants, magic, Snow White, Cinderella, with a boring religious book?"

"You will eventually enjoy reading the Holy Bible as much as you loved to read fairy tales."

"When I was a little kid I did not question the veracity of the fairy tales. Cinderella had a fairy God mother, who created for her a beautiful coach out of a pumpkin and transformed several mice into her coach drivers, servants and horses. I just accepted it without questioning, because it was so likeable, entertaining and an interesting story. Never stopped and asked myself; 'Hold on, why are you reading this fantasy? It is not the truth. It is impossible to transform a mouse into a man, or pumpkin into a coach."

"The Holy Bible talks of God`s message to man. The events and stories in the Bible are told by the writers of the Bible, inspired by the Holy Spirit. The miracles described in the holy Bible are God`s intervention, a temporary suspension of natural order."

"I already read a few verses on the first page. I was curious what the Bible was all about."

"What did you read?"

"I read on page one: "In the beginning God created the heavens and the earth. The earth was void and without form and darkness was upon the face of the deep; and the Spirit of God was moving over the face of the waters."

"Were you confused by this narrative of the first day of the creation?"

"Confused? That is an understatement. It sounded more fantastic than any fairy tale I read."

"Really, why?"

"I doubt any man would believe this description credible, nor would he understand it."

"Boro, you are right; men could not understand this by their mind. Let me remind you what I told you about us angels. Since we have no body like you, we have no mind like you. Our mind works different than yours."

"How can that be? Isn`t mind the same of angel and man?"

"What do you consider the mind is Boro?"

"The mind is an immaterial entity, that directs the entity it belongs to perform certain actions.

"Plants, animals and men, have bodies peculiar to them?"

"Yes, of course."

"Do you think that the plants, animals and man, having bodies all have the minds?"

"The plants having minds? Perhaps some of the more advanced animals like the apes? How can plants have the mind? They have no brain."

"I have no brain, but I have a mind. Doesn't that prove that you don't need to have the type of the brain man and animals have, in order to have a functioning mind?"

"Your mind is different from the earthly concept of the mind."

"You concluded then that the mind can exist without a kind of animal/human brain?"

"I guess I did."

"Since animals, men and angels have a mind, couldn't you conclude that plants have their 'minds,' regardless how primitive and basic they are?"

"How my rose bush displays its 'mind'?"

Stefan smiled, shaking his head: "Are you trying to confuse me Boro, by asking me such a tough questions?"

"How could I, an ignorant earthling, confuse you, an angel of God?"

"That was a friendly, well intentioned joke. Sometimes, guardian angels get a bit unnerved by the behaviour of their protégés."

"Really? That surprises me. I thought you were always in control of your protégés life, and since you know even their thoughts, nothing they do, can surprise, or confuse you."

"Only God is always in control."

"Stefan, the more I talk with you the more amazed I am. We went away from my question; 'How does a rose bush display its 'mind?"

"Sorry Boro, I was not evading your question. Sometimes, one question gives birth to another question and we go off the topic.

God did not give plants and animals of His Spirit, nor did He create them with a free will, but with the impulses they follow to live and to procreate. Your rose bush's 'mind' is expressed by the impulses God built into it. It displays its 'mind' by spreading its roots into the soil drawing water and minerals, and by using sunlight and air grows its stem, leaves, branches and sweet smelling roses. In the fall it displays its 'mind' by withdrawing the life giving juice from the branches and depositing it into the roots, for winter hibernation. Its 'mind' gets rid of leaves, causing them to lose the colour, shrivel, and fall off to serve as the fertilizer."

"Thank you Stefan that was an interesting explanation. We were taught in school that 'mother nature' has set up laws for itself. Everything on the earth must obey natural laws, without exception."

"What were you taught about the nature? What is nature? Who sets the laws that nature obeys?"

"The nature is everything around us; earth, sun, stars, moon, sky, clouds, plants, animals and men. Nature is the boss. It gives itself the laws which everything in it obeys."

"Interesting! Did you learn that this thing, 'everything,' the nature, created itself?"

"Sure, it created itself. This is a normal and logical conclusion. How else could it happen?"

Stefan laughed jovially. "You were taught: Nature is everything existing living and nonliving. It created itself, giving the laws to itself, which are obeyed without exception. Is that a good summary Boro?"

"That is exactly as we were taught and I believe it is the truth, because all other theories and explanations are unscientific and illogical."

"Boro, even if you have not yet read the Holy Bible, you might come to a conclusion that some of these things you were taught in school were pretty ridiculous. I forced myself not to laugh at such naive and silly theories. Evidently, the Enemy succeeded greatly in sowing tares into man's mind and heart."

"I am surprised Stefan you hold these scientific explanations naive and silly. To me, they seem logical and reasonable. Why do you say these are silly and naive teachings?"

"You said you were taught that the nature created itself. Does that sound logical and reasonable to you that something created itself?"

"Our smart people, the scientists figured it out. I cannot explain it, and I don't understand how mother nature created itself. There is no other logical, scientific and reasonable explanation."

"You have big faith in your 'smart men,' the scientists. Don't you question their theory?"

"Who am I to question it?"

"God gave you the reason; you can figure out that some things are possible, some are impossible."

"I am not sure what are you getting at Stefan.?"

"You told me that you had a toy called Mico?"

"Oh yes my little wooden buddy. What about him?"

"Who created Mico?"

"Created? I did not create him. I carved him out of a piece of wood."

"How did you create Mico?"

"You know that Stefan. I explained it before. Why do you ask again?"

"Yes, of course I know, but I love to hear it again."

"I just used a knife and carved him out of a piece of wood."

"Why did you do all this work to make a little wooden toy?"

"My house was not in the village. No kids to play with. I was lonely. So I decided to make me a buddy to play with and to talk to."

"You decided to make company for yourself, a friend?"

"Yes."

"But how did you decide to make him?"

"My friend Pero was sitting on the same bench with me in school. I tried to make Mico to look like him. Pero had a real big nose and long thin legs, so did Mico."

"You had a picture in your mind what Mico should look like, you found a piece of wood, got the knife, did some carving and your buddy Mico was born."

"That is exactly how it happened."

"Was Mico good company for you?"

"He was my real buddy. I talked to him and pretended that he was talking back to me. Sometimes, we quarreled."

"You made, or you could say created Mico?"

"Well, I guess I did make him," said Boro proudly.

"What would you say to someone who would try to convince you that your wooden buddy Mico did not need anybody to create, or make him, that he created himself?"

"I would say that the guy was crazy, and needed to see the doctor urgently."

"You would tell him he was crazy for trying to convince you that Mico created himself?"

"Any normal person knows that a wooden doll cannot create itself. It is required that something, or somebody higher creates it."

"Higher than itself?"

"I found that piece of wood, which eventually Mico was made out of. I was 'higher' than that piece of wood, because I had higher life, energy, and mind. That is why I was able to make Mico."

"When you carved Mico out of that piece of wood, did you give him laws on how to behave?"

"Are you kidding me Stefan? How could I give laws of behaviour to a wooden doll? He could not hear, see, nor reason. I could make all kind of fancy laws, 'do`s' and 'don'ts', but it would be a waste of time."

"Are you suggesting Boro that one given the laws, must have the reason, that is to be a conscious being, to understand the laws and to be able to observe them?"

"Yes, that is what I am saying Stefan."

"What about the law giver?"

"He must also have the reason that is to be a conscious being and have the ability to create, give and enforce the laws."

"Based on what you just said, do you think is it logical and reasonable to believe that nature created itself, and gave laws of its operation to itself?"

"I say that both of these beliefs are silly, naive and baseless. No entity can create itself. The law giver and the law receiver must both have reason, and be conscious beings in order to give the laws and to understand and observe the laws. Nature has no reason, it is not a conscious being, therefore it could not be a law giver, or a law receiver."

"Great explanation Boro. Are you clear now about 'mother nature' and its laws?"

"Clearer, but still have questions. What about these natural laws? How could nature receive them, since it is not a conscious being? Who gave nature these laws?"

"We concluded that 'mother nature,' being an unconscious entity could not receive the laws, but it is evident that it behaves as if it follows certain laws; in procreation, growth, life and death of living organisms, in weather and all other facets of life. Since these are not 'the laws,' what are they?"

"I cannot answer that Stefan. I need your help."

"I will help. The natural law is nothing but the impulses and instructions God built into the nature. God has not given laws to nature, because it is just an unconscious entity. The only laws given by God are to conscious being; man. These are God`s moral laws."

"What are moral laws?"

"These are the highest laws of the universe. God gave them to men through the prophets in the Old Testament and through His Son Jesus Christ in the New Testament."

"Is there any connection between men`s violation of God`s moral laws and the behaviour of nature?"

"God allows nature`s reaction to men`s transgression of moral laws."

"Unbelievable! Are you saying God allows tornadoes, floods, droughts, earthquakes and other natural disasters on the mankind for their transgression of His moral laws?"

"Yes, Boro, that is exactly what I am saying."

"Wow, if I say this to people, they would consider me a nuts, a crazy religious fanatic."

"I know that Boro. The modern mankind sees 'mother nature' as almost an independent god that does its own thing, unrelated to the mankind`s moral behaviour. On its own whim produces earthquakes, floods, droughts, pestilences. Even lot of people who 'believe' in God, don't believe He has anything to do with 'mother nature's' doings."

"It seems to me Stefan that men removed God from any role in the nature. Why is that?"

"The Enemy is never idle. You were taught that man is part of the nature, which created itself. It follows that the nature is your mother. That is why you address it: 'mother nature.' Is that right?"

"Yes, we do call it 'mother nature' because it gave us birth, through our parents."

"Are you saying that nature gave birth to your complete personality?"

"Of course it did. It could not have given me a partial birth. What are you getting at Stefan?"

"Is Boro just a visible body?"

"Is this a trick question Stefan? What you see, that is it, the whole me."

"But what about the invisible part of you? Your thoughts, emotions, your soul?"

"My thoughts and emotions are product of my brain and nervous system. I don't know what soul is and even if there is such thing. Perhaps what is called the soul is our thoughts and emotions together."

"Do you remember Boro when you were a little boy, your mom and baba prayed for the souls of their departed, 'To be in the Kingdom of heaven with God."

"Yes, I remember quite well. Both my mom and my baba believed in that thing you call 'soul.' If you asked them; 'What is the soul, how does it look, has anybody heard it, seen it, measured it? Where is soul located in the body?' They would cross themselves reverently and say: 'We don't know anything about soul, but God does. That is good enough for us.' Us kids joked with baba: 'Hey baba, tell us the secret, where is your soul?' Baba would thump several times in the middle of her chest and say: 'Here, my soul is here."

"Your mom and baba prayed for the souls of your dead family members. What does that tell you about their belief about the soul?"

"They believed that soul survives the death of the body."

"Can we conclude then, that the soul is united with the body as long as the man is alive?"

"But there is no proof for the existence of soul. We were taught that was just a superstition, a priestly propaganda, to brainwash people."

"What kind of proof are you talking about?"

"The proof for the existence of soul, would be If it was registered with our human senses; eyes, ears, smell, touch, or proved to exist by the scientific methods?"

"Let me answer by giving you an example: You are standing in the middle of a room in total darkness. All of a sudden, something hits you on the head and knocks you down. Do you know what hit you?"

"I don't know. I just felt the effect of that something, or somebody's action."

"You have no clue about this force. You just felt the action of this unknown force."

"I agree."

"Couldn't we conclude that magnetism, gravity and electricity are the forces that 'hit you' from 'the pitch darkness.' You cannot see them, but you experience their effects?"

"Yes, I have to admit that."

"Couldn't we conclude that there are other forces invisible and really unknown to men that 'rule' man's world, 'from the unknown,' but men feel and notice their effects?"

"I am still not clear where are you leading me with your questions?"

"I am always leading you to learn the truth."

"What kind of the truth are you leading me to learn?"

"The truth is that you were created a complex being. Your visible part, your body and your invisible part your soul, are in a way unknown to you interconnected. You don't see your soul, but you feel its effects; love, emotions, free will, sense of right and wrong, yearning for immortality. Just as the other invisible forces rule the world, your soul rules your world."

"Wow, this is quite shocking to me. I listened to all your conclusions but still, my reason is still refusing to accept it. It is shouting: 'proof, proof, proof.'"

"It is normal that your reason is refusing to accept the truth about you being created a complex being, a soul living in the body, like in a rented apartment. Your reason is jealous. It wants to be always the judge, the ruler, the decision maker. It wants to be the exclusive channel of acquiring the knowledge and information about everything. That is why it rejects what it cannot comprehend on its own."

"Reason is the product of my brain. Isn`t it logical to conclude that my brain is the only organ processing information from the outside?"

"Don`t you believe you could acquire the knowledge through your soul?"

"What is the role of soul, in acquiring the knowledge?"

"I think we talked too much this time. We got to be careful even in feeding you too much of the spiritual food. Digest what we talked about, so next time we meet, your soul and your mind will be fresh and ready for more. Is this fine with you?"

"Yes, my head and my soul are tired, cannot absorb any more. They need a break."

"We will continue next time. Please read that big book with the hard red covers you found on the train. Don`t start with the first page, start with the Gospel by Saint John. Read as much as you can."

Stefan kissed Boro on the cheek and the next second was gone.

Boro turned on the other side mumbling something in his sleep. He was trying to catch up the last drops of the early morning sleep, before the alarm clock wakes him up. He had to catch the six am train.

## Chapter 12

## *High Learning*

After completing grade twelve Boro had to decide what to study at the University. He narrowed down his choices to medicine or engineering. 'Doctor Boro' would sound glamorous. He could get any girl he wanted. Good money, people give you envelopes with cash. Everybody bows to you. The problem was; he was afraid of seeing dead people, did not like the sight of blood and being a bit clumsy, he thought he would be bad doctor. He chose Engineering. He applied and was accepted at the Electrical Engineering faculty in the real big city.

That year he went to his parents' home for summer break. He had more confidence in approaching girls. He was tall, lean, muscular young man, very romantic and excitable. That summer he kept frequently falling in love. He saw something beautiful and sexy in most of the girls he met. He was always polite and respectful. These were all innocent platonic relationships. They went for walks, swimming, and movies. The benefit was that he was perfecting his kissing skills and the art of talking with girls. Girls were conservative at that time and in that part of the world. Most of them kept their virginity as the biggest part of their dowry to their "prince charming," at the consummation of their marriage.

Summer passed quickly. He had to go to back to the real big city to start his Engineering studies. He was excited about the train ride. "Who am I going to meet this time on the train? Maybe, true love of my life."

## A Kingdom to Buy

To his surprise, he met the wife of his distant cousin. Pera was a plump brunette of medium height, about fourteen years older than Boro. She was living with her husband and their two children in a village on a small farm. She was a simple woman, with only a grade four education. She did what farmers wife supposed to do; keep the house, took care of children, fed the livestock, cleaned stables, washed, and cooked. This was the first time Boro was alone with Pera. As they were sitting beside each other in the compartment, Boro felt her ample thighs. Yes, she was his cousin's wife, but she was also a sexy woman.

A little voice whispered into Boro's conscience: "Don't be a pig. She is your cousin's wife. She is older than you, almost could be your mom. Behave respectfully as a good cousin. Expel these, ugly, sinful thoughts out of your head."

"Good side" was quickly over powered by the lust growing within his body to 'have' this plump, curvaceous, farm women.

"Don't do it" message, was quickly squashed, by the fire of a rising desire.

Boro thought about his encounter on the train with Nada a few years ago. "Incomparable," he concluded. "This is 'forbidden fruit,' which makes it much more exciting and tempting."

They initially talked about regular stuff, families, her children, and his school. Slowly, conversation was becoming more intimate and flirting. Boro suggested: "Let's go out into the corridor to get some fresh air. It is such a beautiful night."

"Sure, that's a very good idea," agreed Pera, flashing happy smile, showing her beautiful, perfect white teeth.

They leaned at an open window. Boro noticed her curves under light summer dress. "She is very voluptuous, like Venus," he thought.

He was surprised when she told him that her husband rarely kissed her.

"Do you miss kissing?" asked Boro, his heart dancing in his chest.

"Oh very much," replied Pera. "Sometimes, just a kiss and few tender words would make me happy."

Not believing his ears, Boro whispered into her ear: "Would you like me to kiss you?"

Her answer was the most wonderful music to his ears; "Would I ever my beautiful boy."

They went to a poorly lit corner near the passage connecting the wagons. It was hard to see who was more eager to engage in aggressive and arousing petting. Pera was such a willing and active participant that a thought flashed in Boro`s mind: "My God, she behaves as if she was a never kissed virgin, not as a middle aged women, married over fourteen years with two children. What am I getting into?"

Repeated warnings and protests from his conscience were quickly dismissed by the burning lust: "Keep quiet, you old fashioned thing. This is life; enjoyment galore, unsurpassed. Nothing is better than this. You have no chance of moralizing now. Do it later."

And they went eagerly at each other bodies, caressing, hugging and kissing. "She is a great kisser," thought Boro. "Perhaps she lied to me; she must have had some kissing experience, with somebody else."

After a very long kiss, Boro asked; "You are an excellent kisser, who taught you?"

Pera answered by hugging him for another kiss; "You are my teacher, my beautiful teacher," she said lovingly, kissing him gently.

"No other teachers?" asked Boro with a note of jealousy in his voice.

"Only you."

"Wow, you learn fast," said Boro with a slight sarcastic smile.

"This is natural. If you like someone, you don't need to learn how to kiss or make love. It comes naturally, like breathing."

Next thing he said, surprised Boro hearing his own trembling voice; "Would you make love to me?"

Putting her head on his chest, she said with her voice dripping with the passion: "Yes, my beautiful boy, I would eagerly, with all my heart."

A mix of crazy emotions hit Boro. His male ego felt like Mount Everest: "I am becoming real man. I am going to lose my virginity. She is going to give herself to me. I can`t believe it. But, this is not right what we are doing. She is my cousin's wife!"

His weak conscience was trying to do its job, but was slapped down by the huge giant of the burning lust, screaming: "Shut up, and go to sleep. Don't you see how big and strong I am. Nothing, nothing can stop me from reaching my goal. I am winning."

Then came the tunnel, first the short one. They smiled big happy smile, and as soon as the darkness enveloped them, continued passionate petting.

Pera had something Boro liked on women; nice, rounded, ample buttocks. Passionate, deep, moist kisses were getting them hot and out of breath. He felt her big breasts, still quite firm, on his chest. They were both breathing heavily as if suffering from a bout of asthma.

Darn tunnel came to end too soon. They stopped and straightened their clothing. Pera combed her hair. They were happy, red faced and exhausted from swollen emotions. Pera looked like a satisfied women in love. She squeezed Boro`s hand: "This was the nicest ten minutes in my life. It was wonderful."

Boro was very proud of himself. He kissed Pera on the chest saying: "I wish the darn tunnel was longer."

"Don`t worry my beauty, we will find a more private place," said Pera.

Boro was eager to make love to her right there, but people were everywhere. They had to suffer and wait.

They repeated passionate petting in the longer tunnel, more gently and with less crazy lust. Pera was getting off the train soon. She went to the washroom, washed her face and combed her hair. She was again just a happy farm woman. They behaved now as two respectful cousins. It was getting brighter on the East. The new day was being born on the Pannonia plains.

"When am I going to see you again?" asked Boro.

"You would want to see me soon my beauty?"

"Yesterday," smiled Boro.

She smiled seductively: "You want me that bad?"

"Worse than that, how soon can we meet?"

"I have to go to Petrovo to visit my cousin. I will visit you and your cousin's family in the evening. Perhaps, you could make me company going to the train station, because I am afraid of dark. Could you be my guide?"

"Yes, I will be your guide and protector, but when are you going to come?" asked Boro impatiently.

"How about in a month. I was away for three weeks. My house is probably very dirty?"

"A month? I am going to burst waiting for you. Can't you come sooner?"

"How about in two weeks. Please understand; I have to take care of my husband, children, house, livestock, and farm work."

"Fine, fine, you busy farmers wife, will see you in two weeks."

"After that I hope you are going to visit me soon. Promise."

"I promise solemnly," said Boro.

He helped Pera with her luggage. Saying good bye to her, he discreetly slapped her right where those two lovely buttocks join.

She jokingly slapped his hand "Don't touch, you bad boy."

Boro watched her walking away, enjoying her buttocks, dancing up and down under light summer dress, as if teasing him. Feeling very tired, not sleeping a minute the previous night he went to rest in his compartment.

Pera came as she promised, in two weeks. His cousin greeted her warmly. Boro, Pera and his cousin enjoyed some bread, cheese and strong Turkish coffee while engaging in a bit of family gossip. After the darkness Pera said that she had to visit her cousin before catching train back to her village. She asked Boro to show her a short cut to her cousin's house. Boro gladly agreed.

He was on pins and needles the whole time during Pera's visit, trying to stay cool and calm. Inside, a volcano was building up, ready to erupt. Pera got up kissed his cousin and thanked her for her hospitality.

The short cut was leading through a corn field. Corn was taller than Boro. As soon as they passed the first houses, he took

Pera's hand leading her into the cornfield. Going through the cornfield, they went crazily at each other's body. Few steps and they would stop and 'attack' each other. Her mouth smelt like a ripe watermelon. She put this time some cheap, but provocative perfume.

"Women in prime, hungry for love and tenderness is in my arms. Unbelievable," thought Boro. 'Am I dreaming?' When he judged that they were far enough from the pathway, he 'wrestled' Pera to the ground amongst the corns.

Almost in a trance, loosing concept of time, carried by the fire of the passion and the lust, Boro realized his long-time dream; he lost his virginity. He became a 'man.' When 'the storm' passed, they lay on the ground among the corns, tired and happy. They turned towards each other and kissed gently, caringly.

"You are my first. You are a beautiful woman. I love you. You are my sexy farm woman," whispered Boro.

She gently kissed him on the cheek "And you are my beauty, my lover. My first love."

Boro was very proud of himself. "Was I good? This was my first time. I was a virgin. Please tell me. Teach me."

Pera laughed heartily. "Give me a nice kiss and I will tell you."

Boro obliged putting his arms around her and holding her tight against himself, kissed her gently.

They repeated the whole thing with less passion, but with much more gentleness. At the end, they both lay happy and tired. Pera really had to go this time. They got up, tidied, and were again an eighteen year old young man and a middle aged farm woman.

"When am I going to see you again?" asked Boro.

She smiled invitingly. "You will see me when you come to visit us. It is not nice to forget your cousins. You should come more often. You are going to like it there: Fresh air, good food, and people that love to see you."

"I will visit my dear relatives as much as I can. I want to say 'bye' to somebody," whispered Boro.

Pera was surprised. "To whom?"

Boro tapped gently on Pera's crotch whispering: "Bye love, will visit you soon."

Pera laughed spanking him jokingly on the hand, "You are a fast learner. She will eagerly wait for you."

After coming back to his room Boro felt tired, happy and guilty. He went straight to bed.

He was not surprised when he sensed Stefan besides his bed. This time, he covered his head with the blanket, hoping that Stefan would disappear, as he did at the end of their encounters. It didn't help. His hand went on its own and uncovered his head.

"Oh Stefan, it's you. Could we postpone this meeting? I am just not up to it this time."

"Boro, if you want me to go away, I will leave. However, as your guardian angel, I would fail in my duty if I don't make it clear to you that we need to talk pretty soon."

"How soon is 'pretty soon?'"

"If there is a problem it is the best to solve it without delay, before it grows into a much bigger problem, which may be harder, or even impossible to solve. The Enemy's most potent weapon is to induce man to delay doing good things. 'Solve the problem but not today –tomorrow. Repent, but not today – tomorrow. Pray, but not today-- tomorrow.' And tomorrow comes the same sneaky suggestion of 'do it tomorrow.' Lot of the time that 'tomorrow' becomes 'never.'"

"Stefan, I am not talking never, or in few years, but just few days, until I get a bit of rest."

"You need to become aware of the events of the last few days, and to get clear in your head."

"How do I become aware and clear in my head?"

"Your soul is stained by the actions of your body. You need to make an effort to remove that stain."

"I am not sure Stefan what do you want me to do?"

"I am asking you to discuss with me the most recent events in your life."

"I agree."

"No hesitation?"

"No, let's talk."

"Relax Boro. This is not a court. Please see me as a friend trying to help you."

Boro felt right away better after Stefan's reassurances. He said with a subdued voice "I did screw up badly this time, didn't I?"

Stefan smiled, "These are growing pains. As long as you live, you will be making mistakes and committing sins. You have to eradicate the effect of the sins."

"Eradicate the effect of the sins, how?"

"There are few essential steps you need to do."

"What steps do I need to take?"

"First you need to become aware you sinned."

"Isn't everybody aware, when they sin?"

"It is not clear lot of times. The Enemy is very sly. His main weapon is the deception. He always tries to convince people: 'Sin, what sin? This is a normal, natural thing you did. Enjoy yourself, don't be silly, this is just a small, insignificant sin. It won't hurt anybody.' Lot of people fall for this deception and sink deeper and deeper sinning."

"Is the Enemy that sly and deceptive? Is that former good angel Lucifer?"

"Yes Boro, I am glad you are aware who the Enemy is."

"I thought that he comes with huge tail, horns and goat feet."

"The Enemy appears to people in any form he wants. He can masquerade even as a bright angel. The Evil ones are very skilful in deceiving people. That is why men should be careful when seeing any kind of apparitions, because most of them are from the Dark side."

Boro listened very attentively. He was shocked by Stefan's explanation. His brain was working in overdrive: "Really Stefan, how could I be sure that you are not an apparition from the Dark side?"

Stefan smiled. "I am glad that you are questioning even me. God has given me permission to let you know He gifted you with a wonderful gift of the discernment."

"Thank you Stefan for explaining this. I am a 'special person,' with the gift of the discernment? How did I deserve that gift? How long am I going to possess it?"

"Let me explain what the gift of the discernment is. It enables you to recognize good from evil."

"I don't see what's the big deal with that? Doesn't anybody with an average brain see the difference between good and evil?"

Stefan shook his head: "No Boro, it is not as simple as you think. The Devil is crafty. He presents a lie as truth, by mixing some of the truth in his deception. He 'dresses' his lies with the 'make up' of the truth. Your gift is to protect you from the Enemy's deception and to help you apply your God given talent."

"Stefan I am aware that some of my actions lately, were not in God's 'good book.' Why do I need to be more aware?"

"Yes, you need to become more aware than what you are now."

"Stefan, I am all ears. Make me aware. I am ready to listen."

Stefan grinned dismissively. "I am sorry Boro, I am not your teacher, nor are you my student."

"Aren't you going to criticize me for my recent inappropriate behaviour?"

"I won't."

"How do I become aware of my sinful behaviour? Please, help me."

"Boro, you said the magic words: 'Please help me.' These words open the gates of the heaven. Unfortunately, many men ignore that and keep wallowing in their sins. I will help you, by talking with you as your friend, helper and trusted confidant."

"Let's discuss it. I am ready."

"I saw everything you did. I acted according to my instructions, helping you to avoid falling into the temptation, while respecting your free will. Your conscience lost hands down in that struggle. There were just too much hormones, lust and passion. Too much fire power."

"You saw that I was giving in to the temptation, and would be committing sin. Why didn't you stop me from doing that. You had the power to do it, didn't you?"

"Power is not the issue Boro. I have the power to do whatever God orders me to. If He orders me to suck the oceans dry, or to level the highest mountain on earth, I can do it in a flick of an eye. The reason I did not intervene to stop you from falling in the temptation and sinning was because that was not in my instructions."

"Instructions, instructions, always those instructions. Wouldn't life be better without them?"

"You may not understand, nor like these instructions, but I am obliged to act according to them."

"This is worse than in the army. You still didn't help me to become aware of my transgressions."

"We are doing it by talking about it. Tell me please, how do you feel about the affair with Pera?"

"I enjoyed the whole thing tremendously. I was amazed at how strong lust and passion were. Nothing could stand in their way. I was willing to do anything to get that woman, anything! It was better and more enjoyable than I ever imagined. I still remember the wonderful enjoyment I had in this affair. I felt it was wrong, but my conscience was defeated by the power of lust."

"Why you think it was wrong for you to have that affair with Pera?"

"I would have to be a real moron not to see that it was immoral, and improper to have an affair with my cousin's wife. They treated me well, like family, and I turned around and betrayed that trust."

"That was a sincere admission of guilt. Was there any other reason you felt was wrong for you to have an affair with Pera?"

"It would be wrong to have an affair with her, even if she was an unknown man's wife, but I would not feel as bad as in this case."

"If Pera was a single girl like Nada, would you see yourself sinning?"

Boro forced himself to laugh: "I see no reason why a single man and a single woman sharing their bodies with each other, should feel guilty. They don't hurt anybody, don't betray anybody."

"Boro you made an interesting statement. I see that the Enemy was not staying idle."

"What does the Enemy have to do with what I said?"

"Devil, the enemy of man and the enemy of God, does everything in his power to corrupt any man and lead him away from God into the eternal damnation."

"C'mon Stefan, you are using big words 'eternal damnation? 'I don't understand what that means, but it sounds like something very unpleasant?"

"Eternal damnation means spending eternity in hell, suffering eternal torture and pain."

"Isn't that a terrible, ugly, hot place reserved for big sinners: Stalin, Hitler, mass murderers, rapists?"

"These guys are in the worst section of the hell."

"What did they do to be thrown into the hell?"

"They put themselves into the hell by doing what took them away from God and into devil's embrace."

"Am I in danger to: 'put myself' in that bad place; hell?"

"Every man has chance to go to hell, or to paradise."

"Who decides that?"

"Every man decides on his own, by the way he lives. If he lives according to God's commandments, he has a greater chance to find himself in paradise. If he rejects God's commandments, does not live according to them, follows the devil in this life; he will be with him and his demons in the world to come."

"It seems impossible for man not to sin. Who is going to qualify for paradise? Few select ones?"

"Men get into the paradise by accepting Lord Jesus Christ as their Saviour, repenting of their sins, and living according to God's commandments. This struggle is lifelong for every man."

"What should I do now? I have sinned. How do I correct this error? How do I repent?"

"The proper way would be to prepare for holy Confession and Communion and get it. This is what the Church prescribes. However, you never had Holy Communion. You don't go to church, therefore you need to ask God to forgive your transgression and help you, not to sin anymore."

"How do I know if God forgave me?"

"Yours is to repent and ask God for forgiveness. You do your best to repent and to live according to God's commandments. Trust God and He will do His part."

"What is God's 'part to do?"

"Seeing your sincere efforts to get closer to Him, He will meet you, helping you in your efforts."

"You said; 'God will meet you.' How is God going to meet me?"

"I am one of the ways God is going to meet you. He will instruct me to help you and guide you in correcting your behaviour, and getting back onto the road that will lead you to the heaven. This will be done by strengthening your faith, helping you to grow in humility, resisting the Enemy's attempts to lead you to his side."

"And what happens if I give in to the temptation and sin again. Am I going to hell automatically?"

"If it were like that, paradise would have lot of vacancies, while hell would be overcrowded. Lord loves you and gives you the opportunity as long as you are in the body, to repent, ask for forgiveness and God's help to resist the temptation."

"What if I sin again and again?"

"Repent, and ask God's forgiveness, again and again, and try to amend your ways. Ask God, to help you, to give you strength and faith to resist the temptation to sin."

"So, there is hope for me?"

"Yes, as long as you renounce your sinful ways and humbly ask God for forgiveness and help."

"Stefan, I am really surprised that God is so forgiving to the sinners."

"Our Lord is loving, and forgiving. He gives every man the opportunity right until his last breath, to repent and come to Him."

"It seems to me that it is proper for a man to sin all his life. Repent on his deathbed, be forgiven, and 'sail' into the heaven."

"This 'cheap way' into heaven is the exception rather than the rule. It would be very risky for man's salvation to rely on this kind of repentance."

"Why would it be risky? Didn`t you tell me that God gives everybody the opportunity 'until their last breath,' to repent, get God`s forgiveness and get into heaven?"

"It is risky because of the way human nature works. The Enemy keeps telling man: 'Enjoy yourself, indulge today. Repent tomorrow. The habit of sinning becomes part of man`s nature. If a sinner repents quickly after committing the sin, it is easier to repent. If he keeps sinning day in day out, he will be able to do it with great difficulty, or not at all. This is why delaying the repentance is a very risky business indeed."

"Stefan, do you think, I am fully aware of my sinning with Pera?"

"Pretty well. It would help if you read holy Bible, particularly the Ten Commandments. We will soon discuss your transgressions in the light of God`s Commandments."

"I am afraid, I will fail these Commandments."

"You are going to fail them many times, but our Lord is a loving and forgiving God. For the spiritually sick, He offers the medication of repentance, fasting and prayer. Do not despair because of the depth of your sin, God`s love is deeper."

"Stefan, this is reassuring and wonderful. I am very glad you came today."

"I am glad too Boro. I will leave now. We covered lot of issues. Your head must be overflowing," said Stefan jokingly.

He kissed the sleeping youth on the forehead, spread his huge golden dust wings and became invisible

## Chapter 13

## *Trouble with Nuts and Bolts*

Two weeks after the encounter with Pera in the corn field, Boro went to visit her. He took the Saturday afternoon train. Within a couple of hours he was in Vrba. He walked about twenty minutes on a dusty rural road until he reached the house of his other cousin. The cousins greeted him warmly. They offered him some strong mulberry brandy, dried ham and hard, dark homemade bread. He ate and drank while chatting with his cousins.

Pera came few hours after he arrived. Boro had to do his best acting, so nobody would suspect their affair. He was just a very polite and kind cousin. Seeing Pera`s happy smile on her face and her gazing eyes on him, he got nervous, fearing that somebody would become suspicious.

She asked him: "Where are you sleeping tonight?"

Getting red up to his ears, Boro tried to act calmly; "I don't know."

"We have a spare bedroom. You are welcome to sleep there," said Pera.

"Well, I guess if you have a spare bedroom that would be fine with me," replied Boro nervously.

He thanked his cousins, said good bye to them and him and Pera walked to her house. There were odd villagers on the street walking, or riding on horse pulled wagons. In few minutes they came to Pera`s big, old house. Boro greeted her children. Her husband was not home yet from the field.

"Excuse me for ten minutes, I have to milk the cow," said Pera, smiling seductively at Boro.

"Can I watch you milking?" asked Boro innocently.

"Sure, come and help," smiled Pera.

The barn was about twenty meters away from the house. As soon as they stepped into the barn they threw arms around each other. Both were eager and ablaze with passion. Pera looked so happy, so hot. She just could not stop kissing Boro. One long passionate deep kiss over, she wanted more, and more, and more.

For a second a scary thought hit Boro: "What if somebody walks in and sees us. It would be a scandal, shame and a catastrophe for both of us?"

That thought of a caution and weak protest of Boro`s conscience were quickly overpowered by huge desire and lust burning in both of them. They threw away all caution. They did it standing against the barn wall. Red and hot, they cooled their burning faces and necks with water from the well. Pera milked the cow and they went back into Pera`s kitchen.

Her husband came a short time later. He greeted Boro warmly. They shared dinner and after a short chat, husband excused himself saying that he was very tired and must go to bed, because tomorrow he has to get up before sunrise to work on the fields.

Pera offered Boro some black coffee. They sipped the coffee and talked with her children about school and their friends. Soon, Pera ordered the children to bed. Then she took Boro to his bed. When they came near the bed Boro grabbed her for the buttocks, "I love this."

Pera gave him silent kiss, whispering: "Maybe, you will get a visitor tonight."

Boro panicked; "Are you sure nobody would surprise us."

"Don`t worry, my husband is very tired and the children are also hard asleep. Relax my love."

There was no way he could sleep. Troubling thoughts attacked his mind. "It is crazy what we are doing. It is stupid, dangerous.

Why did I come here?" His thoughts were interrupted by his nightly visitor, Pera. Boro noticed that she had neither bra, nor panties on. "Wow, did she ever come ready," he thought. They spent the next the few hours in a passionate love making and pillow talk. When Pera left him to go to her bed, Boro was pretty exhausted.

He woke up late in the morning. He was just about to get up when Pera walked in. "How is my lover boy, still tired?" She said flashing him a big, happy smile. Boro was amazed that She didn`t look tired at all. She was a happy and satisfied women.

"I am pretty tired and spent, but I am still hungry for you. Where is everybody?" asked Boro.

"Nobody is at home, but me and you, my beauty. My husband left three hours ago to plough the fields. The kids went to my cousin Vera`s. Her boy is celebrating his birthday today. I got up two hours ago, fed the livestock, cleaned the house, and washed myself, even put on some perfume. Smell me, do you like it?"

Boro`s passions was rising quickly: "I love you regardless of the perfume. Your naked body smells better than any perfume. Come in, rest for a while with me."

"Just a minute," said Pera. She closed the curtains on the windows, locked outside door, took off her shoes and in dress joined Boro in bed.

A thought flashed again in Boro`s mind; "Isn`t this crazy what we are doing. What if somebody comes and knocks on the door? What if her husband comes back from the fields and finds me in bed with his wife? If he does not kill me, I would want the earth to open and swallow me out of the shame."

Pera sensed his hesitation. She kissed him gently and reassured him: "Don`t worry my dear. Nobody is going to surprise us. I told my neighbours that I won't be home this morning. I don't want anybody to bother us, relax." She started a passionate kiss. It looked like she enjoyed it tremendously, for she was purring like a cat.

Boro disrobed her completely. Jokingly, Pera protested: "Hey, this is not fair. I am naked and you are not."

"Well, go ahead and undress me," challenged Boro.

"I am shy, you do it please," said Pera covering her naked body.
"No way, you do it."
"I will do it with my eyes closed," said Pera shyly, starting to disrobe Boro.

She closed her eyes and slid down Boro`s underpants. "Here, are you happy now?" She said seductively.

It was new, wonderful experience to have "full contact," naked body to naked body.

The next hour was spent in passionate love making. They got quite tired and just lay in bed recuperating. Pera got up first, tidied herself, washed her face and made breakfast; a big plate of bacon and eggs, homemade cheese, bread and coffee. Boro got up, washed, dressed and joined Pera for breakfast. She unlocked the door and opened the curtains. Everything was back to normal.

"Your turn to visit me," said Boro.

"Sure my love I will come. I don't want anybody to suspect anything. I have to find a good excuse to visit."

"We must be very careful. It would be very bad for both of us if somebody finds out. Let me know when you are coming," warned Boro.

Pera embraced him: "I wish you were my husband and made love to me every night. Last night was the happiest in my life."

Boro gently touched her crotch: "Bye spring of life, pleasure box, beautiful bush covering the nicest flower."

Pera laughed heartily on Boro`s poetic, long good bye to her femininity. "Hey, what about equality," she protested.

"What equality?"

"I want to say goodbye to my gift. I insist."

Saying this Pera gently touched Boro`s crotch and blushing said: "Bye my best gift, my pleasure stick, my handle of happiness."

Jokingly, Boro protested: "See what you have done. We got to say real good bye now." And they did one more quick, passionate, 'good bye,' against the wall of Pera`s kitchen.

This time, Boro really had to go. He quickly washed up, straightened his clothing, said "bye" to Pera and run to the train station.

In few weeks, Pera came as she promised. This time she came late, and Boro's cousin asked her to sleep in her house. That evening, Boro, Pera and his cousin drank coffee and talked small talk and family gossip. Boro was afraid that his cousin might become suspicious of Pera's second visit. He was 'sitting on pins and needles,' and had to try hard to act cool and respectful to their cousin in law.

Pera was given a spare bedroom to sleep in. It was a silly illusion Boro had that he would be able to sleep. Not a chance. He just thought about Pera, imagined himself holding, kissing, caressing her, and making love to her. His lust made his heart speed up. Adrenalin and testosterone were wreaking havoc of his body.

"What am I going to do? I have got to have her, but how? Is everybody sleeping? Somebody might want to go to the washroom and see me with her. I think I would die of shame. Darn, can't get her, it is just too risky, too dangerous."

This moralizing was helped by the stronger voice of his conscience; "You are crazy to even think of doing such a shameful deed in your cousin's house. How could you even consider betraying her trust? Don't be a sinning fool. Just turn on the other side, and sleep."

Boro heeded the voice of his awakened consciousness, turned to the other side and tried to sleep, closing his eyes and doing fake snoring.

He did not realize the strength of the ruthless invaders; the lust and the passion.

Strengthened by the vivid, seductive, luscious images of making love to Pera, they chased his feeble consciousness into some distant corner of Boro's soul, threatening it: "Stay there, not a word, until we get our jollies, than you can preach all you want."

Taking command of Boro's body, they 'forced' him to get up from his bed and walk very slowly and carefully like a cat, in the pitch darkness, find the spare bedroom and Pera.

Pera was not able to sleep either. She came to be loved, to experience passion and tenderness she didn't share in fourteen years of marriage with her husband.

She whispered to his ear: "Why did you wait so long? You enjoy torturing me?"

Boro whispered back, "I was tortured maybe more than you. I had to wait to make sure everybody was fast asleep."

They lay facing each other. "Where is my gift," joked Pera.

"Don`t be impatient. You will get it as much as you like."

"Is that a solemn promise?"

"Yes it is."

"Don`t torture me please, I want the gift now."

Boro teased her a bit. "Don't rush; let them get warmed up a bit."

"You are a bad boy," complained Pera, kissing him passionately.

Boro readily replied engaging in long, passionate love making.

Tired and happy, they listened; no sound in the house. Everybody was asleep. They relaxed and talked whispering:

"Do you enjoy making love to me?" asked Boro.

"More than anything, don`t you see that?" complained Pera.

"I just wanted to be sure. Is your husband bugging you to make love to you?"

"Since I met you, I managed to avoid him. One week I had a headache, the other week I was too tired. I can`t refuse him for long time. Luckily, he has been working on the fields from sunrise to sunset, so most of the time; he was too tired even to ask."

"But eventually, when you consent how does it happen?"

"Why do you want to know? I love only you."

"I am curious."

"After the kids are asleep, he comes to my bed. I am already prepared, just in my pyjama, bra and panties off. He kisses me on the lips and usually bites me at the neck, puts me on my back and makes love to me for a few minutes until he reaches his orgasm. I had orgasm with him only a few times, but I pretend that I have it every time, just to make him happy, and not to hurt his ego."

"And then, what happens?"

"He gets up and goes to his bed. I go to the bathroom, wash myself and go to sleep. The end of the love story."

Pera lovingly stroked Boro's face. "I am glad I was on that train. First time in my life, I experienced real love. I wish we met years before."

"Hey, you would seduce a boy of sixteen," joked Boro.

Pera stroked him gently on the back. "I think you could have done it at that age. I would train you."

"You are teaching me now. And I must say you are an excellent and dedicated teacher. How am I as a student?"

"You are talent, a natural talent. God gave you the ability to make women happy. Any brute can jump on a woman, but it takes, caring, loving man, to share tenderness, respect and love. Most men are very selfish in love, like my husband. Not you. I believe you care to make me happy and satisfied, more than you care to make yourself happy and satisfied."

"I think you are overdoing with the compliments. I was a virgin until a few months ago. One thing you are right about; I really care about making you happy."

Boro thought that he heard somebody in the house getting up. He was horrified expecting someone to come in, switch the light on and see them together in bed. Oh shame, oh catastrophe! The sound died.

Pera whispered; "This was probably one of the kids, dreaming something and suddenly turning in the bed. My kids do that too. Relax my love."

They continued caressing and kissing quietly, enjoying each other's body. Boro's strength was slowly coming back.

"Unbelievable that one can enjoy love making this much," whispered Pera kissing him gently on the cheek. Are you tired?"

"Yes, I am quite tired. You sucked all the life out of me."

"I am tired too," said Pera. "Do you want to go to sleep?"

"I need few more minutes to rest before I go to my bed, otherwise I could stumble in the darkness, fall and wake up everybody

"I won't touch you anymore. We sure don't want wake everybody up. Rest." She detached from him.

"It's all right. You are safe, you drained all my power."

Pera could not stop laughing. "That is very funny; I drained you out."

"Yes you did, but that is fine. There is some reserve power."

"We have to say good bye and go to sleep. The morning is coming soon."

"I can't move, I need a week to recover," sighed Boro.

Pera kissed him gently. "You are kidding me. You get tired, but your strength returns quickly. If you had a young, beautiful eighteen year old virgin beside you, I bet she would not be virgin too long."

"You give me too much credit. The way I am right now, even if Miss World was beside me, I would kiss her on the forehead; turn to the other side and sleep. By the way, were you a virgin before you got married?"

"You bet I was. I grew up in the village. Virginity was girl's biggest capital. If husband found out the morning after the first night, that the linen was not bloody, he would return the bride in shame, to her family. The marriage would be over."

"How was your first night?"

"Why do you want to know that? I don't remember. It was long time ago."

"No girl forgets her first night and the loss of her virginity. Please tell me."

"I hardly knew my husband before we got married. He saw me once during a festivity in our church. He liked me. Our families arranged everything. My father asked me if I wanted to marry him. I said; 'If you think he is good man, I will marry him.'"

"What happened the first night?"

"We did not have a separate room. Our bed was in the corner of the house. They put some wooden boards making something like a small room. There was no door, just an opening about three feet wide. We didn't have much of the privacy. I was ashamed that the family sleeping around us would hear us. After we entered our "honeymoon" enclosure, my husband undressed to his shirt, lay in bed and whispered to me; "Come on, undress and join me."

"I was scared and ashamed. What is this big man going do to me? Is he going to hurt me? I took off my skirt, shoes and socks, and was left only in my long shirt. Clumsily, shyly, I climbed on the bed, covered myself and turned my back to my husband. I was hoping he would have mercy not to touch me that night. But, he grabbed me, turned me over on my back and said; "Don't be afraid; it might hurt a little a bit, but you will like it and wish for more." He pulled my shirt up to my neck and climbed on top of me. I thought he was going to crush me. He started kissing me. My response was to suffer and bear it, letting him do his thing"

"And then, what happened?"

"Still biting me on my neck and chest, he spread my legs, and feverishly tried to deflower me. He hurt me quite a lot, but I just cried silently, without tears. He was getting frustrated for not being able to penetrate me instantly. He spread my legs more and attacked me at the most sensitive point. I felt something in me giving in, was being torn. Next moment he was in me. I was shocked; it was a foreign body within me? Pain, fear and shame were mixed with some strange feeling of pleasure. He was huffing and puffing and with big push he filled my inside with something warm. I realized I became a woman. He got off me and lay on his back to recover his strength. Soon, he was snoring. I was hurt, wet between my legs. My blood and man's seed intermingled inside me."

"Was there lot of blood?"

"Not that much, just a fair size blood stain on the linen."

"Did he spare you the next night?"

"Are you kidding me? He was proud like a peacock, because I came to him as virgin and he deflowered me, made me a woman. The following night, it was easier for him. It was less painful to me, but I did not participate. I just laid there like a good submissive wife and let him have his pleasure. He spent more time making love to me the following night. When he climaxed, I felt some kind of pleasure, when he discharged his seed into me. Perhaps that was when our first child was conceived, for I had him about nine months later."

"Morning is coming; we will have to split soon. Somebody might wake up," said Boro worriedly.

"Oh honey, let's just enjoy few quiet moments," sighed Pera.

They just lay there. Happy, tired, silent. Pera broke the silence first. "Are we going to survive this?"

"Hardly," said Boro. I have to catch the early train to school. My brain will be useless today. Next time, I will visit you."

Pera teased him. "Are you really dry now."

"Don't challenge me," whispered Boro.

"Let me not wait too long for your visit," pleaded Pera.

"As soon as I can."

"Give me one more kiss and hug honey, one for the road."

They engaged in a deep, loving kiss. "Are you sure no more power," joked Pera.

"No, this time not a gram, you got it all. Don't tell me you want more."

"Oh I had enough honey, she wants a kiss her gift good bye."

"Ok let them kiss. It is getting late."

This time, Boro knew it was dangerous to stay together any more. He crawled of the bed, somehow found way to his bed, crawled in covered himself, laid on his back, waiting for his, breath and energy to return to him.

For a few days Boro felt spent physically and emotionally. His conscience recovered after serious beating and started to bug him: "You are killing yourself. See, you are so tired, can't study, can't do anything. It was immoral what you did. God will punish you; you did an ugly, despicable thing. You must stop doing this. Cut off the affair. Pera is a married woman, your cousin's wife. Shame on you."

One Sunday, he was home by himself. His cousin and her family went visiting their friends in the neighbouring village. He got up late. It was a beautiful sunny, chilly fall day. He had to prepare for exams, but was too lazy to study. He looked by chance at the bookshelf. Big red book attracted his attention. Almost as if by someone's order, he got up, took the book, and went to bed again.

## A Kingdom to Buy

"Hmmm, the holy book," he murmured. "I wonder if there is anything interesting inside."

He opened it at the first page and started reading: "In the beginning, God created heaven and earth."

"Hey, wait a minute; I discussed this chapter with Stefan. Didn`t he tell me, not to start reading at the beginning, but closer to the end. He said to begin at the Gospel by John."

He found "The Gospel by John," and began to read: "In the beginning was the Word, and the Word was with God and the Word was God. He was in the beginning with God. All things were made through Him, and without Him nothing was made that was made. In Him was life, and the life was the light of men."

"Wow, this is amazing, like a riddle, but it sounds beautiful. It sounded like a mysterious poem or fairy tale. What is this; 'The Word,' which was 'with God,' and was God. Let me read some more." He read until he came to the spot where Jesus was at some wedding performing His first miracle by making water into wine.

"Everybody knows it is impossible to turn water into wine. Not even the best chemist in the world could do it. How can people believe this? One has to be super naive and gullible to believe it. What does it mean: that everything was made through 'the Word?' No sense for me to read it any longer. Stefan does not exist. I just dreamt about him and made this up convincing myself, that I have some friend and protector, my personal guardian angel, whom I named Stefan. How naive was I? If anybody hears about my alleged encounters with Stefan, they might think I went crazy, and needed to see a doctor. I should live 'normal' life like everybody else: Enjoy myself, finish school, get a good job, get rich, have lot of women, see the world. Why do I need to worry about these 'high' things, which I can do nothing about?"

He got up and put the Bible back on the top of the clothes closet at the corner of the room. He put it there so that it would be out of his sight. Almost as if he was afraid that he might again get curious and open it. A quick thought hit his mind; "Throw this useless book away. Why do you need it? You, future engineer, reading about these fantasies and fairy tales. Get rid of it, or give it to some old baba, who believes in these fables."

This thought was for a brief time attractive to him. It seemed logical and practical. What caused him to reject it, was the thought of his mom and baba praying, and reverence they had for: 'The holy Evangelion. "No, I won't throw this book out; this would be insult to my two dearest persons. Regardless if they were naive and believed with all their hearts in these tales, I respect their naive, simple faith."

For first time in his schooling Boro found some subjects were not fun to learn, but just unpleasant chores. In his second year he had a terrible shock; he failed a subject. This seriously shook his confidence in his intellectual ability. It did not help that within three months he passed the same exam with excellent mark. The damage had been done. He lost a year. He was ashamed for allowing this to happen. He was also upset because his elderly parents had to support him one extra year.

Due to huge stress caused by failing the exam he got terrible stomach pains. The only free doctor available was at the student polyclinic. An old, miserable lady doctor examined him. "I think I know what your problem is, but I will send you for a test to confirm."

They gave him a big glass of thick, creamy liquid to drink. After he drank it, they checked him on the x ray machine and told him to go back to see the doctor. Old miserable doctor was holding x ray shot of Boro`s stomach. "Young man," she said with a bored voice, "You have a bomb inside you, a nasty stomach ulcer. You must follow a very strict diet. Avoid anything fried, spicy, too hot, or too cold. I will prescribe you some pills, which might help."

It was awful; two terrible things within one year. Boro started questioning again: "Why do these things happen to me? If I really had a protector and guardian angel, he would not allow such bad things happening to me?"

One night, after particularly miserable day in school, sharp pain in the stomach and bitter cold weather, Stefan appeared.

Boro was ashamed, because of his continued affair with Pera, and now the sickness and failure in school. He felt miserable.

Stefan was his usual angelic magnificence. He kissed Boro on the forehead like his mom used to do, after she would tuck him in the bed. "How are you Boro? I missed you. We have not met for long time."

"Well, I could be better," replied Boro with a noticeable presence of shame in his voice.

"I can tell that by your voice and by the way you look. What caused the problems?"

"You said you know everything about me. Why do you ask me what caused my problems, when you know that better than me?" complained Boro.

"Yes, I know what happened, but you need to verbalize it, so you are aware about your problem."

"Problems, problems? Why things like this happen to me. I choose the profession that does not suit me. Then, I fail an exam, which never happened before. And to top it, I got an ulcer to torture me, and make my life miserable. Couldn`t you, my guardian angel, prevent some of these bad things from happening to me. You care for my well-being, don`t you Stefan?"

"Lord gave me job to protect you, guide you and guard you, so that you could fulfill the mission destined to you by God."

"You are talking, as if I will be some prophet, or Superman, that will change the fate of the world. Good prospect material I am; choosing the wrong profession, failing in school, and on top of that getting an ulcer, as that miserable old doctor told me that I had 'a bomb' inside me. Please don`t joke with me anymore and mention some fancy, glorious mission, some wonderful gift from God. I don`t believe in that," complained Boro bitterly.

"Boro, I understand why you feel like that. Our heavenly Father helps you on the way of reaching your destiny. To keep you on the road of your destiny, He uses some 'sticks and carrots."

"What in the world are you talking about Stefan? God using 'carrots and sticks' on me?"

"When you were little boy, you did not understand that some things could hurt you. Your parents punished you for doing bad or dangerous things. Punishment might be; getting hit with the belt, being left without meal, or denied something you liked. Did something like this happen to you when you were little boy?"

"Many times."

"Did you like to get punished?"

"Nooo, nobody likes to get punished."

"After being punished, did you repeat the thing you were punished for?"

"I avoided repeating it, because I was afraid of the punishment."

"After you grew up, did you realize that the punishment your parents exercised on you, was actually beneficial to you?"

"Yes, it is true. When I grew up, I understood why they punished me and I was thankful to them. They did it out of love and for my well-being."

"Your parents taught you to do good things, by promising you rewards like toys, cookies, ice cream. These were 'the carrots."

"But, how does this 'stick and carrot' method apply in my situation. There are no 'carrots,' just lot of 'sticks?"

"As your parents used both 'carrots' and 'sticks,' depending on the situation, our Heavenly Father uses, His 'carrots and sticks.'

"What are the sticks God used on me?"

"God's sticks are unpleasant things that God allows to happen to you: pain, sickness, failure on the exam, shame, humiliation, embarrassment."

"I got it. God considered me a very bad sinner, because He used big arsenal of sticks on me: bang, bang, bang, bang. Couldn't He use one by one? Not like this, to cause me so much pain and shame?"

"Sticks very rarely come single. One stick is accompanied by more of its companions. Your failure on the exam caused you shame and embarrassment, and was conducive to the appearance of sickness and pain. God decided that it was a necessary intervention to keep you on the road of your destiny. It is painful, unpleasant and humiliating now, but in due time you will realize, that it was all for your benefit and you will thank God for that."

"Are you saying Stefan, that in, say ten or, twenty years I will thank God for failing the exam, for all the shame and embarrassment it caused me and for the ulcer, that caused me terrible pain?"

"Your parents punished you, when you were little boy. When you got older, you realized that they punished you out of love and for your well-being and thanked your parents for applying these sticks on you?"

"Yes, it is true .I admitted that, but this is different. God`s 'sticks' are very bad, very painful."

"Every person of authority uses different sticks."

"Stefan, what's the reason that God used such heavy 'artillery' on me. You know that as my guardian angel, don`t you?"

"Of course, I know this Boro, but my instructions don`t allow me to go in details with you. All I can tell you is that by using His sticks, God is giving you the message that the way you acted lately was leading you off the path to your destiny. That is the reason for this unpleasant intervention."

"Mildly said 'unpleasant', it is horrible, it is crushing me. Don`t you see that?"

"I see that you are suffering, but our Lord does not give men bigger temptation, then what they are able to bear. And another good thing is: there is always a way out of the suffering. 'God closes the door, but opens the window of opportunity."

"Well Stefan, I am glad to know Lord thinks I am tough enough to bear and withstand these sticks, but I don't understand this about; 'The window of the opportunity.' What opportunity? I see no opportunity."

"Most of the time, the opportunity does not knock at your door and says: 'Hi, I am your opportunity, please use me.' It comes camouflaged. You need to recognize it. I am sure that with your effort and with my help, you will in time recognize the opportunity to get out of these troubles."

"Please tell me if these troubles dumped on me because of my affair with Pera?"

"What do you think?"

"I have a feeling the troubles I am in and the affair with Pera were connected."

"Congratulations Boro. Your guess was right on."

"Why didn`t you tell me that right away, instead of beating around the bush?"

"It is within my instructions to help you verbalize the cause of your predicaments. You just did that."

"I realize, I did an improper thing, but I did not hurt anybody. Actually, I made Pera and myself quite happy. Isn`t that good by itself?"

"Being happy and making somebody else happy, is not automatically a good and proper thing. You can get drunk, or use drugs to make you happy, steal something and make you and your accomplices happy, be involved in adulterous relationship and make yourself and your lover happy. You can commit very bad things and be 'happy.' Happiness is a lousy justification for doing something improper and immoral. This is the snare of the Enemy, one of his most powerful weapons."

"Are you saying it is wrong to want to be happy and make others happy?"

"It is natural for you to search for happiness, but without violating God`s laws."

"And what happens if I violate God`s laws?"

"What happens if you violate human laws?"

"The law punishes me."

"Likewise, you get punished for violating God`s laws. It may not happen right away, it may not happen in ten years, it may not happen to you, but it will happen eventually, if not to you, then to your descendents."

"You told me; God is love. What kind of love is it if He punishes for the smallest violation of His laws?"

"When you parents disciplined you, did they do it because they hated you, or because they loved you?"

"I think they did not hate me, but they hated what I did. They disciplined me out of love."

"That is how our Heavenly Father disciplines you as His child, His creation. God always loves you, but He does not love the sin you are committing. He disciplines you out of love, to keep you on the road of salvation. Do you understand that?"

"Yes, I understand it now. I need to know: which one of God`s laws did I violate?"

"You violated several God`s laws. I don`t want to go into details now, because you should read in The Holy Bible, about God`s Commandments."

"What happens if I sin again? Will God permit more troubles coming my way?"

"Yes, that might happen."

"I thought you told me when I violate God`s law, punishment follows."

"God decides what kind of trouble He is going to allow going your way. Remember, when you were little boy and you did something wrong. Your parents decided the punishment. Sometimes, it was very harsh and painful, while other times it was mild and painless. Wasn`t that the way it happened?"

"Yes, it did. Sometimes I was surprised how mild the punishment was, while other times, I was shocked being subjected to an unexpectedly harsh discipline."

"Our Heavenly Father also decides what kind of trials to allow, keeping you on the road of salvation."

"What do I need to do to avoid these trials?"

"Very simply: do not violate God`s Commandments."

"If the temptation is strong I just can`t resist it. When a woman is near me, I just forget all God`s laws. I lust to have her. Lust and passion overwhelm me and enslave me."

"These passions are extremely strong with young people. It takes great deal of the struggle to overcome them. You need to fight against your passions as much as you can."

"Stefan, you have no body, so you don`t experience the violent struggle us men have to fight against our passion and flesh. Our flesh is selfish. It just wants satisfaction of the senses. Why did

God give us such strong passions, which we have a difficult time to control?"

"God gave you all healthy desires, eating when hungry, drinking when thirsty, desire to procreate and have children. All of these desires are God ordained if they remain in a normal frame. But if taken to the extreme they become man's god and he becomes their slave, removing himself from the road of his salvation."

"Are you saying that some desires, say; eating, could become my god?"

"God gave you normal desire to eat to feed your body. But if you gorge yourself, eating more than you need and making food and eating focus of your life, then the food and eating became your god. It rules you and your life."

"Can sex become my god?"

"Yes, it definitely can. Sex within marriage is blessed by God, outside of the marriage is not. If sexual desire occupies man's mind incessantly, if he tries to have sex with as many females as possible, that is not normal and not blessed by God. That man has sex for his god. He does great harm to his body and to his soul if he does not correct his sinful way."

"You are talking about me Stefan, aren't you?"

"I am talking about any man abusing his body and soul by being promiscuous."

"Why God gave me such a strong passion, which I am often powerless against?"

"God made everything to measure. He made no mistakes. He gave you the talent. With that talent came some strong passions. God provided every man with the tools to control these passions."

"Tools? are you talking about some mechanical or electronic gadgets?"

"I am talking about two mightiest tools at Christian's disposal, prayer and fasting."

"Are you talking about prayer and fasting my mom and baba practised?"

"Yes Boro, that is what I am talking about."

"How do I use these tools, or as you say, 'weapons', to curb my lust and passions?"

"Do you remember when your mom and baba fasted, and why?"

"My mom and baba fasted every Wednesday and Friday and all other Church appointed fasts. I think they fasted for two reasons: to get confession and communion, and because Church prescribed these fasts.

"Did you ever fast?"

"No, this was done mostly by older women, very few men."

"How did your mom and baba fast?"

"They abstained from eating dairy products, eggs, or meat. They decreased the quantity of the food, and prayed more and helped people."

"What do you think is the purpose of fasting?"

"I have no clue. It seems unnatural to me to avoid so much good stuff and starve yourself. Besides simply obeying Church order, I see no other reason for fasting."

"Enemy propaganda," murmured Stefan.

"What enemy are you talking about? The bad guy with horns and goat feet?"

"Yes Boro, I am talking about the Devil, the enemy of your soul, the destroyer of your salvation."

"Why would the Devil try to persuade me not to fast? What does he gain if I don`t fast?"

"I am going to answer your question with a question. Is that Okay?"

"Sure."

"When do you think your passion and lust are stronger, if you eat just a small piece of bread and drank water, or if you had a huge meal with lot of meat, cheese, wine, sweets?"

"My passion and lust would be much stronger, if I had a big meal with meat, cheese, wine, and sweets."

"Couldn`t you conclude then that it would be harder to fight your passion and lust if you ate rich food in abundance, then if you had a basic, simple, small meal?"

"Yes, I think one could conclude that."

"Could you figure out from our conversation what the purpose of fasting is?"

"The purpose of fasting is: by denying the body an abundance of rich food one curbs the bodily passion."

"Excellent summary Boro. Your talent just cannot be kept dormant, it shines."

"What talent are you talking about? If it exists it is sleeping comatose sleep, like beauty in the fairy tale."

"But, she woke up at the end of the story, married the prince and they lived happily ever after."

"She got a prince to kiss her and wake her up, but who is going to kiss my deeply sleeping talent?"

"Boro, a 'princess' will do that at the right time."

"When I am eighty and a crippled old man?"

"Much, much sooner than you think Boro."

"Stefan, I see why Devil is sabotaging our attempts to fast, because fast is a real weapon against that freak. That is why; he wants us to throw it away, so that he could boss and enslave us easier."

"Are you clear now about the importance of fasting?"

"Even though, I don't like to fast, I see that fasting is a mighty weapon in fighting passion, lust and Devil."

"Eventually, you will see that it is a very pleasant experience. You will enjoy fasting."

"I doubt it! I love meat, eggs and cheese. I am not happy unless I have them every day."

"Boro, part of your talent is the ability to renew your mind."

"When is that day going to come when I don't care for good ham and cheese sandwich, or an omelette with bacon and eggs?"

"It takes renewing of your mind Boro. It does not happen overnight, but gradually. Patience."

"Nobody has patience in our time Stefan. It is 'in' to be impatient."

"That is another snare of the Enemy," murmured Stefan.

"That guy is full of tricks, isn't he?"

*A Kingdom to Buy*

"He is evil, super intelligent, experienced deceiver. Man is no match on his own against him."

"Who can help poor man in the struggle against such a powerful enemy?"

"When you were little kid and threatened by a bully, a bigger and older boy, whom did you ask for help?"

"Whoever was closest to me? My older brother, a friend, my father."

"You had conflict with human; you called another human to help you. But, if you faced an enemy that was a spirit, would you ask your brother, friend, or your father to help you in that fight?"

"Yes, of course, I would ask them for help."

"Bear in mind Boro; The enemy you faced was not a boy like you, but an invisible, evil, experienced, super intelligent spirit. Do you think your friend, brother or father, would be able to protect you from this invisible spirit?"

"They would be as helpless as me fighting Devil. Who can help me?"

"Pray to God to help you. Also to Godmother, angels and saints to intercede on your behalf."

"Thanks Stefan. I know now where to ask for help."

"We are going to cut our meeting short today. I hope that you are going to read the Holy Bible. I am sure that eventually you will enjoy reading it."

Boro wanted to ask Stefan a question, but he just said: "Bye my friend," and was gone.

# Chapter 14

# *Getting Up*

Boro recuperated from the shock of the exam failure and pain from the stomach ulcer. The pills doctor gave him were easing the pain. He concentrated on his studies and passed all of his exams. He visited Pera a few more times. It was wonderful every time. The "chemistry" between them was amazing. They were taking crazy risks, but were lucky. Nobody ever saw them in a compromising situation.

One date remained in his memory. It was a hot July weekend. He came to Vrba in the afternoon to visit his "dear relatives." He knew that Pera was working at the cornfield, about half an hour away from the village. There was no way Boro could wait that long.

The sun was mercilessly hot. Boro was tired, perspiring and dusty when he came to Pera. This time corn could not hide them; it was not high enough. They were on the flat open plain. Boro suggested to have a break, drink some water and relax a bit in the shade of a big tree, close to the railway tracks. They walked, hot and excited right close to the railway line. A large ditch was running alongside the railway tracks. It was quite deep, with lot of grass on the bottom. Nobody could see them there, not even the people from the passing trains.

Pera was working all day in the field. She was dusty and sweaty. That would be repulsive for some 'cultured' Westerner. Not to Boro. It excited him. Since they were both hot and tired, they did not spend lot of time lovemaking; they left it for the night in the cool and comfort of the spare bedroom.

Boro did not see Pera any more after his graduation. Their affair was over. She would always be a special woman in his life. He was thankful to her for making him a "man."

Soon after graduation, Boro went to a small city to begin his working career. He rented a room, sharing washroom with his landlady, a middle aged divorcee and her son, few years younger than Boro.

He was now free like a bird. No more exams or stress. He could spend time on his favourite hobbies: girls, soccer, and reading. And he engaged enthusiastically in all three.

The little town was an important railway center. Boro loved to go to the railway station and watch people. It was good place to meet women. Walking one evening through the waiting room at the railway station, he met a lady that reminded him of Pera. In the conversation, he found out that she was from a little town about an hour travel by train and was divorced with five year old son.

They agreed to meet in her house the following Sunday. That Sunday Boro had a passionate and tiring lovemaking experience. When he came to his room, he had only one thing in mind: sleep. To his surprise, he found a bowl of the almonds, dry figs and a bowl of honey with a spoon. He figured out that it was his landlady that left him these treats. Before going to bed he ate it all. The next morning he was good old Boro, full of power and vigour.

It was late in the night the next day. He was coming to his room after a date. He passed by his landlady`s bedroom. The door was slightly ajar. A small night table light lit the room. Boro wanted to pass by silently, without disturbing the landlady.

"Is that you Boro?" he heard her voice.

"Yes it`s me, good night."

"Good night," replied the landlady.

"Oh by the way, did you leave those treats for me yesterday. It was delicious. Thank you very much."

"Who was the girl that sucked out all your power?" joked the landlady.

Boro opened her bedroom door. Landlady was lying in bed reading a magazine. Her barren shoulders attracted Boro's attention. 'Hmm, not bad,' he thought.

"Oh no, I went to visit an old school friend. We played lot of soccer and that's how I got tired."

Landlady laughed. "You can't fool me. That was not soccer tiredness, that was girl tiredness."

Boro smiled back blushing. "Anyway thanks for the treats, they helped me great deal to regain my strength. Good night. Have pleasant dreams." Saying this, he was turning around to exit the landlady's room, when he heard her groaning.

"What is the matter? You don't feel good?"

"Just a headache, I will be okay I just need to massage my neck."

"Would you like me to massage your neck?"

"That would be nice, but I don't want to impose on you."

"Oh, no trouble at all. You are so nice to me." Saying this, Boro knelt beside landlady's bed and started gently massaging her soft, warm neck.

"Would you like me to massage your back?" asked Boro, getting hot.

Landlady was 'catching fire' "Oh, please, that would be great."

"Lay on your stomach," whispered Boro, breathing heavier.

Landlady gladly obliged. Still kneeling beside her bed, Boro went with his hands down and up at her back all the way to the ample sized round buttocks. They were now both hot, with only one thing on their minds.

Boro undressed and joined her in bed. He took off her pyjama, leaving her naked. The light was off. Pitch darkness in the room."She is a little plumper than Pera," thought Boro.

Landlady was about fifteen years his senior. The age was already showing on her, but she made it up, by sincere enjoyment and passion. She was a happy and satisfied woman. "You are a tiger young man. I am too old for you. You need a virgin to make you real tired."

"You are very nice and sexy. You are better than many twenty year olds," complimented her Boro.

Landlady was pleased with Boro's flattery. "I know you are just flattering me, but it is nice to hear."

Among a number of affairs, one failure stuck in his mind. The girl was a young divorcee from the neighbouring village. He heard that she had a brief, unhappy marriage. She was tall and dark, not a particular beauty, but he fell in love with her smile and vulnerability. They just exchanged few amateurish kisses. That was as far as she allowed Boro to go. "She is afraid to get hurt again," thought Boro.

Boro loved her enough to let her know that he will soon leave for America, and he wanted her to come to America and get married to him. She refused, because she was not willing to leave her parents, village, nor her job. Boro was hurt. He cried for two days, not being able to get over the unanswered love. He finally consoled himself by thinking: "She probably hopes to get back with her husband."

His American visa approved, Boro was ready to make a big step in his life. He was sorry for leaving his elderly parents, but America was calling. 'Better life' was seductively smiling at him. His mom and dad cried a lot saying 'good bye,' so did Boro. Looking at both of them saddled with old age and failing health, he wondered: "Am I ever going to see them again?"

On the train he travelled so many times and had few exciting adventures, Boro was this time sad and withdrawn. He was leaving his country, parents, and friends, for a strange land.

In July 1969, Boro landed at an American airport. He met for the first time his older brother who left their village in 1944, three years after Boro was born. He stayed at his house.

That night, he was very tired from a long trip. He fell asleep almost instantly. Soon after he fell asleep, Stefan came. Boro was glad to see his old friend.

"Stefan, you found me even in America. How did you arrive, wings, or no wings?" joked Boro.

"Travel is the easiest thing for me. Directing my protégés on the right path of salvation is a touch harder," replied Stefan with a gentle smile.

"Stefan, you look majestic. That must be wonderful; to be young forever."

"My job is to help you in this life to deserve life in God`s Kingdom. You will be there above angels, because your soul will be reunited with your resurrected and un-corruptible body. You will be young forever."

"That is a pie in the sky for me now. I have to find a job, and I need a car. Can you help me?"

"It is not in my instructions to help you find a job, or buy a car. I work through other people; 'behind the scene,' so that you are unaware of my work. As I told you before, have faith."

"I cannot live on faith, nor can I buy a car with faith. I need dollars."

"I know that you cannot eat faith, nor buy a car on faith, but faith is your guide, which will direct you what to do in order to get the job and buy a car."

"Are you refusing as my guardian angel to help me at least get a job? I am disappointed."

"Please Boro, don`t get disappointed. I never refuse to help you, except when you ask me for something not permitted by my instructions. I am God`s faithful servant and I obey His instructions, not ninety nine, but one hundred percent."

"Okay Stefan, it`s fine. Thank you for watching over me and protecting me."

"Are you homesick Boro?"

"I am homesick, because of leaving my parents, friends, my country. But I am excited about life in America."

"Were you sorry for leaving women you had the affairs with?"

"Just a bit sad for leaving, ones closer to my heart."

"Who were these women?"

"Pera, as my first lover and the divorcee that rejected my invitation to come with me to America."

"Is your conscience bothering you for having these affairs with divorcees and married women?"

"I am not boasting about, but I had an affair with a girl who was a virgin. You knew that, didn`t you?"

Stefan smiled, "I was aware of Milena. What happened between you two?"

"I am not proud with my behaviour in this case. Why do you want me to talk about it, since you know what happened?"

"I know everything, but I would love to hear it from you."

"I was not excited by Milena. She was good looking, but there was no 'chemistry' between us."

"Why didn`t you end the relationship?"

"It was that stupid male pride. There was a girl, a virgin. How could I miss that opportunity, to have one more 'conquest,' virginity coming as 'the whipping cream' on top?"

"And, you 'got the girl."

"Yes, I did. I was her first."

"Why did you feel bad because of the way you behaved with Milena?"

"Because I was dishonest. She wanted to get married. She thought that 'going all the way,' would make us closer, and we would commit to each other."

"Obviously, you did not feel as her?"

"I lost interest and didn`t even say, bye, to her before I left for America."

"What do you think would have been proper way to treat Milena?"

"I should have told her, that I was not ready for a committed relationship, but was interested in just having fun."

"It is good that you feel remorse for your improper behaviour. God will forgive you this sin."

"Am I going to succeed in America Stefan? Are you allowed to reveal that?"

"It would be damaging to you to know your future."

"Why would it be damaging to me if I knew my future? I think it would be good."

"It may look like that, but it would be bad and contrary to God`s providence."

"Contrary to God`s providence? What do you mean by that?"

"If you knew your future, wouldn't that mean abrogation of your free will?"

"Why would it mean the abrogation of my free will?"

"If your future was revealed to you, wouldn't that mean that nothing you do could change your future?"

"Yes, if you put it like that. I could not change it."

"Don't you see that if you cannot change your future by your free will, you have no free will."

"Couldn't I still have my free will, just for 'the small stuff."

"Free will is free will. It applies to big and small decisions."

"I think it would be better if God took away free will to do bad things, giving us only free will to do good things. Wouldn't that be a perfect world?"

"Free will implies; good or bad choices, moral or immoral decisions, stupid or smart decisions."

"I can see now what free will is and why God chooses not to allow us to know our future for our own benefit. What about you Stefan. You have no free will, since you always do only good things?"

"I had a feeling you would ask that question. When God created us spiritual beings, He gave us free will. Using free will, the fallen angels with their leader Lucifer decided to rebel against God, while the good angels decided to stay in obedience to God. Angels made that choice once and for all time."

"It's not fair Stefan. God gave you angels a choice to decide, but denied choice to men."

"Boro, that is God's will. He created the world the way He wanted. Man is a special creation of God, a being created from the union of soul and body. God gives man opportunity during his life on earth to use his free will, chose to follow God or the Enemy. Depending on the choices man makes while in the body, he is preparing himself for Kingdom of heaven, or for Hell."

"Thank you Stefan. That was a beautiful explanation. I did lot of bad things. Am I in God's 'black book' because of that?"

"Boro, you are not in God's 'black book,' because He does not keep such a book. God loves you and wants you to 'qualify' to spend eternity with Him in His Kingdom of heaven."

"Does that mean that God already forgave me all my sins?"

"Did you ask God to forgive you your sins?"

"No, I did not. What do I say?"

"Admit that you sinned, and are repenting and asking God to forgive you and help you not to sin anymore."

"Is there another way to ask God for forgiveness?"

"The best way is to get confession and communion, as the Church prescribes."

"I remember my mom and baba were preparing for confession and communion. They were like changed persons during these preparations."

"What changed?"

"They become more at peace, kinder, gentler, and humbler."

"What happened at the end of the preparations?"

"They went to church, had confession and after that received communion."

"You told me that you never went for confession and communion."

"I never did."

"Would you like to have confession and communion in the church, before a priest?"

"I don't think I am ready for that yet."

"Why not?"

"I couldn't fast seven days to deny myself all good, normal food. I don't know any people of my age that had confession and communion in the church. It would be very awkward for me to do that. I would be ashamed to tell the priest all the bad things I have done."

"Are you talking about the Church in the old country?"

"Yes. Is it different in America?"

"There is quite a difference between young people in America and in the old country, regarding the attitude towards the Church."

"What kind of difference?"

"A lot of young people here have confession and communion several times a year."

"Are you saying that I should do it in the church?"

"That is the best way."

"A question Stefan: once I confess my sins and ask God to forgive me, what is the purpose of having the communion?"

"Do you know what holy communion is Boro?"

"I think it is small pieces of bread soaked in wine. Priest gives person one small spoon of that. Everybody gets it from the same chalice and with the same spoon."

"Do you know why the Holy Communion is given?"

"I don't know. But, I know that my mom and baba had enormous reverence for it, as something holy. I heard the priest calling the communion; 'The body and blood of Christ."

"Holy communion is essential for every Christian to partake. The sooner you get it, the better."

"Stefan, I really liked your visit and our talk today. Good news: I have been miraculously cured from my stomach ulcer. I am perfectly healthy again. Did you have your hand in this miracle?"

Stefan smiled, "Boro you are tempting me to bend my instructions. I will leave it to your budding, growing faith to figure it out. You should thank Lord Jesus Christ for restoring your health. It was wonderful graduation gift, a very nice 'carrot,' wasn't it Boro?"

"I thank God and I thank you my guardian angel, for a wonderful gift of healing my body. Thank you, thank you, thank you."

Stefan smiled shyly. Kissed young man on the cheek and disappeared.

The dawn was breaking over Jonesville. Life in the Promised Land was smiling to Boro.

## Chapter 15

## *America, the Blessed*

Boro was smart enough to prepare himself and learn English, before coming to America. He used a small book: "English in one hundred lessons," pretending to be an English gentleman, "Mister Brown." That provided him with basic knowledge to go to job interviews, and hold a conversation. He found out quickly that his chance of landing engineering job were slim, since his English was awkward, and he had only one year of engineering experience.

His brother helped him to get a job in the steel mill as electrician apprentice. At the same time, Boro applied to the Engineering Association to grant him his Engineering designation. About a month after this interview, Boro received a diploma confirming that he was granted 'Designated Engineer' status. Armed with his diploma, he applied and got engineering job in the steel mill. He got a pay raise, and now had a 'shirt and tie' job. He was very proud of his achievement.

After about nine months of working as an engineer, Boro decided to go back to school, to get some more education. He applied and got accepted at the local university in a Master's degree program. He was lucky to obtain the scholarship, which was just enough to cover his living expenses. He lived with his brother`s family, even managed to buy a small car. Boro was getting Americanized. Life was good.

During his studies at the University, he met a girl who came from Holland, the same year he came to America. They became lovers. Elizabeth was interested in marrying Boro. She was expecting him to 'kneel down' and ask for her hand. Boro hesitated. He was in no rush. While going out with Elizabeth, he had on the side a few short affairs. One of those encounters with a married women resulted in her pregnancy. She claimed that it was Boro's child, but he had a good alibi; her husband. She told Boro that she had an abortion. "It was a boy," she said. Boro felt no remorse. He never saw the woman again.

A few months after this incident Elizabeth told him that she was pregnant. Boro froze at the thought of ;marriage, baby, diapers, and obligations. He did not want any of that. He told Elizabeth that he was not ready for marriage, babies and commitment, and that she should have an abortion. After she had an abortion Elizabeth told him, 'It was a boy." The romance was over. Boro felt bad, but found consolation in the arms and beds of new lovers.

One day, Boro 'woke up' and took a picture of his life. He was approaching thirty. He decided that he had enough of the bed jumping affairs. It was time to settle down, find a good girl and get married. He did not tell his family, but they figured out that Boro was changing, and that his wandering days were coming to an end.

He figured out that the best place to meet a good 'marrying kind' of girl was to visit places where they went, in the church, and picnics. A girl he knew introduced him at a dance in the church hall to her friend, Jelena, tall and slender girl with a Hollywood smile. At the first sight of Jelena, a tiny voice from within whispered to Boro: "This girl is not for a 'quick love affair.' She is the girl to have a family with, to be a life companion."

Boro asked her to dance. They were both lousy dancers. They danced slowly, trying not to step on each other's feet. Right then and there, after the first dance, Boro decided: "The search is over. It is her. I am going to marry this girl. I've had enough of the affairs." Before the dance was over, they set up a date to meet again.

When he came to his little room and lay in bed Boro started analyzing the events of that life changing day. Thinking about it, and being tired of contradicting emotions, he fell asleep. He had no clue, how long he was asleep, when he noticed a visitor beside his bed.

"Who could that be?" He asked himself with trepidation. A beautiful, melodious 'out of this world' voice solved the mystery.

"Hello Boro, you forgot your old friend."

"Stefan, it's you. Sorry I almost forgot you. It has been long time since we met, seven or six years?"

"It's been almost four years."

"But, why does it seem to be much longer."

Stefan gave him a short, sad smile. "Boro, you are in America now, 'The land of freedom and opportunity.' Everybody, including you, is too busy chasing their American dream."

"I saw that most people were busy pursuing that dream, but it seems that people in America are much more religious than in the in the old country. They go to church more often, celebrate religious holidays, and keep traditions. Isn't that what God expects them to do?"

"God wants them to do all of that, but He is jealous God. He wants to be the focus of their lives, on the top of their priorities, not only on their lips, during church Sunday service, or other religious festivities, but in their hearts, all the time, always."

"Wow, that is a tall order Stefan. Not even monks in the monasteries are like that. What you are saying is impossible for us regular men, working for our living and struggling to improve our lives."

"What is impossible to man alone, is not impossible to men helped by God. Do you believe that?"

"I guess God can do anything He wants. What I am talking about is normal every day needs for any man; a good paying job, nice house, good car, money in the bank, being able to have decent vacations. I don't see that God is involved in these little 'trivial' details that are essential for every person while living on this small ball racing through the space."

"I think you are overlooking one essential fact Boro."

"Please tell me what I overlooked."

"If God did not give you living force that keeps your lungs breathing, blood circulating, cells working, brain operating, heart beating, mind thinking, emotions feeling, do you know what you would be?"

"I don't know what I would be without that living force?"

"You would be just a lifeless, rotting cadaver."

"That does not sound very nice."

"God sustains man's life. Man who thinks that he can exist, live and function on his own is a fool."

"I never heard you before being so critical of people in the old country Stefan. Why are you so critical of America? Do you dislike America?"

"I don't dislike America. Many Americans are dear to our Lord, keeping His commandments and having strong faith in His Son. Many of them are very charitable helping less fortunate people worldwide."

"I don't get you Stefan. First you criticized America, then you said that you don't dislike American people, and you even complimented them that many of them are 'dear to our Lord'. Can you explain this controversy?"

"There is no controversy. It is true and for good reasons that I criticized America. I complimented many of them as being believers in Lord Jesus Christ. Do you want to know why I criticize America?"

"I am anxious to hear that."

"America got seduced by the Enemy to gradually renounce Our Lord, and bow to gods of world power and supremacy, competitive struggle for materialistic success, and hedonistic pursuits of all kinds of deviant pleasures."

"Is God having the same opinion as you?"

"Angels are God's messengers and helpers. When I tell you something, it is what God wants me to tell you. Remember; the instructions."

"How could I forget these famous instructions that you mentioned so many times. Tell me please: Why would you criticize America for being the world power and leader. Isn't that normal thing that every nation strives to be? Do you see anything wrong, or immoral in that?"

"I see plenty of wrong and immoral in the pursuit of world supremacy and hegemony."

"I see this as a natural tendency, since they are the strongest, the richest nation on earth. It is normal for them to have main voice in world affairs. Didn't God give them all that, wealth, power and might?"

"God allowed America to amass huge wealth, army, economy, but it was American ruling class's choice to seek supremacy of the world. That was an exercise of their free will, not ordained by God."

"Anything wrong with that?"

"Plenty. America is putting itself in the place of God, deciding fates of people around the world."

"Yes, but you can't deny that America helps freedom and democracy all over the world. America gives huge amounts of money, food and other forms of aid to poor and developing nations around the world."

"That is true Boro, but it is also true that America does not do it just out of its goodness of the heart. America won't help unless it has benefits, market, cheap resources, and land. Americans have a good saying: 'If you want to find out the reason for the interventions--follow the money.'"

"I got you Stefan. You are warning me that even in America I can go wrong way and lose my salvation."

"More subtle dangers and seductions are waiting for you in ambush in America. They are usually disguised. You won't recognize them as the threats to your salvation, because they will appear so normal, regular and innocent."

Boro changed the topic all of a sudden. "How do you like Jelena, the girl I met at the church dance? Should I ask her to marry me? Are we a good match?"

"Glad you asked Boro. I am going to step on the very edge of my instructions and divulge a secret to you. Yours and Jelena's meeting was not an accident. It was arranged as the step in your life to prepare you for the calling God ordained for you."

Boro laughed loudly. "Again that talent of mine, that gift from God. Where is it? What talent and gift are you talking about Stefan? You keep talking and promising, but I see no trace of the talent. I sometimes think that you are just teasing me, or joking with me."

Stefan scolded Boro: "Please Boro, get that thought out of your head. I told you many times; guardian angels never lie, joke, nor tease."

"I am sorry Stefan. I did not intend to insult you, nor question your character. I just got a bit frustrated. Please forgive me. Anyway, it would help, if you could open the veil from that secret of my talent."

"Do not worry Boro, I don't feel insulted. I am aware of your impatience and frustrations for not knowing much about your gift from God and your life calling. You are now being trained to learn to be patient. As I told you before, you will hear about your gift when ready."

"Is there anything I can do to speed up uncovering of that mystery?"

"Of course. It is your life and you are the main player. You can reject that gift of God, or speed up its disclosure."

"What do I need to do to speed up uncovering of that secret gift?"

"It is not one single thing."

"Could you be bit more specific please?"

"I will, as much as I am allowed to."

"Instructions again?"

"Of course. Strive to live good, honest, clean, and moral life. You found the girl you are going to marry. You must be faithful to her from the moment you make up your mind to marry her. Lord has forgiven you your former sexual indiscretions and affairs, but any future ones would be extremely threatening to your salvation, particularly to your God given talent."

"God is very kind for forgiving me all the bad things I have done. Please thank Him for me Stefan."

Stefan smiled, "I just did Boro. Lord is pleased with your repentance."

"Does that mean that Lord is going to forgive me easily any future sins, as He forgave me the past ones?"

"It is very dangerous idea to believe: 'I am going to sin as much as I like. Not to worry. God is going to forgive all my sins, no questions asked.' This would be mocking God, or bargaining with Him. Both are bad ideas. Lord expects when temptation to sin attacks you, fight it, but also invoke God`s help in fighting it. If after genuine fight, you still succumb to the temptation, Lord will forgive you, if you humble yourself before Him and repent."

"I got it Stefan. I need to try to go straight, resisting the temptations. I got to 'turn the page.'"

"I am with you always. I will be the power behind the scene, an invisible guardian, helper and secret organizer. Before I leave you I will introduce you to the guide, which will help you to go 'straight and narrow."

"What kind of the guide is that?"

"It is Ten Commandments of God. Do you know what they are?"

"I think I know most of them, but I am unable to recite them all in a proper order."

"Would you like me to recite them?"

"Yes please."

Beautiful angel began proclaiming God`s Commandments. Boro listened to Stefan`s recitation in awe. "Stefan, this is beautiful. I have never heard anything so pleasing to my heart and to my ears."

Stefan smiled. "Thank you Boro for the compliment. You now know all the Commandments."

"I don`t think I broke any Commandment."

"Can we check one by one?"

"Sure, but I told you I am clean. No Commandments broken."

"That would be great, but let's check. How about the first one? Did you ever violate it?"

"I don't believe I did. What is; 'the other gods?'"

"The other gods' could be anything, or anybody you worshiped instead of God, such as power, money, glory, your own body, a person, false gods."

"What if someone does not believe in God? Is that person violating this Commandment?"

"Yes, he does."

"How?"

"This Commandment also requires 'Not to have other gods besides Lord God,' which implies that if you don't 'have' God, you are clearly violating the first commandment. Do you see now that you broke this commandment?"

"I understand this commandment now. I have broken it because I did not 'have' God, but had other 'gods' like sex and soccer. I am guilty. How do I insure that I don't break this commandment?"

"Believe in God. Don't put anything or anybody on the pedestal as god."

"What about the Second Commandment?"

"This one is almost the same as the first one. I don't see how could I have broken that one."

"This commandment is similar to the first one, but it goes further forbidding worshiping anything that is not of God."

"I heard some Protestant Christians here in America are very much against icons, saying that we worship icons as 'graven images' and pray to them. They see it as idol worshiping. What about that?"

"In Orthodox Church you do not worship icons, you worship only God. You revere icons as bearing images of the saints, God Mother, angels and Lord Jesus Christ. When you kiss an icon, bow before it and pray, you are not worshiping the saint depicted on the icon, you are just showing him reverence, asking him to be your intercessor before God. Icons help you to focus on the prayer and worshiping God."

"Are icons Okay?"

"Yes, they are. What about the Third Commandment Boro?"

"One about not taking Lord`s name in vain?"

"Yes."

"Neither me, nor anybody in my family liked to swear, taking Lord`s name in vain."

"Very good Boro. What about number four?"

"Is that the one about not working on Sunday?"

"Yes, it is."

"I have broken this Commandment many times. I think this is one of the most violated Commandments. Present way of life forces people to break this Commandment."

"Men really went overboard breaking this Commandment. God is displeased with men, because they so brazenly and openly violate this Commandment."

"It is very hard to avoid breaking this Commandment. If your job requires you to work Sunday, or if you are a farmer and must harvest, or plough fields on Sunday; what do you do?"complained Boro.

"God is forgiving and merciful, but will be displeased with you if you choose to work on Sunday, although you didn`t have to, or you attend various sporting events and godless entertainment, instead of dedicating Sunday to God, and your family."

"I will do my best to dedicate Sunday to God and my family."

"God will reward you for that. Let`s go to the Fifth Commandment. How did you do on that one?"

"That is one about honouring my mother and my father. I really loved and respected my mother and father. I don`t remember when I insulted or disobeyed them. I am sorry for not helping them and visiting them more in their old age. Particularly, that I did not go to be with my father when he was terminally ill. I light candle in the church every Sunday in his memory."

Stefan kissed Boro on the forehead. "Boro, you were a good son. Lord is pleased with your obedience of this Commandment. Let`s see the next Commandment."

"Thou shalt not kill.' I am clean on this one."

"Just a minute Boro, when you were single, two of your lovers got pregnant by you. They had abortions, killing these unborn children. Didn't you encourage the mothers to be, to commit these murders, and thus you were an accomplice in killing of these two innocent, unborn children?"

"I am surprised Stefan that you call these surgical procedures killing and murder. These were not children, just fetuses, parts of their mothers, who should have absolute control of their bodies, shouldn't they?"

"Do you believe that absolute control woman exercises over her body, includes the right to kill the child growing within that women?"

"But, that was part of women's body. That was a fetus, not a child, it is just a surgical procedure, like removing an unwanted growth from woman's body."

"Really? Could you please explain how do you kill a person?"

"Everybody knows that Stefan. Is this a trick question?"

"No trick questions from guardian angels. Could you answer please?"

"Killing means taking a person's life."

"Does it matter when in his life the person is killed? Ten years old, twenty five years old, or ninety five year old?"

"Life is life at any age. Killing is killing regardless of the age of the killed person."

"I love your clear, precise answer Boro. You told me killing a person at any time in his life is killing."

"Yes, that's what I said."

"Thanks for confirming that. Could you please tell me when did your life begin?"

"What a ridiculous question? My life began when I was born."

"Guardian angels don't ask neither ridiculous, nor tricky questions."

"Sorry Stefan. I was shocked by your question."

"Were you alive five minutes before you were born? three month before you were born? or nine months before you were born?"

*A Kingdom to Buy*

"I was not alive as a person, because I was not born yet. I was alive in my mother's womb as a fetus, a part of her body."

"What would happen if there was a complication five minutes before you supposed to be born and fetus, that supposed to become you, died in the mom's womb, before being born. Would you still be alive and talking to me now?"

"Of course I would not be alive. How could I be, if I was not born?"

"You were born, but not alive."

"What is your point Stefan in this questioning?"

"My point Boro is to raise your awareness of the vital truths. This is an important one."

"What am I supposed to become aware off?"

"You said that if the fetus that supposed to become a person dies or gets killed in the womb, 'the person to be' will not live, because that person was the fetus that died, or was murdered."

"Are you suggesting that the fetus in my mom's womb was, me. Killing that fetus, meant- killing me."

"Excellent Boro! You formulated the question and you provided a concise answer."

"But, how far back do you go? Do you go all the way to the formation of the embryo; the conception, which is, as I learnt in school, just a blob of the biological material."

"Is it true that without conception, no child would be born? What does that tell you when your life began?"

"I must say, life begins at the conception."

"What do you believe is an abortion?"

"Are you suggesting Stefan that the abortion is killing of an unborn person, a murder?"

"I prefer Boro that you draw your own conclusion, based on our discussion."

"It is a heavy saying Stefan. I could be in trouble for saying something like that, I could go to jail."

"I am aware of that Boro, but I am asking you is that the truth?"

"Well, it could be the truth, but perhaps, it should be softened a bit, formulated in a more politically correct manner in order not to offend people and cause trouble with the law."

"How could it be said in a different, non-offending, politically correct manner?"

"There are quite a few different terms used to describe killing of a child in the womb of its mother: 'Unwanted pregnancy termination, family planning procedure, population control measure.'"

"What is the purpose of these politically correct wordings for killing of unwanted children?"

"I think it is to placate people. Most women, who had abortion, would be mad at you if you told them: 'You had your child taken out of your womb and killed.' They would protest: 'You are mean. Nobody was killed. It was just a surgical procedure to remove an unwanted fetus, which is part of my body, and I can do with it what I want without asking anybody`s permission.'"

"Are you aware Boro of the sin you committed by inducing your lovers to kill theirs, and also your children?"

"It is heavy saying Stefan. Are you accusing me of being an accomplice in the murder of my own children?"

"Don`t you see, that by realizing what a terrible thing you have done, you are accusing yourself of the participation in the murder of your children?"

"You are right Stefan," said Boro his voice trembling with sadness. "When I did these things, I didn`t realize what I was doing. I was a selfish pig, thinking only about satisfying my lust."

"Are you sorry for what you have done? Did you ask God to forgive you?"

"I am scared to ask God to forgive me. What punishment awaits me? Will God forgive me this ugly sin?"

"God forgave those who crucified, mocked and tortured His Only Begotten Son. He will forgive your sins, if you repent and ask Him for forgiveness."

"What should I say Stefan? I don`t know any prayers for this occasion. Please help me," panicked Boro.

## A Kingdom to Buy

"Just say: 'Lord I have sinned greatly. I am sorry for sinning. I am repenting and asking you to forgive me these sins, and please Lord help me to sin no more."

"That is a wonderful prayer Stefan. Do I need to repeat it, after you?"

"No, your prayer was received by our Merciful Lord. He has forgiven you. Sin no more."

"Thank you Stefan. I love you; you are the best guardian angel."

"Thank you for the compliment Boro. How about number seven."

"The one about not committing adultery?"

"Yes, that one."

"Doesn't adultery apply only to married people?"

"On technicality you are clear of breaking this Commandment."

"How about the next Commandment?"

"That is number eight. 'Thou shalt not steal."

"How did you do on this one?"

"We were taught at home from very young age that stealing was sin. God would punish us for stealing, and our parents would too. Clean hundred percent on this one."

"Excellent Boro. Our Lord is pleased with you. How about number nine?"

"Is that the one: 'Thou shalt not bring false witness against thy neighbour?"

"Yes, it is. How did you do on this one?"

"I am clean as a whistle. I cannot recall that I ever purposely did a bad thing to my neighbour. Baba told us many times: 'Have fear of God and shame of people."

"You are doing great Boro. Only number ten left. Clean on this one too?"

"This is the long one, saying that I should not desire things that belong to my neighbour such as; his house, land, servants, and livestock. I never wished any of that stuff from my neighbour."

"That's great Boro, but didn't you miss an important belonging of your neighbour, that you should not desire to have?"

"No, I included them all. Let me read it again: 'Thou shalt not covet thy neighbour's wife. Thou…I got it; I missed 'the wife.' But I think I am clean on this one. I never wished any man's wife to be my wife."

"Did you ever have an affair with a married woman?"

"Yes, I did. But that has nothing to do with this Commandment. I never stole any wife from her husband, nor forced them to have an affair with me."

"Were you aware that they were married women when you met them and had an affair with them?"

"Of course I was aware, but it was their choice."

"It was their choice, they were committing adultery. Didn't you also break this Commandment by desiring other man's wife, your neighbour's wife?"

"I don't see what could I have done if woman consented of her free will. She was sinning, committing adultery, but I can't see how I was sinning?"

"God commanded you not to desire other man's wife. So what did you need to do not to break this Commandment?"

"Are you suggesting that if I had an affair with a married woman, I have sinned and broken God's Tenth Commandment."

"Brilliant conclusion Boro, brilliant. You are aware now that having an affair with a married woman, was sinning and breaking God's Commandment. Are you sorry you committed such sins?"

"Yes, I am sorry. Do I need again ask Lord to forgive me?"

"Lord has seen into your heart that you had sincerely repented, and He has forgiven you."

"Do I need to thank God for forgiving me my sins?"

"Always. Every moment of your life you should be grateful to Lord your God, your Creator and Redeemer."

"These are very hard commandments to keep. Almost impossible to keep them all. How did I do overall?"

"Pretty good, except in sexual behaviour. You did lot of sinning there, but you did some good things."

"What good did I do in my love adventures?"

"You had many affairs; single girls, married women, divorced women, widows. How did you behave towards these ladies?"

"I was always polite, discrete and respectful towards my lovers."

"Were you dishonest with any of your lovers?"

"I was. I behaved dishonestly with few of them. I am sorry that I did not asked them to forgive me."

"Did you ask God to forgive you these transgressions?"

"Yes, I did, but I don`t know if God forgave me these sins."

"God forgave you all your sins. Lord saw your clean heart, though it was stained by the passion. He saw that you will renounce your sinful ways and become His faithful follower. Remember the incident you had, when you beat Eros hands down?"

"Was I ever able to do that?"

"It was about a year before you came to America."

"I remember now. That was Nevena."

"Please tell me what happened."

"Why…not much to tell; Nevena was working in the plant as a machine operator. She was twenty years old, beautiful brunette. We talked and flirted at work and in the company cafeteria. I persuaded her to come to my rented room one evening, 'just for a drink.' She came. Clean, healthy, gorgeous young girl. I was sure that she was aware of my intentions; otherwise she would not come alone to my room.

After small talk and few strong drinks, I moved toward my goal starting the foreplay, but when I was just getting ready for 'the real thing,' trying to undress her, she gently held my hand, giving me a signal to stop. To my surprise-- I stopped."

"Boro, listen to me please. I am still a virgin. I like you. I will consent to whatever you want if you promise me that soon after this we will get engaged."

"I was ambushed. Mr. Eros was shouting through my excited body: 'Go ahead, promise anything to get her. They all say; 'no, no,' but really expect you not to listen to that. You will easily find an excuse to get rid of her. Don`t be a chicken. Go for it, lie, get her."

I listened to the convincing words of Mr. Eros and almost decided to follow his urgings, but, something unexplainable happened, as if a 'Counter Eros' took over my mind and warned me: 'Don`t be a dirty, lying hypocrite. Don`t ruin this young girl`s life for a few minutes of your selfish pleasure." I stopped disrobing her, got up and sat in the chair beside my bed:

"Look Nevena,' I said,' you are young and beautiful girl, and I am excited about you. I like you,but I don`t want to lie to you and hurt you. I am not ready to get engaged yet. The best is if you go home now. Nobody will ever know what happened between us tonight."

I saw that Nevena was disappointed and sad. She got up straightened her clothing, combed her hair and quietly left."

"Wonderful victory Boro! Eros ran with his tail between his legs. Did you feel good about your behaviour?"

"Most of time. Occasionally, Eros would tease me: 'Ha, honest man, you could of had her, you chicken, missed one more conquest, a true virgin."

"This will be a bright shining light for you in this and in the life to come Boro. That was a significant victory over Mr. Eros, over your lust, your flesh. More victories will surely follow."

"I sure hope Stefan. I still have a question for you. What is the role of Eros in an intimate relationship?"

"God created Eros to be a 'fire starter, in the relationship. Since you were born in the village you knew how to start a fire?"

"I started fire many times, roasted corn, or potatoes, while tending sheep, or cows."

"How did you make the fire?"

"I collected dry wood. Thick branches were needed to provide the heat and the cinder for baking, while very thin branches or dry leaves were needed to begin the fire and to spread it to the thicker branches."

"What did you use to start the fire?"

"We usually used matches."

"Are you saying that the matches started the fire?"

"Yes. Are you suggesting that the matches were; "the fire starter?"

"It is obvious, isn't it?"

"I don't see what matches and Mr. Eros have in common."

"Matches are used to start the fire. What does Eros start?"

"Hmmm, I see what are you getting to. Eros starts the relationship."

"Do you see how Eros is similar to the matches?"

"It starts the fire of a relationship. It quickly burns. It cannot sustain the relationship on its own, just like matches cannot sustain the fire."

"You are aware now Boro that God created Eros to start 'the fire' of the relationship. He is not the sustainer, just the fire starter."

"Yes, I am fully aware now. You are great teacher Stefan. Thank you!"

"You did it all by yourself. I just helped."

"Yes, but without your guidance and direction, I could not figure this out by myself."

"You are making good progress Boro. You got an honest and beautiful girl. Your marriage will be blessed and long lasting."

"Thank you Stefan. I have to ask Jelena to marry me. You think she is going to agree?"

Stefan smiled, "You have an excellent chance, unless you do something stupid to turn her off."

"Don't worry, Stefan. I have matured. I am not going to do anything stupid, immoral, or improper. That is 'water under the bridge' for me."

"I believe you Boro. Always remember; you are not alone. I will be watching you. Just be aware of that and be aware how I work. That is very important."

"Should I pray to you Stefan?"

"You can pray to me as you would pray to God Mother or saints to intercede with our prayers to God on your behalf. I am a created spiritual being. Don't pray to me, pray to Holy Trinity, or any of the members of the Holy Trinity, Father, Son, and the Holy Spirit."

"Thank you Stefan for clarifying this. Do you have any other suggestion for me before we part?"

"You will be entering a different phase of your life. There will be various temptations and challenges. Do not repeat the sins from your past, the sins of sexual passion. Lord has forgiven them all. Do not even mention these sins ever in your confessions. Consider them gone, wiped out, forgiven forever. If you get entangled again in the net of Mr. Eros, getting involved in an adultery, your life will be miserable.

When temptations attack you, remember your childhood; see yourself sleeping in bed with your mom, listening to her prayers. Remember your baba praying and fasting. These were good seeds sown into your soul. Your memory and remembrance of them will be to your faith, like sunshine and rain are to a flower. This will strengthen your faith, helping you to resist the temptations. I could suggest many, many more things, but I think it could be counterproductive. The important thing is that you made the decision to change your life and your behaviour. You will 'know' what to do. Your conscience and I will be your guides and watchmen. Enjoy the journey."

Stefan knelt beside Boro's bed gently caressing his face and said: "Yes Lord, I understand, I will." The next moment he was not there anymore. It was just a young man sleeping with a mysterious, happy smile on his face.

# Chapter 16

# *Tying the Knot*

After spending more time with Jelena, Boro concluded: "Surely, Stefan arranged for two of us to meet. She is almost the perfect girl for me to marry. I've had women sexier than her, but overall she is just what I need: same upbringing as mine, religious Orthodox family, moral, most likely still a virgin, healthy."

Boro attempted to consummate his forthcoming marriage, but was gently, yet firmly rejected every time he tried. That frustrated him a bit. He was a healthy young man used to have women regularly, but now, he was forced to be the abstainer. On the other hand, he was glad Jelena rejected his advances. He reasoned: "If she gave in to my advances, who is to say that she would not do it for some previous boyfriend. She is a good looking girl, and has likely had boyfriend before me."

His failure to convince her to "go all the way" actually made him respect her even more, and assured him that he made right choice of his life partner.

He did not even formally ask Jelena to marry him, nor did they have the engagement. "Why bother," he thought. "Let's just get married as soon as possible." They both had to have confession and communion before their wedding in the church. This was the first time for Boro. He did not feel any special emotions, or enlightenment after getting communion.

Boro was eagerly awaiting to consummate his marriage. The first night after the wedding they spent in a local motel. Fate was cruel to Boro. Jelena had her period and was safe from the advances of her passionate husband.

"Another blank, looks like bye, bye good times when I could have it whenever I wanted. Rationing seems to be the way from now on. Poor me."

They had some money left over from the wedding reception. Not having American passports they could not fly to the sunny islands and sandy beaches of the Caribbean. They decided to drive along the East Coast, visiting Boro's school buddies from university.

Boro realized years later how stupid that idea was. It was the middle of cruel, cold American winter. Within a few days they packed up their winter clothing and went on their way: honeymoon driving in the American winter. The car was good; he had some money, good looking virgin wife (hopefully). Boro was a happy man. He had everything a young man needs.

They stopped often for coffee and food. Not a boring moment. Finally, after driving through a blizzard for hours, they arrived at their destination. It was bitter cold in that northern town. They rented a room in the motel and ordered Chinese food.

That night, lady luck smiled to Boro. Jelena's monthly was over. No more excuses! Boro was gentle with his bride. She truly was a virgin. It took a bit of extra effort and a few painful sighs from Jelena, but their marriage was consummated. They were now husband and wife.

After the honeymoon was over a normal, family life began. They both found jobs in a nearby town. Boro was working as an engineer, Jelena worked in a local factory. They rented small apartment on the second floor of a house owned by an elderly childless couple. The apartment was furnished, except one minor item, it was missing a bed. That did not bother young couple. They bought a mattress and had a good time sleeping and making love on it. They talked about saving money and buying a house first, and then starting a family. It sounded like a good, logical idea, because a baby would "disturb" their plans. Jelena would not be able to work, plus all those extra expenses connected with a baby, diapers, formula.

For about a week, they practised a primitive form of contraception. Boro hated it. But, he said to himself: "There is no way we can save enough money for a house down payment only on my salary."

One night, after vigorous love making, they both quickly fell asleep. That night his guardian angel appeared. Boro greeted him :"Stefan, my friend. I am glad to see you. I need your advice."

Stefan smiled greeting his protégé: "I sensed you needed me Boro." He turned towards Jelena who was sound asleep besides Boro. "She is beautiful?"

Boro replied with a happy smile; "Yes Stefan she is beautiful. I am happy. Thank you for arranging for us to meet."

Stefan smiled back. "It was my pleasure. I did exactly as per my instructions. The Lord thought it was a good match for a man He bestowed a special gift upon."

"Are you talking about me Stefan? For a moment I thought you spoke about somebody else. Am I that guy with a special gift from God? Are you talking about that talent that I have, but I still have no clue what it is?"

"There is no 'somebody else' Boro. You are the man that God bestowed special gift upon. I told you that numerous times. Do you doubt my word?"

Boro shook his head left and right; "I am trying to believe in that talent, but it is like trying to see a ship in a dense fog. I tell myself: "Stefan said I was gifted by God. He is God`s messenger and helper. He is my guardian angel. I must believe him.

But, then another voice, mocks me. 'Special gift? What is so special about you? Are you good looking? No, definitely not. Are you especially smart? Not at all. You failed in school. You are a mediocre engineer. Are you smart businessman? Not at all. You are too shy and timid. Are you athletic; strong, fast, tough? No, not at all. You are an average 'Joe Blow,' one of the five billion-- nothing special about you. Somebody is giving you false hope, raising your tail. He is deceiving you. If you had that special gift, what did you do with it? Did you become rich, famous, an important person? You did not. Why? Because, you have no gift. Stop living in the delusion. Wake up. Cut that fantasy short."

Stefan was listening with astonishment to Boro's monologue.

"Boro, I am glad that you opened up your heart and told me very precisely what bothers you."

"Perhaps I should have done it much sooner. You knew about it Stefan didn't you?"

"Yes, of course I knew. It is important that you become aware of that disbelief and that you verbalize it. It is like going to a doctor. More precisely you describe your health problem, the better chance is that the doctor can make a correct diagnosis of your ailment, and prescribe a proper medication to heal you."

"Are you in this case 'the doctor,' and I am the patient?"

"Boro, real doctor of human soul and body is God. I am just an assistant helping with the patients, carrying out 'Doctors' orders."

"Doctor's assistant, what is the diagnosis and is there medication to cure my sickness?"

"There is diagnosis and medication to cure your illness."

"Well, what is the diagnosis, what is my illness?"

"Your illness is disbelief, caused by the Enemy's attack on your mind by swamping you with thoughts you described as 'an another voice."

"The Enemy? Are you talking about The Devil, alias Lucifer, that is messing up my mind?"

"Yes, Boro. He is God's enemy and your enemy."

"I see no reason for the Enemy trying to mess me up and confuse me. Who am I? I am not important person for him to pay so much attention to me?"

"The Enemy tries to mess up and confuse every human being. His biggest targets are men God gave special gifts to serve Him. The Enemy will persistently try to convince them that they have no special gift, and that this is 'just a fantasy, an illusion' of person thinking that he, amongst billions, was selected by God to receive that gift."

"Stefan you made a correct diagnosis. Those were exactly the thoughts drilling into my head. But, I am still confused why me as a special target."

"The Enemy knows what your gift is. He is trying, to prevent you from ever applying your talent."

"Why is the Enemy concerned of me using my talent?"

"Because, knowing what that gift is, he knows that by applying your talent you would help people to abandon Devil and become Lord Jesus Christ's servants and followers."

"Is my gift that big Stefan? It is hard for me to believe."

"Believe, believe Boro, it is big gift. God gives big gifts."

"Does the Enemy have a chance to destroy my gift, or convince me not to use it?"

"Oh yes, he does have that opportunity."

"He cannot destroy the gift God bestowed on me, can he?"

"No, the Enemy is unable to destroy the gift God gave you, but he might succeed in convincing you that you actually don't have it. Even if he admits that you have it, he will attempt to convince you to use your God given talent 'not today, but tomorrow."

"Does the Enemy ever succeed to confuse people that have special talent from God?"

"Tragically, he often persuades people gifted by God to use that gift against God. They help the Enemy to seduce more people and turn them away from Lord Jesus Christ."

"Why is the Enemy able to do that? Why God allows him to do it?"

"You are asking a 'loaded' question. Only God knows the answer to that question, not even us angels."

"I am puzzled why God would not allow you, His helper and faithful servant to know all the mysteries?"

"Does not the Creator have a right to decide about His creation? He is the absolute Master of everything. You could ask again and again: why? And still would not get the answer that your human brain would be able to comprehend. Our Heavenly Father in His wisdom allows you to grasp by your mind some things. As you grow spiritually, God may increase your comprehension, but some things will be out of the bounds to you. This is all for your benefit. You need to accept it."

"Thank you Stefan. I won't display my unbelief in the gift God gave me."

"You need to understand some basic truths Boro. Nothing happens if God does not will it to happen, or allows it to happen. God never violates man's free will.

Man is free to choose to follow God, or Devil. Devil cannot force man to do anything unless man consents to Devils suggestions.

And the answer to your other question, 'Why God allows the Enemy to attack men,' is given already, because this is all part of God's plan of men's salvation."

"How do I fight such a powerful enemy as Devil?"

"Boro, this is a lifelong struggle for every man. No man can avoid that struggle."

"Not even saints?"

"Most saints went through horrific struggle against Satan and their own passions and flesh."

"Saints fighting against their own passions and flesh? Why would anybody fight against his own flesh?"

"You would understand this, if you read the Holy Bible."

"I am sorry that I have not read Holy Bible, but why don't you explain this assuming I was an illiterate peasant that doesn't even know the Bible exists."

"Do you know what I mean when I say 'the flesh?'"

"Well, I know what the flesh is. We eat the flesh of the animals. I am made of the flesh and bones, but I am not sure what kind of 'the flesh' you were talking about."

"Instead of saying 'flesh and bones, the word flesh is used. Flesh is man's body. Do you understand this?"

"Yes, I do"

"Do you know what the passions are?"

"I am not sure."

"What do you love to do in your spare time?"

"I love to go fishing, as soon as I have some free time. I grab my fishing gear and supplies and head to the lake, or river. I find nice spot by the water. Just sit there and fish. I really enjoy and love it."

"Boro, you just described a passion, your passion for fishing."

"Are you saying Stefan that my fishing passion is sinful and I need to fight against it?"

"I am not saying that. But let's assume that this fishing passion becomes so strong, that you neglect your job, your family, your faith. All you want to do is: Fishing, fishing, and more fishing. Don't you think that you would have to fight this fishing passion, before it seriously made a mess of your life?"

"Naturally, I would have to fight it."

"And how would you fight it?"

"Do less fishing, so that it does not ruin my faith, family and my job."

"Well said Boro. There are many other passions."

"Like what?"

"What happens if you meet a good looking woman?"

"Oh, I got you. I might get the desire to make love to her."

"What would happen with your life, your health, your mind, your family, if this passion to make love becomes your obsession? You want to make love to every good looking women you meet?"

"I mighty go crazy, damage my health, and ruin my family, my work."

"And what would you need to do with that passion?"

"I would have to control it."

"How would you control it?"

"I am a happily married man. I should make love only to my wife."

"Can you think of any other passions?"

"How about passion for alcohol, drugs, food?"

"These are the big ones. What if you desire to wash five times daily, wear always fancy, expensive clothing? Or the desire to get rich at any cost?"

"I see these are the passions as well. Each one could make my life a mess if I indulge in it excessively."

"Do you understand now what it means to, struggle against the passions and flesh?"

"I understand why I have to struggle against my passions, but why should I fight against my flesh?"

"Where do the passions originate? For instance, the passion for excessive food, drugs, alcohol?"

"From my body."

"What about the other passions?"

"I think they also have the source in my body."

"Do you understand now what it means to struggle, against flesh and passions?"

"Yes, I understand. Thank you Stefan. You are a great teacher."

Stefan was very pleased. "Thank you Boro. If I had a body, I would be blushing now. I have a great Teacher and Master, our Lord."

"I see that I really have to educate myself about these things. I have to find the time to read the Bible."

"I am sure Boro that you are going to start reading the Bible. You will read many books not quite in accordance with the Bible and you would get engaged in some practices not exactly proper for an Orthodox Christian."

"I always read all kinds of books. I see no reason to stop reading them now."

"I know that Boro, but these would be different kinds of books, so called, Christian and spiritual books, but actually might be dangerous to you, leading you astray, and jeopardizing your salvation."

"How do I know if a book I read is dangerous to my salvation?"

"This is quite big, and as you say in your world, controversial subject. I could give you a list of books 'not to read,' or give you a lengthy lecture: 'How to spot the book dangerous to your salvation', but I am not going to do that."

"You will let me make my own mistakes, and learn from them?"

"Almost right. I will not abandon you. Remember, I am on guard always. I will be watching over you and protecting you."

"I am surprised that one can lose his salvation as easy, in rich and free America, as in communist dictatorships in the old country. How can that be? People are free here to worship whichever way they like, attend any church they like, believe whatever they choose to believe. Isn`t that beautiful; true freedom and democracy?"

Stefan was shaking his beautiful angelic head. "Boro, you just summed it up almost unconsciously, giving the reasons why man can lose easily his salvation in free, democratic America. Your talent cannot be hidden, even if you try to hide it."

"I need to know what the dangers are here in America, for my salvation."

"Boro this is a complex issue. My suggestion to you: keep your faith basic, simple, and childlike. Remember what your baba and your mom taught you. They have sown good seed of faith in your soul. Allow it to germinate. When the time is ripe it will blossom. Patience is a great virtue; practice it as much as you can. That is all the direction and instruction I am going to give you now. You conscience will guide you. You will know when you do something wrong against God`s Commandments. We will talk soon."

After gently kissing sleeping young man and his bride, Stefan spread his huge golden wings and was gone in a blink of an eye.

# Chapter 17

## *The Enemy`s Plotting*

Boro worked in the plant where the workforce was mainly women.

He was thirty two years old, tall, and pretty good looking. His job required him to do frequent tours of the plant. Being a nice guy, he greeted all ladies politely, with a pleasant smile. Few of the ladies responded with very friendly smile, signaling young man; 'I like you."

The sweetest, the most flirtatious smile came from a married woman a few years his senior. She reminded him of Pera. The same build, just better looking, like an actress. Their greetings and talks became more frequent and more and more friendly. Boro was finding any excuse to go by her workstation, to see her and talk to her. A bond was developing, a mutual feeling of liking, growing stronger and stronger. Boro was aware that he was happily, just married man, but Ivona was such a sexy woman.... He started imagining him and Ivona in a passionate embrace in a motel room.

After three months spent at the plant Boro was fired. The plant manager decided that this young, intelligent engineer did not pay attention to small, important details in his work. Boro was hurt and upset. Just married and no job! Being unable to find another job in the town, they had to move to the bigger city, where he got a job. They found a small apartment on the second floor of a house.

## A Kingdom to Buy

The job Boro found was just opposite of his previous job. No women working. He had to work lot of overtime, supervising repairs of the equipment by the contractors. One night he came home very dirty and tired. After a long shower, he had something to eat and went straight to bed. He sensed soon that he had a visitor. It was Stefan looking unusually stern and serious, almost angry.

Boro broke the silence: "Hello Stefan, how are you? You look so stern and serious. Something bad happened?"

"Boro, you see projection of your conscience on my face."

"I have no clue why my conscience would be stern and serious. I have not done anything improper."

"You have not committed any immoral action, but you contemplated to do it."

"What was I contemplating of doing?"

"The Enemy attacked you, filling your head with the thoughts of lust. You started fantasizing of committing adultery with that good looking woman that reminded you of Pera."

Boro blushed. "I cannot hide anything from you Stefan. Few times I did have thoughts like that. Nothing happened. No harm was done. I don't know why you make a big deal out of bit of my fantasizing?"

"You don't realize how close you were to commit a sin that would ruin your life in this and in the world to come."

"But, I didn't do anything. How could I be guilty of something I have not done?"

"Would you like to know what would likely be the next step in your fantasizing?"

"I am eager to hear it."

"Did that good looking lady, Ivona remind you of Pera?"

"Yes, she did."

"Did that arise in your mind the memory of your affair with Pera?"

"Yes, it did."

"Pleasant, lustful and passionate pictures in your mind?"

"Yes, very much so."

"Did the fantasy stop there, or did you go a step further."

"Step further? Nothing happened. Just a bit of fantasizing."

"Was Ivona the object of your erotic fantasies?"

"Yes, she was."

"You began imagining yourself having an affair with Ivona?"

"Yes, but that was only innocent fantasy. I did not do anything immoral or improper."

"Did you believe Ivona liked you?"

"I don`t know. She was very pleasant to me. Always nice, big warm smile."

"Wasn`t that, a message; 'I like you, I am thinking of you?"

"Perhaps it was."

"It seems there was mutual attraction between you and Ivona?"

"I think you are right Stefan."

"And what would be the next step in your relationship?"

"Nothing. We were attracted to each other. Many men and women are attracted to each other. They just fantasize for a while, but do nothing."

"Did you imagine yourself with Ivona, in a secret date in a motel?"

Blushing, Boro said quietly; "Yes, I did imagine us having an affair in a motel on the outskirts of the town."

"It seems, both of you were ready for the action. Wouldn`t the next step be to arrange that clandestine date?"

"I don`t think that would happen. Ivona would refuse to jeopardize her marriage. Do you think I would do that, to ruin my marriage?"

"Do you believe nothing would happen between you and Ivona, if you stayed there few more months?"

"I don`t think Stefan I would have an affair with her. It would be risky for both of us. It would be very hard to hide."

"Both of you wanted to have an affair, but were hesitating to do it, because you were afraid of the consequences?"

"Well, I would not put it exactly that way Stefan. We were just fantasizing about an affair."

"Every action you contemplate begins in your mind as an idea, and then you create a picture in your imagination of that action, and finally do it?"

"I don`t see what are you getting at? What is the connection?"

"The connection is: You and Ivona had pictures in your minds of an affair. You were afraid to do it, but as your desire and lust grew, it would overpower any caution and fear. You would find the way to do it. Does that seem likely scenario to you?"

"I hope nothing like that would happen. We would be crazy to do it. We could not hide it for ever."

"Before you got married you had affairs you knew were improper, but you did get involved in. Do you remember why?"

"I certainly do. My lust overpowered my conscience, which capitulated against much stronger opponent."

"Don`t you think in this case with Ivona, your fear of consequences and your conscience might be overpowered by your lust, once it grew very strong?"

"You put it in an interesting way Stefan. It could happen the way you suggested."

"You said that it could happen, both of you would throw away all fear and caution and silence your consciences. The only thing necessary for that to happen was 'more fuel on the fire' of your lust, and that would be achieved if you stayed longer in contact."

"Stefan, you put me 'in the corner.' Surely, it could happen as you just said, but I hope it would not."

"It was my goal to put you 'in the corner,' so that you understand the severity and danger of that potential sin. The temptation was strong. The Enemy fed your male pride, and your sexual appetite, which was always strong. You were resisting the temptation, but your resistance was getting weaker. I saw that it was just a matter of time, before you would gave in to the temptation. I checked my instructions and decided that the least painful way for you and Ivona was to cut your contact. That is why dismissal from your job was arranged."

"I thought that was not in your instructions. Why could you not arrange something nicer? Say, that Ivona had to move back to Europe, or that plant manager orders me not to contact her. Wouldn't that be fair and less damaging to me?"

"I do not go into details how I do my job Boro. That is not necessary for you to know."

"Why did you disclose to me that you intervened in my life, by fixing the loss of my job.?"

"Before you got married, we met and I pointed out to you that Lord forgave you all your sexual transgressions, but that you must be absolutely faithful to your wife. If you commit adultery, your life would become hell. Lord would be very displeased with you. You were acted upon by the Enemy. He would succeed, providing you stayed there longer and fed the fires of your lust. That is the reason why this 'radical surgery' had to be performed. Remember the Lord has a special job for you. That is the one you are going to apply your talent to. My instructions were to intervene and to keep you going straight."

"I may not understand it, nor like it, but I believe you acted for my good."

"The Enemy is going to continue attacking you, inducing you to sin. Resist the temptation. Be aware that you cannot fight the temptation on your own. Ask for help. Lord Jesus will help you in your struggle. I will be there to carry out His instructions, to guide you, help you and protect you. I will leave you now. When you need me call me."

Saying this, the mighty angel spread his golden dust wings, kissed Boro and Jelena, and vanished.

## Chapter 18

## *The Family*

The meeting with Stefan had strong influence on Boro. He never again allowed himself to even think about being unfaithful to his wife. Stefan`s stern, message and warning worked very well.

After moving to the bigger city, Jelena discovered that she was pregnant. This was big life change for Boro. From a "free hunter," he was becoming a family man, with wife and child to take care off. He was very respectful of his wife. They did everything together. They were growing in love, which was not without passion, but devoid of the crazy: 'Eros only' kind of the relationship. Eros stepped in frequently, but it did not play principal role in their relationship. He was just a pleasurable component of the committed relationship, 'a fire starter.'

The birth of his son was a life changing event in Boro`s life. It was a unique, eye opening experience to see his first born, little helpless crying human. Boro was proud for procreating life, continuing his family. He almost felt as a co-creator. Holding his son, touching his tiny hands, kissing him, feeling his soft, smooth skin, was his great pleasure.

He did not mind to get up in the middle of the night, to change his son`s diapers, feed him and carry him around until he fell asleep. Then, there were visits to doctors; for regular checkup, and when baby was sick. The inconveniences of parenthood were rewarded richly by their baby boy. His first smile, first 'mama,' first tooth, first step, were unforgettable moments of happiness for Boro and Jelena.

Their son was baptized when he was about six months old, in the local Orthodox church. Boro was intensely watching the whole ceremony. First time in his life he tried to understand symbolism and meaning of the baptism. Several actions in the christening ceremony stuck in his mind.

One of them was when the priest using some swab immersed in the oil, anointed his son on his ears, eyes, hands and feet. Priest was doing baptism in the ancient church language: Church—Slavonic. While he was anointing baby he kept repeating: "Pecat dara Duha Svjatago."

"Boro knew enough of the Church -Slavonic to translate this as: "Gift of the seal of the Holy Spirit."

He remembered when priest was chanting; "Vo Hrista krestitesja, vo Hrista oblekostesja." He translated this --"You, who were baptized in Christ, you were dressed in Christ."

Back, in the old country Boro was 'kum' (the godfather), a few times, at the baptism of babies. He was just a young kid at that time and was not interested in the meaning of that strange ceremony. It was entirely different now. He was grown man, it was his son being baptized.

Though, he did not understand the symbolism and meaning of the various chants and acts in the baptism, it intrigued him. For the first time in his life, he felt vaguely that there was more to the Church rites and ceremonies than mere religiosity, that there was a world, unseen, unheard and unimaginable to even the sharpest human mind, that was announced by all of these Church rites, symbols and ceremonies.

It seemed to him that in some mysterious way the door to this invisible, unimaginable world was behind the altar of the Church. He felt that the Church opens that secret door leading to the world "without pain, sickness, worry and death."

Attending the baptism of his son, Boro felt that a desire was born in his heart to learn about the mysterious door connecting the seen and the unseen world. After the baptism, he started occasionally opening his big red book. To his frustration, there were no easy and quick explanations he expected. It was almost like trying to row the boat with an oar only on one side, just going in circles.

A few times he watched American televangelists on TV. It was a glamorous show. Some of these sermons were made in huge cathedrals, seating thousands of people. The preacher was just a guy, looking more like a businessman, politician, or high pressure salesman, selling his wares to the crowd. No priestly vestments, no icons, no confession, no communion. Nobody ever crossed themselves, while preacher talked all the time about "Jesus." Some of these meetings, or revivals were like a Las Vegas show with musicians, entertainers, invited celebrity guest speakers.

This was quite different than the Liturgy served by monks in ancient monastery near Boro's village. The monastery was built in the fourteenth century. It had stone walls, stone floors. No heating, no air conditioning, no electricity. The walls and ceilings of the monastery church were covered by frescoes, depicting biblical events and saints. The sanctuary and the altar were separated by a wooden partition called iconostasis, also depicting biblical events and saints. A bearded monk dressed in priestly robes, served liturgy, quietly, deliberately slow and very seriously praying to the Creator and Redeemer of the world. The monk was using censor, censing all around in the church several times. Boro remembered sweet pleasant scent of the incense in the small clouds of smoke floating from the censor.

There was a definite schedule to the liturgy, which was followed by the monk at all times. Many candles lit by people burnt in the church. All this was giving impression that this was a holy place, not just a regular building. Even though, lot of people did not understand the liturgy, they felt fear of God and awe before something higher, eternal, out of this world.

Comparing the old monastery service and modern American revival service Boro wondered, "Who is right? Who does it the right way? To whom is God listening? To this polished successful looking American televangelist, or to the simple, bearded monk in the monastery?"

He concluded that the evangelist was speaking more to his reason. He could understand better about the Bible and Jesus Christ, listening to him, than to the simple, bearded monk. But, at same time, he also realized that the monk, icons, frescoes, incense, cross and slow ceremonial service were speaking directly to his heart. It helped him to believe, without knowing the intricacies of the Theology.

Boro and Jelena went to some of the evangelical meetings. Once, there was preacher, who was also a healer, doing miracles, and healing people just by touching them, or praying for them to get rid of various ailments. Boro was always sceptical about these miracles. He thought; "Too easy to manipulate and use even for ungodly purpose." He saw on TV and on the revivals people rejoicing and thanking Jesus for the healing they received. Even some people from his church were seeking healing going from one revival to another. On one of these revivals, the preacher called everybody who wanted to 'dedicate their life to Jesus' to come forward. Out of curiosity, Boro stepped forward. The preacher led them in the prayer of the dedication.

As people were coming to be touched by the healer, He would say some short prayer, and touch the person's forehead slightly pushing him backwards. To Boro's amazement the person would fall backward. Two ushers would hold him and let him drop gently on the floor, where he would remain lying on his back in some kind of spiritualised state. Boro 's turn came. The preacher said the prayer, pushed Boro slightly on the forehead with his right hand. The ushers were standing on Boro's sides ready to help him fall back on the floor gently. Boro just stood there, a bit confused. He felt fine. No need to fall back. The preacher was a bit embarrassed, but quickly, as a real pro, collected himself, motioning Boro to move forward.

Another time Boro attended service in a Protestant church. This time there was another surprise. All of a sudden a person in the audience stood up and started shouting, crying laughing and singing in some strange language. People in the audience were overjoyed that brother was 'in the Spirit' and was 'speaking in tongues.' "What kind of spirit is causing a person to do that? Or was that just a 'show' and acting to excite people in the audience,' wondered Boro."

On some of these events, the Preacher was preaching 'the prosperity gospel,' sermonizing to the excited audience that God wanted all of them to be rich, drive big fancy cars, even planes, be super confident, healthy and always happy and smiling. All one had to do was: 'have faith, trust Jesus.' God was obliged to provide all those goodies to his devout people. It sounded so simple and easy, like stealing candy from a baby.

A couple people at these meetings asked him: "Are you saved? Have you been born again?" Not to look like an "infidel" Boro said modestly, yes he was 'saved,' and was just recently 'born again.'"

Coming home, and cooling down his head, he accused himself: "Why did you lie? You have no clue what they mean to 'be saved.' You have no idea what is the sign that you were actually saved. Saved from what?" And that 'being born again', that was silly talk. How could you even ask a person that kind of question? It is not nice, not proper at all."

Attending all these revivals and watching them on the TV encouraged Boro to buy the books that were recommended. He read many of them. He understood the Bible better after reading these books. One thing he benefited from these events was to acquire a praying habit. He rarely prayed before, so this was a good habit he was building. The prayers he was praying were not the Orthodox Church prayers, but self-made prayers, mostly consisting of; 'Jesus give me this, Lord give me that' demands.

He was going to the Orthodox Church more often with Jelena and their son. He became a church member and got involved in several parish boards.

Boro confirmed his old fear that he was not "made to be an engineer." After losing several jobs, he quit engineering entirely. This was a big change in his and family`s life. Engineering provided a steady monthly income, but becoming a commission salesman was entirely different. Some months, there was hardly any income. Boro would get depressed, and complain: "Why do these things happen to me? Why I am not like other guys. They get a steady job in the steel mill with guaranteed income, good benefits, and good pension." He tried some investments, real estate, stocks. The results were mixed. On some he lost, on the other made some money, but nothing to brag about. Jelena was working also, but at a low paying job, that did not make them rich either.

"I need to talk to somebody I can confide in, somebody I can trust." Boro's message was heard. Stefan appeared the same night.

"Why didn't you visit me for so long time Stefan?"

"I was always near you. I watched you all the time."

"Why didn't you come to talk to me and help me in my struggles?"

"Were you aware Boro that I would come any time you wished to see me?"

"Well, being very busy, I forgot about you."

Stefan smiled; "That is the American dream for you, busy, busy, like a bee. Trying to get ahead to acquire 'things' and you forgot your guardian angel."

"I did not forget you Stefan, but, there were big changes in my life: new land, new customs, new people, getting married, having family, job problems. Pressure and stress were my steady companions."

"Your 'dormant' talent is waking up. You described 'the American dream,' or 'the American nightmare,' as it can turn to lot of times."

Boro smiled tiredly, "Stefan, there is no use for my talent here in America, unless it is a way of 'selling anything to anybody.' Americans are pragmatic people. What could I offer people like them? Nothing, I am telling you nothing."

"Pardon me Boro, but allow me to disagree with you. I am going to share a little secret with you: America is where you are going to apply your talent. That is the reason you came to America."

"I came to America in search of better life, as millions of people did before me."

"People came to America searching for a better life. So did you. However, along with your plans, God has plans for you. A part of this plan is that you come to America. Eventually, you will conclude that nothing happens in life accidentally. Meeting new people, getting jobs, losing jobs, moving to another city or country; it all fits into the picture, into a mosaic of life."

"Are you saying that God arranged things so that I come to America, to serve whatever purpose He has for me?"

"It is little more involved then that Boro. God has plans for you, but you have free will. You can reject God`s plan."

"Are you saying that I can disregard God`s plan, without any penalty?"

"You can reject God`s plan, just as the first man and women, Adam and Eve ignored God`s warning in the Paradise, not to eat the fruit from the tree of life. If you read Holy Bible, you would know that God told Adam and Eve what the consequences would be if they ignored God`s warning and ate the forbidden fruit."

"You are saying that I can reject God`s plans, but I would suffer consequences for rejecting God`s plans?"

"You put it perfectly Boro. Your talent is getting through more and more, like a chick breaking the shell of its egg."

Boro smiled sarcastically. "Again that talent of mine, that shell is very thick, when my poor talent was unable to break through for so many years."

"Do you know Boro what would happen if chick breaks the shell of its egg before its time?"

"I think the chick might not be able to survive out of the shell, if it left it prematurely."

"That eggshell of your talent has just started cracking. God, in His wisdom has ordained the time for everything: Your talent has to 'ripen,' before it will come out of its shell to the light of the day. Premature birth could kill it, because it just would not be ready to face life outside of its shell."

"Stefan, that was nice sermon. If I can reject God's plan for me, couldn't I conclude that God is not omnipotent, if anybody can reject His plan?"

"My explanation would be much easier for you to understand, if you read the Holy Bible. I told you before, no angel or man can understand the nature of God. He created the world and everything in the world. He keeps heavenly bodies in motion, winds blowing, snow and rain falling. He sustains all life on earth; grass growing, animals living and procreating and of course, the man, the crown of God's creation living a short time in 'the exile' on earth, preparing for the eternal life in a different world. God is all powerful and all knowing. There is no power stronger than Him."

"If God is, as you say, all powerful, why does He tolerate man, ignoring and rejecting His plans?"

"God did not create man to function like a robot, but as a personality, a being that has a free will to love God or not, to obey God, or not."

"But, if man by his free will decides: 'I want to fly like an eagle, and dive deep into the ocean like a fish,' why can't he do that?"

"In this life and in this earthly body he cannot do it."

"I know that, but why God gave man this yearning, if man is unable to fulfill it?"

"Man is unable to do it in this life, but he will be able to do that in the life to come."

"Are we going to have wings like birds and bodies like fish, so that we can fly in the air and swim into the deepest ocean in that 'other world'?

"It is not given to man to know the nature of his resurrected body. It will be like the body Lord Jesus Christ resurrected in. It will be incorruptible body, not chained by the forces human body is subjected to in this earthly, temporary life. The resurrected body will be able to do whatever man conceived, while in his corruptible earthly body."

"Thank you Stefan for the explanation. If I could have one more question please?"

"Sure."

"You said that since man was given free will, he can exercise his free will to reject the plans God had for him. Is that correct?"

"Yes it is. What is your question?"

"Does God punish man if he refuses to accept God`s plan for him, If he refuses even to believe in God?"

"When Adam and Eve exercised their free will and broke God`s warning not to eat the forbidden fruit, they were severely punished," said Stefan.

"Why God gave them free will if He punished them for exercising it?"

"No angel nor man, knows the depth of God`s wisdom and providence. God could have created man without free will, like a robot, but He decided that it was worth the risk to give man the most glorious and at the same time the most dangerous gift; free will."

"That sure was a huge risk. Just wonder if God was ever sorry for giving free will to man."

"God does no wrong. There is nothing for Him to be sorry about. He does what He wants. He creates the way He decides."

"If I understand you correctly Stefan; you are saying that there is no contradiction in having free will and in paying the penalty for the actions done, exercising free will."

"This is exactly what I am saying. I can see that you still don't quite get it."

"I don`t understand how this works in my life?"

"Here is a true story: A happily married man; wife, children, house. Good comfortable life. He hires a beautiful young secretary. She likes him and flirts with him with her smile, body language, little signs of care for her boss. His male ego is fed by her attention. He compares her to his middle aged wife, who put on forty pounds in the last five years. She is often tired and unkempt, struggling to take care of her job, house, and children. She does not think of him anymore as a good looking man.

But, his secretary is so sweet, so tender, so caring, and then her smile, a tight miniskirt, her curvaceous young body, slim, fresh, seductive. Not to be rude, the boss returns favour for favour, smile for smile, kindness for kindness. Coffee together, lunch together, walks together. Man feels rejuvenated. Testosterone runs through his veins. He dreams about his secretary. Has a film in his mind about his imaginary passionate encounter with her. But on the other side: wife, children, family. Man is severally tempted.

The choice is: to sleep with his secretary, or cut off the relationship with her. He is aware that their affair would be hard to keep secret. Even if nobody finds out he would have a very unpleasant witness, his own conscience, which would stick to him night and day, torturing him, scolding him: "You are a sinner, betrayer, and adulterer. You will suffer, suffer, suffer, pay, pay, pay."

If he decides to cut off ties with his seductive secretary, he would suffer, because his sexual fantasy was not fulfilled. His male ego would be bruised because Mr. Eros would dress him down: 'Chicken, you are not a man. You missed such an opportunity, such a beauty. She is worth the risk of the shame, divorce, lost family and career, look at her, like a goddess."

Man sees clearly what the consequences are in each case. He exercises his free will. He is punished or rewarded, depending on the choice he makes. Man sows the seed of his future reward (punishment), whenever he makes a decision. It says so beautifully in the holy Bible: 'Whatever man sows that he shall reap.' Did you understand this Boro? Do you need any more examples?"

"I understand this quite well now. I just thought that our lives would be much simpler, if God gave us free will, but without the opportunity to make the choice leading to evil and breaking God`s laws. Wouldn`t that be nice?"

"But, if you have only one choice that is not free will."

"So what? If my free will was limited to do only good things, wouldn`t that be great?"

"Don`t you agree Boro, that the world with the real personalities, having choice of doing bad or good, moral, or immoral, God pleasing, or God rejecting, is much more interesting than the world of the programmed robots, that always and predictably do only what they are programmed for.

We touched many important issues today. Perhaps you need a break to digest this. I am leaving you now. Please do not wait again years, before calling me. Remember I am on guard, but it is always good and necessary for you to check up the way you are conducting your life. Bye my friend."

The angel bent down and kissed the sleeping man on the forehead, and in the next second he was gone.

## Chapter 19

## *Visiting "The old country"*

"The American dream" seemed to be slowly happening for Boro and Jelena. Both were working. Jelena`s cousin, an older widow, watched their son.

Boro discovered a new joy: watching his son growing. His favourite time was playing with his boy. He would come home from work, lie down on the floor and have wrestling match with his son.

One year they made a family trip to the old country. Boro met Jelena`s family for the first time. He liked them, particularly her parents. They reminded him of his parents. They went to visit Boro`s family. His mother was overjoyed to see her youngest son, and the youngest grandson.

They visited the monastery and the nearby cemetery, where his father was buried. It was very strange feeling standing by the tomb covered by a black marble plate with the pictures of his father and mother on the monument.

Silly thought; "did my father really exist?" crept into Boro`s mind. "Is this it? Just being put in the coffin and stuck into the darkness of the tomb to disintegrate, become a stinking mess, and eventually just a skeleton. My father was big strong man. Now he is, just a bunch of bones. It scares me to think that one day I will go the same way. I will disappear like a cloud from the sky, like a wind that blows, and is no more."

He asked a monk from the monastery to hold a prayer at his father`s grave. Holding a burning wax candle, watching his little boy and wife holding candles, Boro felt a great sadness enveloping him. There was life and death one besides the other. His father grew old and died, his son was renewal of life. It was a unique experience standing beside the grave of his father, watching the flame of the candles flickering in the slight breeze, listening to chants of the monk. Boro had sense of an unseen power holding all this in its hand: the death with dead decaying bodies, life in young bodies, grass and trees, the wind, the sky, the birds nesting in pine trees in the cemetery. He felt belonging to this system of intermingling life and death.

They went into the monastery church. There, Boro saw old icons, which his mom and baba kissed reverently when they went to the church. Boro remembered his mom used to lift him up, and told him to cross himself and kiss all the icons. His favourite icon was silver plated "Three handed Mother of God." Kissing this old, famous, revered icon, Boro felt as if seriously looking Theotokos was calming him down. She held baby Jesus, young God, in her arms. The Creator of the world growing as, a weak, little boy.

After the cemetery visit, they went to Boro`s village. Everything looked small and poor, houses, school. He had trouble recognizing villagers, but they recognized him and greeted him warmly with bear hugs and traditional triple kisses. He was glad to see them, but somehow he felt detached. They felt like relics from the past. He was already in a different new world, in America.

A lot of people left the village after the flooding of the river valley. Mostly older people remained in the village. There were a lot of abandoned houses, and uncultivated fields and very few children. The village was slowly dying. That night after returning to the city, Boro went to bed early. He was emotionally exhausted. Visiting his father`s grave, prayer at the cemetery, meeting with villagers and seeing slow death of his village, all that drained him emotionally. He felt the need to talk to someone, a trusted and loyal friend.

"It would be nice if Stefan shows up," he thought. His trusted friend and guardian appeared that night.

Boro was glad to see him: "Stefan, my friend, my counsellor, my advisor, I am glad to see you."

"Glad to help Boro," replied Stefan.

"I had very tiring day Stefan."

"What made you so tired?"

"It was first visiting my father's grave, seeing his and my mom's pictures on the tombstone, flickering candle in my hand, monk's prayer over the grave, and after that visiting my village full of old people and abandoned houses. All this invoked thoughts of stupidity and meaninglessness of life, and drained me emotionally."

"When did your father die?"

"You know that Stefan. Why do you ask?"

"You know that I know and it upsets you that I 'needlessly' ask that question."

"I am sorry Stefan. It was a long day. I am very tired. My father died about five years ago."

"No problem Boro. When your father died, were you already in America?"

"Yes, I was already in America. I was studying at the local university."

"When you heard that your father was going to die soon, what did you do?"

"I had no money to go see him and attend his funeral. I was also very busy in school."

"Did any of your brothers go to see father at the end of his life?"

"No, they did not. They had obligations, family, and jobs. The trip was expensive, time consuming and tiring."

"Anybody went from America to visit your ailing father?"

"Our sister went few months before father died. She took care of him and was at his funeral."

"How did you justify in your mind not going to see your father in his last days?"

"I told you already: I had no money, had school obligation and …"

Stefan interrupted him: "I heard all these reasons Boro. Was there another real reason, why you did not go to see your father at the end of his life?"

"Why is it important for me to disclose that to you?"

"I am sorry Boro, if I resemble a police inspector questioning you. This is strictly 'no, no' in my instructions. You can at any time flex your 'free will muscle' and refuse to answer any of my questions. As always, the purpose of my question is to help you become fully aware of your actions. This again would help you to adjust your life and behaviour accordingly."

"Sorry Stefan. I was annoyed by your questioning."

"Why were you annoyed by my questioning?"

"I was annoyed because even after I gave you the reason why I didn't go to visit my father, you still pressed me for 'the real' reason. Apparently, you didn't believe I gave you the real reason. Indirectly, you told me: 'You were lying.That is what upset me."

"I am sorry Boro if you felt upset. Believe me that was not my aim. I knew that it was very important for you to be fully aware what the real reason was and I was prodding you to disclose that."

"I don't understand why is that so important?"

"It is important for building of your character."

"I see no connection between my character and reasons for not visiting my father before he died."

"Let me help you to understand the connection between your character and the true reason why you did not go to see your father before he died. The character of a person is built on his beliefs. If person believes it is quite acceptable to lie, steal and cheat, this shows that his character was built on lies, and thus his character will be defective."

"Fine, but I still don't see the connection in my case."

"Would you agree Boro that the character should be built on truth, not on lies, or half-truths?"

"I have agreed that it is important for character to be built on the truth, but half-truths? What is a half-truth?"

"Lot of devil`s deceptions are based on half-truths. He tricks people much easier on half-truths, then on the open, brazen lies."

"I don't follow you Stefan, isn't truth on one side and lying on the other side? Something is true, or false. There is no in between?"

"There are many half-truths Boro. It is as if an old ugly woman puts on lot of makeup, fancy jewellery and expensive clothes to cover her age and ugliness. She looks good, just like a lot younger women. When she washes off all makeup, she is again just an old ugly woman."

"So, what is half-truth there?"

"Full truth is that she is an ugly old woman. With all makeup, jewellery and fancy dress, she looks like good looking younger women, which is a half-truth and the deception."

"Would Devil use this kind of deception on man?"

"He has tremendous imagination. He presents evil covered by a sliver of the truth, ugliness with thin layer of a beauty as cover, hate covered by thin layer of love, pride masked by false humility."

"But Stefan, you still didn't say, how half-truth relates to my case?"

"You gave an official, reasonably true sounding reason for not going to see your ailing father. 'I was busy in school, I just did not have the money. I had my obligations. The trip was expensive, long and tiring.' Isn't that right?"

"Yes."

"Was there any other reason that you didn't share with anybody else but yourself?"

"No, there was no other reason."

"Please Boro try to remember. Isn't it true that you gave one explanation to others and another explanation to yourself, to your conscience?"

"Well, kind of. But that was not really an explanation."

"What was it then?"

"That was just my thinking. I did not try to explain anything to my conscience. There was no need for it."

"What was your thinking about not going to see your ailing father?"

"I was thinking: 'What would help my father if I went to see him. I could not take his pain away, could not cure him, and could not prolong his life. I probably would get depressed seeing him weak, sick and bedridden. I might have to clean up the mess he made. That would be awful. I could not do that. I could not watch him dying. I am afraid to be so much around death and dying. From here at least I don't see anything and it is easier to bear it and forget it."

Stefan was smiling while listening to Boro's explanation. "That was well said Boro. Your talent is just about to break its shell and walk out on the light of the day. Are you now aware of the real reason why you did not go to see your dying father?"

With a sound of guilt in his voice Boro whispered: "Yes Stefan, I am now fully aware of the real reason. Thank you very much for helping me to uncover it. I must admit that only after I became father, I felt guilty, for not going to see my dying father, to make his death less awful, easier to face."

"It is all right to be afraid of death Boro. Even saints, God's favourite people had fear of death. You need to make yourself conscious, and know that death is not the end. It is just the end of the man, the composite being, made out of union of immortal soul and mortal body. Death just breaks that union. The body decomposes and becomes the elements it was made from. The soul, freed from the body, joins the other world."

"The soul joins another world? What kind of world?"

"My instructions allow me to uncover just a small peek of this world to man while in the body."

"You are very secretive Stefan. These instructions tie your hands, I mean mouth. What could be the harm if you tell me what awaits the soul in the other world? It won't scare me. I am a grown man."

"I am sorry Boro, but I must follow my instructions without exception. As you grow in faith you will be able to understand more of God's mysteries. As your spiritual eyes start opening, you will begin to see the things with the eyes of the spirit."

"The eyes of the spirit? What are you talking about?"

"Eyes are man's main sense of communication with the world surrounding him. Since the soul has no body, it has no senses as body does. But soul still can communicate with the world and 'see' that world. The eyes of the spirit are not like man's physical eyes. They are different, sharper, and more powerful."

"I hear what you told me, but I am still wondering how the soul can see without eyes."

"To help you understand, I am going to give you an example."

"Sure."

"You are travelling on a road. It is pitch dark and you have difficulty walking on the road. Your friend gives you something and says 'Here, put this on your eyes, it will help.' You take this gadget, and put it on your eyes. You see almost like in the daylight. What happened? What made you see in the darkness?"

"The night goggles. It is not a miracle."

"It is awfully close to a miracle. You could see nothing with you 'normal' eyes, but with this gadget, you acquired 'better eyes.'"

"Well, goggles are the gadget, my eyes are the same."

"Do you know of any other of man's inventions that can sense things much better than bodily senses?"

"There are many; radar, x ray, microscope, telescope, binoculars, lasers."

"Don't you see Boro, how much more powerful these gadgets are. Such is the spiritual eye; much, much more powerful and sensitive than any man made contraption."

"We see all these gadgets working, but nobody was able to see and experience how the soul 'sees' and communicates. We really have to accept it on a blind faith."

"What is in your opinion a blind faith?"

"A blind faith is belief in something without any proof, that what you believe is true."

"Is there any difference between 'the faith' and 'blind faith'?"

"A blind faith is the faith not based on any proof, that what one believes is true. The faith is based on some kind of proof that the belief is true."

"Which one is; the faith, which one is; the blind faith?"

"I am on top of a hundred metres high cliff. I jump, believing that before I hit the rocks at the bottom, something would happen and I would not get smashed to bits. That is a blind faith."

*A Kingdom to Buy*

"What about ;the faith?"

"I am jumping from the plane with a parachute. Many people before me used the parachute and landed safely on the ground. I have faith that I will also land safely on the ground."

"Excellent comparisons Boro. Is it a blind faith believing, that after separation from the body the soul continues living, and is able to communicate on a much higher level than bodily senses were able to?"

"This is a tough one. It would be blind faith, if there was not any kind of proof, or probability that what we believe about the soul is true.

"You introduced a new word ;probability. Why?"

"Because it is similar to jumping with a parachute: There is a good probability that my parachute will open and I will safely land on the ground. However, I won't know that for sure until I land on the ground. Likewise, I believe it cannot be proven that the belief about the soul is true, until I die."

"What kind of 'the parachute,' you have believing in soul`s continuing existence after the death of the body, what gives you; 'a reasonable probability' that your belief is true?"

"I am not sure about that Stefan. Please help me with this."

"What is the biggest source of information about man, his creation, fall and redemption?"

"I think it is the Bible."

"You have not read the Bible yet?"

"I just read some chapters: The book of Creation, some Gospels and one Epistle of St. Paul."

"You are not an expert on the Holy Bible?"

"I am not. But what I read convinced me that this is the book about man and God, their relationship, and about man`s eternal life."

"Is there any other source, any other proof to support belief of the afterlife of the soul?"

"I think another important source is The Church, which interpreted Holy Bible and formulated the dogmas of Christian fate."

"What do you understand is: 'the Church?'"

"I need your help Stefan. I have not read very much about the Church. I hate to give you wrong answers. Please tell me what the Church is?"

"If you insist I will help you. I would appreciate your opinion what is, the Church. You are learning. There is no wrong or inappropriate answer."

"You are putting me on the spot Stefan. Please don't get upset at me and don't laugh, if I say something stupid."

"My instructions strictly forbid laughing at my protégé and putting him down. As I told you, this is a learning process. What do you believe 'the Church' means?"

"I think the Church means a building where people get together with their priest to pray to God."

"Good answer Boro."

"Thanks Stefan. I feel though that my answer is incomplete?"

"Your answer was correct, but it was incomplete. Why do you feel like that?"

"As little as I read the Bible, I concluded that meaning of the word 'the Church' is much wider than just the building where the worship is held."

"What is the wider meaning of the word 'the Church?'"

"I think the Church means assembly of people worshipping. All of them together make the Church."

"Who are people worshipping?"

"I think that is everybody that believes and lives according to the dogmas of the Church."

"Could an atheist, Muslim or Buddhist be in the Church?"

"No, to be part of the Church, or in the Church, you need to be a baptised Orthodox Christian."

"How about a Protestant, Roman Catholic, or Mormon. Are they in the Church?"

"No, they are not in the Church. Only baptised Orthodox Christians are."

"But even among all baptized Orthodox people, who makes the Church?"

"Women, children, men, deacons, priests. They all together make the Church."

"Anybody else in the Church?"

"Bishops, Patriarch."

"And who is the head of the Church?"

"Patriarch is the head of the Church."

"How is Patriarch the head of your Church?"

"He is elected by all Bishops of the Church."

"Is there anybody higher than Patriarch in the Church?"

"I think he is the top guy. There is nobody above him."

"Boro, do you know who established the Christian Church?"

"I am not sure. Saint Paul?"

"Why do you think it was St. Paul."

"Didn`t he write most of the Bible?"

"He wrote most of the New Testament in the form of letters to individuals, or groups; the Epistles. Did you read any of the Epistles?"

"I think I read one Epistle."

"Do you recall whom St Paul called 'The Head of the Church?"

"God."

"You are very close to true answer. To your recollection did he say: God the Father, God the Son, or God the Holy Spirit, is the Head of the Church."

"I believe it was The Son, Jesus Christ, that Paul called 'the Head of the Church."

"Excellent Boro, you guessed right. Jesus is the Head of the Church. Who makes the body of the Church?"

"Stefan, you are asking me some tough questions. I have very poor knowledge of the Bible. How do you expect me to answer all these questions?"

"Not a big deal if you make a mistake and give wrong answer. It is amazing that even with your rudimentary knowledge of the Bible you gave almost all answers correctly. Your talent is impatient to come out. Who do you think makes the Body of the Church?"

"Jesus is the Head, and then the body must be all believers."

"Who are the believers?"

"I said that already. These would be all baptized Orthodox Christians; people, clergy, Bishops, Patriarch."

"Anybody else in the body of the Church?"

"No, this is it."

"You told me before, when you were little boy, your mother allowed you sometimes to sleep with her?"

"Yes, she did, but why are you asking that now?"

"Your mom was praying, before falling asleep. Do you remember what kind of prayers she was saying?"

"She said: Lord`s prayer, Hail Mary, Creed of Faith, and prayers for the living members of our family."

"Did she say one more prayer?"

"Oh yes, I remember now. She prayed for the deceased members of our family."

"She was praying for the living and dead members of the family?"

"Yes, she was."

"You told me that the body of the Church is made of all baptised Orthodox Christians."

"Yes, I did."

"Your mom was praying for living and for dead. Why?"

"I don`t know where you are leading me?"

"The living are members of the body of Church, but she was praying for dead as well. What does that indicate to you?"

"Oh, I am getting it now. She prayed for the living and dead, because they all belong to the body of the Church."

"Excellent Boro. See, you got all answers right. You figured it out yourself. Should we quit for today?"

"Yes, I think my head is full. You were like a professor, or lawyer cross examining me, I am tired."

"Things will start developing faster in your life pretty soon. Let`s keep in touch. Bye my friend."

The mighty angel enveloped sleeping family under his golden wings, and kissed them all on the cheeks. He disappeared into the starry night.

# Chapter 20

## *The American Dream Hobbling*

Boro purchased several small vending businesses. The idea was to have extra income without spending lot of time. Initially, he made some money, but then problems started. Equipment breaking down, increasing rent, heat, hydro, decreasing revenues. Another unsuccessful venture, the American dream was eluding him.

Then came another child, a beautiful girl. Boro and Jelena decided that they had completed their family. A boy and a girl was enough. More children would just 'spoil' their plans. Jelena would have to take time off the job; a problem with babysitting.

God apparently had different plan. Boro took Jelena out for dinner for her birthday. They enjoyed dinner and bottle of good Italian wine. Several weeks after this dinner, Jelena told Boro that she missed her monthly. Doctor confirmed that Jelena was pregnant. This was a shock to Boro and Jelena. All their plans 'spoiled' by this unwanted child. Stupid! They should have been more careful. The wine did it. Boro decided :"We cannot afford this child."

They went to their doctor and told him that they didn't want this child, cannot afford it, and if he could please arrange the abortion, as soon as possible.

Doctor Kumar listened carefully and said, "I can arrange for the abortion, but I am advising you not to do it. Have this baby.

Do not worry, God will take care of it. Go home, discuss it and let me know what you decide."

Doctor`s words were like ice cold water on their heads. They discussed this again and again and finally decided to take doctor`s advice, to have the baby.

In due time, their girl was born. When Boro saw her first time, he started crying. "My God, I could have caused the murder of my daughter. Thank you God for helping us to make the right decision and have this baby."

"What would Stefan say about all of this," thought Boro. "Perhaps, I should talk to him."

Stefan appeared that night.First thing he said to Boro, "I want to see your new baby and give her the blessings of our Lord."

When Stefan, saw the baby in her crib, he was all smile. All his body radiated some unworldly light. He bent down and kissed little girl on both cheeks. He then put both of his hands on her head and said solemnly: "Blessing on you child of God from our Lord Jesus Christ."

Boro cried.

"Are you interested in a nice ride? asked Stefan.

"Where to??"

"I got the permission to take you to see a place out of your world."

"You have permission now, but when I asked you before, you refused. What changed?"

"Many things changed. Your personal growth, your character development, you maturing as a person."

"Is it dangerous where you are taking me Stefan?"

"Not to worry Boro. I am your guide, and guardian. I will protect you."

"Fine, Stefan I trust you. Is this far away?"

"In man`s measure it is, but in our world no, It is in the neighbourhood."

"How far in man`s measure?"

"Your concept of time, space and distance, does not apply in our world."

"You won't tell me?"

"It is not that I don't want to tell you, but my answer would make no sense. Are you ready?"

"Yes, I am."

"One more surprise. Lord is pleased with you and He instructed me to offer you a heavenly meal?"

"Well, I am not really hungry. I had a good dinner, sauerkraut and ham."

"This food is different. It won't fill you, but I think you will enjoy it more than sauerkraut and ham."

"Fine, Stefan. I will try this heavenly food."

In a moment Boro was under Stefan's wing sitting on a soft cushion. In front of him was a beautifully set table, decorated by exotic flowers of a delicate fragrance. In the middle of the table was huge round dish in rainbow colours full of different fruits; figs, watermelons, apples, peaches, plums, grapes and many other fruits Boro never saw before.

"Wow, where did you get all these fruits?"

"From our heavenly gardens."

"You have gardens in heaven?"

"Sure we have. God placed your ancestors Adam and Eve in the Garden of Eden. All these fruits are from that garden."

Boro could not decide which fruit to try first, gorgeous looking reddish peaches, huge green figs, or delicious looking white and pink grapes.

Stefan saw his confusion. "You have difficulty deciding which fruit to try first. I will help you to decide."

"What do I need to do?"

"Thank God our for this heavenly food, and your indecision will vanish instantly."

"I am not sure how to thank God. What do I say?"

"Simple, straightforward words are the best."

"Are you saying that just a simple; 'Thank You Lord' would do?"

"It could be, but I would add a few words: 'Thank your Lord for this wonderful feast of heavenly food."

Boro crossed himself and repeated the words Stefan suggested. His indecision was gone immediately. He picked a peach and then had some figs, grapes, mango, and plums. He stopped eating saying to himself: "I am overdoing it. I will for sure overload my stomach, and have a huge indigestion."

"You had enough already?" asked Stefan.

"I ate too much. It was so good, so delicious, better than any food I ever tasted. I guess Lord does not appreciate me overeating."

"Don`t worry Boro. This is heavenly food; it won't fill you up, nor cause indigestion, regardless how much you eat."

Boro felt great, full of energy, peace and love for God and the whole world. "Are we close to these heavenly gardens Stefan?"

"We are almost there. I gave you some time to enjoy the heavenly feast. We will land shortly."

Boro looked from his soft comfortable seat under Stefan`s wing. He was expecting to see a small garden, like fruit farm on the earth, but to his amazement he saw an endless green jungle with huge mountains extending in every direction, up, down, left, right. Innumerable rivers and streams also were flowing up, down, left and right, in all directions. He was totally confused and scared: "Stefan, am I hallucinating? Do you see what I see? Everything is upside down. Mountains rise up and down and in every direction. Rivers flow up, down, left, right?"

"Boro I see the same thing you see. You are seeing this with your spiritual eyes. You are not hallucinating."

"But how is that possible? There is no 'up' and 'down' here?"

"You are not on the earth, you are in the Garden of Eden. The laws that apply on the earth do not apply here. It is an entirely different world."

As they were getting more and more into the garden, Boro saw the trees growing at random, in all directions. There were figs, peaches, plums, oranges, lemons, pomegranates, and endless fields of pleasant looking, sweet smelling flowers. He didn`t see any being, animals, nor man. It was as if huge endless garden was prepared for its future inhabitants. It was ready, waiting for them.

*A Kingdom to Buy*

Finally, they landed on a beautiful soft green meadow, right beside a meandering creek. It reminded Boro of Pridraga Creek, back home, and of the meadows he was running on as a boy. This was incomparably more perfect. Grass was intermingled with meadow flowers of the colours of the rainbow. The scent of the meadow grass and flowers was discrete and pleasant. Boro just kept filling his lungs with this clean fresh air and delicate, tender scents of the Garden of Eden.

Boro and Stefan walked on the meadow beside the meandering creek which was gurgling, going over stones in its bed. "Just like my Pridraga," thought Boro.

"This is beautiful Stefan. This beauty is hard to describe in man's language. I thought there would be birds and bees and butterflies and all kind of other animals in the Garden. Why is it that there are none of them, just plants?"

"God planted Garden of Eden for Adam and Eve and their descendants. Since Adam and Eve were expelled from the Garden of Eden, it has been vacant. Lord placed an angel with a flaming sword at its gate to guard the entrance."

"Is this beautiful garden to remain without its inhabitants forever?"

"God prepared it for man. Men will eventually come back into the Garden."

"How is man to come back to the Garden. The angel with flaming sword is guiding the entrance?"

"God will allow some of Adam and Eve's descendants to enter into the Garden and to reside there forever, as it was God's plan for Adam and Eve."

"Does that mean that not all of the descendants of Adam and Eve will be allowed to move in?"

"Only those who qualify would be welcomed into the Garden of Eden."

"What about the rest of Adam's descendants? Where would they go?"

"They will go into an ugly garden, very much different than the Garden of Eden."

"What is the purpose of that place?"

"Its purpose is opposite of the Garden of Eden. That ugly, horrible place, called Hell, is the place for Adam and Eve's descendants that did not qualify to be received into the Garden of Eden. Hell is the garden of damnation, pain and eternal misery. Garden of Eden is blessed place, the garden of eternal joy, without pain or suffering."

"When will these gardens be filled with the inhabitants?"

"Only God knows that time."

"Not even angels?"

"God keeps many things hidden from man, some hidden even from angels."

"Could you tell me what is going to happen at that time?"

"Judgment Boro, Final Judgment."

"Somebody will be accused and go on trial?"

"The accused,' is everybody."

"What do you mean, everybody?"

"Everybody means, every human being ever born."

"Will everybody be charged with violation of some law?"

"The Final Judgment could be called 'Sorting,' or 'Separation,' because the Judge would be doing that, separating people to go to Garden of Eden, or to Hell."

"Who is the prosecutor in this Final Judgement?"

"The prosecutor is person's sins. They are pushing them towards the Hell."

"Who defends them?"

"Their Godly deeds, thoughts, and beliefs. They push them towards the Garden of Eden."

"And who makes the Final Judgment."

"Our Heavenly Father is the Final Judge."

"God sentences person to the torments, pain and misery of Hell, or to the joy, pleasures and blessings of the paradise?"

"Yes, that's how the Final Judgment works. There are different gradations of joy and bliss in the paradise, as well as different gradation of torments in the Hell."

"How long are these sentences of the Final Judgment?"

"Very, very long; forever."

"If a person is unhappy with the Judges sentence, can he appeal?"

"There is no higher Judge above God. The sentence is final, without the appeal."

"When am I going to stand the Final Judgment?"

"When you die your body will be deposited into the ground. Your soul will continue its existence containing all traits of your personality. Your soul will undergo partial judgment (temporary one). It will be decided on a pre-trial, where your soul is going to await the resurrection of your body and the unification with it.

When God decides to 'wrap it all up,' Jesus will come second time on Earth. All dead bodies will be resurrected and all souls (good and evil) will be reunited with their resurrected bodies. Everybody will have the body that will not die ever more. God will then Judge everybody at the Final Judgment, determining the place for everybody where to spend the eternity."

"Eternity! Such a heavy, heavy word. I have no clue, what that is. Can you help me to grasp this concept."

"No Boro. You are creature chained by the time and space. Your mind has no ability to comprehend concepts of eternity, infinity, limitless. Do you want to go home?"

"I enjoyed myself tremendously. First heavenly feast, than the Garden of Eden. My heart and mind are full. Let`s go home. How long is it going to take us to get back?"

"No time at all Boro. Will use 'God`s speed'. We will be back instantly. Here, we are back in your room."

"This is amazing. We might have been millions of light years away, and we came to my room instantly. We were perhaps faster than the light. How is that possible?"

"We are now in a different world, not subjected to the laws applicable in your world. That is the way Our Lord, 'the Designer' of the Universe created it."

"I don`t understand it, but I accept it Stefan."

Like a caring mother Stefan kissed Boro, Jelena, all three children, kissing last newborn baby, tenderly caressing her soft, rosy cheeks."

"Bye my friends" said Stefan with big smile. "We will meet soon."

The family was sound asleep when the beautiful angel made another disappearance into the budding dawn.

# Chapter 21

# A busy, Busy Life

Boro's life was getting more and more busy; wife, children, business. His life habits and priorities were changing rapidly. They started going to church, almost every Sunday. Even the kids started liking it. It was fun for the whole family to go the church hall after the liturgy, have coffee and cookies and do bit friendly gossiping, while kids chased each other in the hall.

He began to read Bible every week. He fall in love with it very gradually. He found out that reading the same chapter second or third time "changed" the meaning of that chapter.

Boro's mom decided to come once more to see her children in America. There were more of them over there than in the old country. Marko prepared a passport and visa for mom and purchased her airline ticket.

Mom went by train to her oldest daughter who was living near the airport. She was bit overweight and needed a cane to help her walking. A week before she was to board the plane for America, she suffered a huge stroke. Her left side was completely paralysed. She had no more use of her left arm and left leg. Her speech and mind were also affected.

Marko came the next week. They managed to bring mom back to their house in the big city on the Adriatic. She was now confined to bed. Marko was her nurse, cook, doctor. Boro's oldest sister soon came to stay with mom to take care of her. Soon, the other sister came from America to be with mom and to help out.

Boro and his older brother decided to go to see their mother. They found their mother in bed. She recognised Boro immediately, her older son too, but next day it seemed that she was not quite sure, who that stocky, middle aged, bald man was.

Boro brought his big red book with him. He loved to be on guard for his mom. He loved praying with her and reading her the Bible. "This is in a way a payback my mom 'invested' in me by sowing the seed of faith in my heart when I was a little boy. Now, in a small way I am paying her back."

His mom told him during long nights about the dreams and nightmares she had. She slept mostly during day. The night was the worst. Pain and insomnia kept her awake. Occasional slumber into the dream world brought strange images into her tortured mind.

"My mother and brother Miro visited me yesterday. They told me; 'Joka, what are you still doing there. Come on over to us. It is much nicer here. There is no pain.' But honey I am afraid of these images and their invitation. I want to be with you, regardless of my pain and suffering."

One night, Boro was alone watching his mom. She had difficulty speaking and was able to communicate with him only by squeezing his index finger with her good hand.

"Mom do you hear me?" Light squeeze meant "yes."

"Mom, do you have pain?"

No squeeze. Mom had no pain.

"Mom, do you want me to pray for you?"

Quite a strong squeeze. Mom wanted her boy to pray for her.

Boro turned toward the icon of God Mother and baby Jesus on the night table. He crossed himself three times, bowing each time before the icon. He did not know a Church prayer for this kind of the occasion. He made it up. "Lord Jesus Christ you know my mother well. She is your old warrior, your faithful follower and servant. Be merciful to her dear Lord in these hours of pain, torment and humiliation. Please, forgive her sins. Be merciful to her, ease her pain, and if it is Your will give her a peaceful death."

# A Kingdom to Buy

He was praying this prayer in a low voice. He could see no reaction on mom's face. Her breathing was getting shallower. He thought: "this is the end". He woke up brothers and sisters, and all five of them sat around mom's bed, talking about the arrangements for the funeral. But mom won the reprieve. Her breathing improved and at dawn, she was alive and awake.

She was quite cheerful and said that she was hungry and asked them to prepare her favourite breakfast; bacon and eggs with 'cafe au lait.' After breakfast she asked them to take her out on the terrace to get some sunshine and fresh air. She wanted to see the city, the sea, the mountains.

Everybody was surprised and pleased by mom's sudden recovery, except Marko.

"It happens very often in situations like this. People seemingly recover, want to eat or drink, are cheerful. But, this is most likely just a short lived recovery. The end usually follows quickly."

Marko was right. The miraculous recovery ended the next day. Mom would go into sleep-- wake bouts, apparently bothered by some images appearing to her. After having a few hours sleep, Boro took the night shift to watch his mom and to pray with her. The next day, Boro and his brother had to catch the plane going back to America. Mom was able to speak, but in a low voice and very short sentences. Boro asked her to pray all the prayers she prayed, when he was little boy clinging to her back in the ice freezing room, in their small stone house in Pridraga.

She began; "Our Father," then "The Creed of Faith," "Hail Mary." Her voice was barely audible. Boro wanted to save her the trouble of saying other prayers. "Mom it's enough. Don't strain yourself. Relax. Try to get some rest."

"There is more," she whispered and very slowly started: "My dear departed ones..." and she finished whispering the prayer for her living family invoking God's blessing on all of them.

He squeezed her good hand and kissed her on the cheek: "Thank you mama that was the nicest prayer I ever heard. I want to tell you about something that happened long time ago."

Mom looked at Boro: "Nice story?" She asked barely audibly.

"Yes mama, the nicest thing that happened to me."

Mom nodded her head asking Boro to continue.

"I was about eleven years old and away from our home, attending public school in the town. One Saturday you came to the fruit market in the town bringing few baskets of our peaches to sell. After you mom, my second love were the peaches from our vineyard. After school, I came to the market to see you. You kept hugging and kissing me, while I was, with hunger in my eyes, looking at the peaches in the baskets. I thought, 'I could eat the whole basket.'

You picked up the three the best, the biggest, the most seductively smelling peaches, handed them to me, and kissing me said, 'Here honey, enjoy.' I felt like I won a lottery, by getting three; 'The best, the juiciest, the sweetest, the biggest peaches in the whole world.' Women selling her fruit besides you looked at you astounded and scolded you. 'Don`t be crazy woman. Why didn`t you give your boy few smaller bruised peaches; those would be good enough for him. You could get nice money for these three big peaches.' You just dismissed her by hand; 'I don`t care. He is my best customer. He deserves the best. He is more important to me than all the peaches, customers and money.'"

"I was very proud of you mom while biting into the first of 'the best peaches in the whole world.' I ate these three peaches that day. Never, in my life had I eaten better, sweeter, juicier peaches than these three. I know why they tasted so good. They were blessed and soaked by your motherly love."

Mom motioned him to bring his head closer to her. Very slowly she embraced him around his neck and kissed him on the cheek. A tear was slowly sliding from her good eye. She whispered: 'That was a beautiful story. Thank you honey.'

Boro wept.

After Boro and his brother got out of the plane in America, Jelena, coming to pick them up at the airport, brought them the news: "Your brother Marko called this morning. He told us that your mom died several hours after you boarded the plane."

Boro and his brother crossed themselves saying, "May God be merciful to her soul and the earth be light over her body."

The following Sunday all of them went to the Church, lit the candles and gave donations to the church in mom's memory. They all got together in Boro's house, had light lunch in memory of their mother, reminiscing about the time when their mom was strong, energetic, God fearing Christian woman.

When his sister came back to America, she gave them details of mom's funeral, with a few pictures. All of them joked that they felt first time in their lives as orphans; no father, no mother.

Death of his mom was life changing event for Boro. He thought about sharing his thoughts with a trusted friend.

Stefan obliged by appearing that night.

"It would be nice to be like an angel," thought Boro, seeing majestic, beautiful, always young, always healthy, always happy face of his mighty guardian angel.

"Hello Boro, my dear friend. How are you?"

"I am good Stefan, and you? Redundant question I suppose. You are always good, always young always healthy, always happy."

"Thank you for the compliments Boro. I am always just as you said, but I still like when you ask me how I am. It shows me that you care for me and I appreciate that."

"There were some life changing events in my life lately, births of my children, death of my mother, problems with jobs and business. I felt the need to talk to you, to put some order in my mind and soul."

"I am aware of all these issues and events. I am giving you compliment for the way you have behaved lately."

"Thank you Stefan. I am not sure if I deserve such a generous compliment."

"It is nice of you to be humble, but you really deserve a; 'job well done, congratulation."

"I humbly accept the credit. Please tell me what I did to deserve these compliments."

"It was not one single thing you have done. It is the change in your outlook on life, your maturing, moving in the right direction for your salvation. It is finally step closer to getting ready to use the talent God gave you."

"I did all that? I was not aware of all of these things you mentioned."

"I know that Boro. Child is not aware of its growing. Only after longer time the growth is evident. It is similar with spiritual growth."

"Please tell me what was the result of my spiritual growth in the right direction."

"I could tell you Boro, but it would be much better, if you uncover it yourself."

"Boro smiled in; 'I give up' motion. Go ahead Stefan cross examine me."

Stefan smiled back disapprovingly. "I am not a lawyer trying to trick you into giving me the answers I want. I am helping you by jogging your memory, so that you become aware of the reasons you acted as you did."

"Sorry Stefan. Please jog my memory."

"No problem. We need sometimes, to break the tension, to relax."

"Do they have any good jokes in heaven?"

"Angels tell no jokes. There is no need for jokes in heaven."

"Not allowed?"

"There is no instruction 'Joking strictly forbidden, jokers will be prosecuted.' Nobody in heaven thinks about jokes, nor is there any need, or desire to tell jokes. This is strictly an earthly phenomenon."

"Is everybody always serious in the heaven? No jokes, no laughing. Must be boring?"

"Boredom is an earthly phenomenon. In heaven, everybody is happy, because they are near the source of life and happiness, Our Lord."

"Stefan I want to find out what good things I did."

"We will get to that. We discussed about the real reason why you did not go to see your father before he died. Remember?"

"Yes, I remember that discussion."

"But, you went to see your mom when she was gravely ill. What changed?"

"I changed. When my father was dying I was single man, 'a free hunter.' My priority was: 'Me, me, me.' When my mother was about to die, the situation was different. I was a family man; wife children, responsibilities. Taking care of my own children I started appreciating the parenthood and sacrifices parents make for their children. I was also closer to my mom than to my father. She left the biggest influence on my character and life."

"I see no need to jog your memory any more to increase your awareness. God is rewarding you for your spiritual growth and inner change."

"I am getting some kind of award?"

"Lord instructed me to disclose, what is the gift He gave you."

"Is that what you refused to tell me for a long time, saying that I was not ready. You think I am ready now?"

"Yes, you are ready. You will be still undergoing tremendous spiritual growth, all the way until you die."

"What is the talent, the secret gift God gave me?"

"Boro, God gave you the talent of word sowing. He elected you to be His word sower."

"Word sowing? What does that mean? One can sow corn, grass seed, wheat, but sowing the words?"

"You cannot sow the words into the soil, but you can sow the words into men's hearts."

"What kind of words are you talking about Stefan?"

"It is rather the message."

"I am not an expert on theology, didn't even read the whole Bible yet. Don't you think I am rather a poor candidate to be word sower. I bet God could find many better qualified men to be His word sowers."

"God makes no mistakes. He elected you to be His word sower. He gave you all necessary talent to become a successful specialist word sower."

"I am specialist word sower. Sounds great, but why 'specialist'?"

"There are many specialist word sowers working for God, utilising their God given talents to spread the word of salvation to men. Some do it through music, the others through icons, paintings or sculptures. Some do it by preaching, some by healing."

"What is my specialty?"

"What do you think?"

"I see no special talent in me. I think even your friendly prodding with questions won't work this time."

"Have faith Boro. When I helped you in the past you always found the answers, you asked me to give you. You were successful every single time. Isn't that right Boro?"

"It is right. By you asking me the right questions, I found the answers myself. I guess my lazy nature is pushing me to get things with as little effort as possible. Please go ahead."

"What were your best subjects in school? The ones you really excelled in and enjoyed studying."

"My favourite subject was always the language and literature."

"Your first love was the language, literature and ability to communicate with people. Did I guess right?"

"You guessed right. My first love is the language, literature and communication with people."

"What's your second love?"

"I don't grade my 'loves' as first, second, third …"

"What is the other love you feel strongly about?"

"My other love is; to help people, to care for them, to bring a ray of sunshine and joy into their lives. I always wanted to do that, even since I was a little boy."

"That is wonderful Boro. Only rare people are blessed with this gift. You are doing great un-wrapping your gifts."

"Are we done now with the gift unwrapping Stefan?"

"Almost, almost done Boro. Let's just throw 'the wrapping paper' away, so that you clearly see your gift."

"What paper? There was no paper."

"There was no real paper. I call 'paper' the secrecy that was covering your gift until today. I helped you take it off your gift, to unwrap it. We need just a bit more to complete that un-wrapping."

## A Kingdom to Buy

"What else were you going to ask me?"

"You first love is languages, literature and communication with people. What grades did you have in languages and literature during your schooling?"

"I always had top marks, usually one of the best in the class."

"Have you tried your luck in writing?"

"I wrote some poetry, which was published in several magazines. When I was in fifth grade I tried to write a book."

"Did you get positive review of the poetry you wrote?"

"Yes, the commentaries were very flattering. I really enjoyed them."

"What about the book you wanted to write?"

"I was just eleven years old, living with my brother in the little town in a one bedroom apartment. Since my brother was away on business most of the time, I was chief cook and cleaner. My staple food was ham and cheese sandwiches. I made sandwich and ate it carrying it all over the apartment. This invited uncalled guests, the ants. Their armies invaded my apartment. I watched as their 'soldiers' gathered and carried the crumbs from my sandwiches. It seemed to me that whole divisions of the ant`s army were hunting in my apartment and disappearing loaded with the spoils of their raid, in a small hole near the kitchen window.

They had no permission from me to hunt, so I declared them war. My weapon was my writing pen. I brought the chair near the window and sat there in ambush, waiting for the little raider's army to show up loaded with the 'illegally' collected crumbs. When little guys showed up, I squashed them and kept on doing it, until the supply of the victims was exhausted.

There, in front of me on the window sill were laying squashed, brave, tough little warriors, their mutilated bodies mixed with the spoils of their expedition, sandwich crumbs. I sat there looking at dead invaders, proud like Alexander Macedonian after defeating king Darius of Persia.

And then, I got a brilliant idea in my eleven year old head. "I am going to write a book about this encounter between me and ants. I will call it: "The ant's cemetery." Excited about the idea, I got me new pen and started writing; "The ants cemetery." I fell asleep after I wrote half a page.

"I cannot write this stupid book," I said to myself. "I have to study, go to school, movies, play with my friends. I got no time for this. Besides, who in the world would read about a massacre of bunch of ants on a window sill, written by an eleven year old boy?' And that was the end of my earliest dream of the literary glory."

Stefan was listening to Boro's history of the Ants Cemetery smiling. "You have a sense of humour Boro. That is great addition to your gift. That is a precious gift in communicating with people. You love writing and you already did some writing with success. Don't you think that this shows that you have the gift of writing?"

"I did very little writing so far. Isn't it premature to conclude that I have the gift of writing?"

"It is not premature at all. Your literary gift has proven itself. What is important is the impact your writing had on the people who read it."

"If I had as you said 'the gift of writing, 'why didn't I write more? Wouldn't that prove that I really had the ability to write?"

"Since we met first the time you were being prepared for your calling, specialist word sower. It was not only the skill that needed to be developed, but more importantly your character. People you met, situations you found yourself in, pleasant and unpleasant, successes and failures, good health and sicknesses. All that served God's purpose to prepare you for use of your talent. The quantity of your writing is less important than the quality. Lord knows that you are just about getting ready to do the job you were being destined for."

"It seems to me Stefan that Lord has much more confidence in my abilities and talent, than I have myself. I never thought in my wildest dream that I would be capable of undertaking such a monumental task as you explained God wants and expects from me."

"I am aware of that Boro. In man's criteria you lacked confidence in your ability. 'You sold yourself short.' That is the biggest reason you did not achieve material success. Your weakest link becomes your strongest when it comes to working on the God`s field, where success and failure are measured by the entirely different criteria."

"There is a contradiction between these two statements you just made. Did you make a mistake?"

"I did not make mistake. I said that lack of self-confidence and belief in your own abilities prevented you from achieving a material success?"

"It is true that the lack of belief in myself kept me poor. You are saying now that the same lack of confidence in my own abilities is a great asset working on 'Lord`s field'. How can that be?"

"It seems to be a paradox but, actually it is not."

"I am eager to hear your explanation."

"What kind of attitude would you need to have in order to be materially successful?"

"I can do it on my own. I have the ability to do it."

"In this 'winners' attitude where is the emphasis, on which person?"

"On 'me' of course?"

"Who gave you the ability to think, to see, to hear, to work?"

"My parents and God?"

"Your parents gave you birth. God gave you soul which makes you alive and able to see, hear, think, work. Saying that all abilities are yours, without recognising they are gifts from God is a deception, which leads to pride, the worst vice."

"I see what you are getting at Stefan. Can I say it?"

"Please say it."

"Thinking that I achieved material success on my own ability and hard work without God`s help, is insulting to God and alienates me from Him. If I am humble and give credit for all my gifts and abilities to God, it brings me closer to God. The lack of material success means that my ties to God will strengthen, while my ties to material world will weaken. It seems to me that Lord 'conspired' to keep me poor, to loosen my ties to the world, so that I could fulfill my mission better."

"That was perfect. I have nothing else to add."

"I know my destiny now. What do I need to do Stefan?"

"Keep building your character and keep sharpening and fine tuning your God given gift."

"How do I build my character?"

"Keep God`s commandments. Love God and your fellow man. Do good deeds. Acquire habit of praying."

"How do I sharpen my God given talent, or as you said fine tune it."

"Read and study Holy Bible and other books of the Church Fathers. Practice writing again and again and again."

"I do all this and then what?"

"That`s it."

"That`s it? I thought I had to do something big, something special."

"You will."

"I will, but when?"

"You will do it when ready. When your character and skill are mature enough, you will decide it and do it."

"What am I am going to do?"

"You are the word sowing specialist. You will decide when, and what to do. Remember, I am with you every day and every night. I am just a thought away. Use me."

"I will use you Stefan. I need lot of help."

Stefan went from room to room, kissed all children, caressing them on the head. He kissed Jelena on the cheek and then Boro. Saying "bye my friends," the mighty angel disappeared.

# Chapter 22

# *Word Sowing Business*

With wife, three children, job and side business, Boro's life got quite busy. He got involved with the local parish, becoming member of the Parish Executive Board. He was astounded at the level of ignorance of most parishioners of basic dogmas of the Orthodox Church. Most people thought that the most important purpose of the Church was to preserve tradition and their ethnic identity. Getting involved with people in the community was a valuable training to Boro in his calling of word sower specialist. He still was not sure what exactly he supposed to do with his talent. He decided: "I got to talk to Stefan." When Stefan appeared that night, Boro greeted him enthusiastically.

"You look wonderful Stefan, mighty and beautiful."

"Thank you Boro. You are looking good too. How are you?"

"You know Stefan that we are all well, but you still ask me?"

Stefan smiled. "Do you remember what I always replied to your questions like this one?"

"You told me that you know everything about me, but you wanted to hear it from my mouth."

"Thank you Boro you said it very nicely."

"You told me that Our Lord gave me the gift to be a specialist word sower. God expects me to sow the words. I frequently have doubts if this was just a figment of my imagination, wishful thinking, an illusion?"

"Let me first congratulate you for recently writing fine poetry. Your talent came on the light of the day brilliantly."

"Thank you Stefan. I was pleased and flattered at the reaction of people who read my poetry."

"Be always modest and humble. Remember; your talent is a gift of God to you."

"I will try to be modest and humble, but I am not quite sure why is this important?"

"We discussed before how Lucifer and his demons became the enemies of God. Do you remember that?"

"No, I don`t recall that."

"I will help you to remember. Was Lucifer always an evil angel?"

"No, He was not. He was created as a good angel."

"How did he become an evil angel?"

"He became an evil angel due to his rebellion against God. He wanted to be God himself; self-sufficient, self-made, rejecting God`s authority and Supremacy."

"Why did God allow him to rebel?"

"Because He created him with free will."

"What do you think drove Lucifer to rebel against his Creator?"

"I am not sure. Jealousy against God?"

"That too, but what do you think was the main driving force to cause him to rebel against God?"

"What else besides his jealousy would prompt him to rebel?"

"When you were a little boy, did you have to obey your father?"

"Yes, I had to obey."

"Suppose one day, you came to your father and told him: 'Listen old man I am not going to listen to you, nor obey you any more, because I am as good as you are. I am my own boss.' What would cause you to do such a foolish thing?"

"Sheer stupidity."

"That too, but what else would incite you to rebel against your own father?"

"Wait a minute. It is the pride that would push me to rebel against my own father. Pride also caused Lucifer to rebel against his Creator, Almighty God."

"You got it Boro. It was the pride that made Lucifer a personification of evil from a bright Archangel of God."

"How does that relate to me. I am not an angel. How do I rebel against God?"

"Very simply: if God is not 'number one' in your life, you have already rebelled against God."

"God as 'number one' in my life? I don't understand what you mean by that?"

"Who is right now the 'number one' person in your life?"

"The most important people in my life are my wife and children."

"Are you saying that your wife and children are 'number one' in your life?"

"They are. Anything wrong with that?"

"What do you think Boro?"

"I see nothing wrong in that. It is quite normal, isn't it?"

"I agree with you. It is quite normal to have your family as 'number one' in your life."

"I foresee a 'but' coming in. Am I right?"

"You are right. Though it is normal for man to hold his family as 'number one' in his life, this is not what God wants. He wants to be in the first place in your life. He wants to be your 'number one.'"

"I don't understand what are you trying to tell me."

"I will help you to understand."

"Thank you Stefan. I really appreciate it."

"We discussed before that man is a complex being. He has a soul, and by his immortal soul he is similar to immortal, bodiless angels. At the same time, he has a body, and he is similar to animals that have body, but not an immortal soul. Since you have body, nobody is closer to you in the body than your wife and children. Your children are 'the flesh of your flesh, the bone of your bone. By marrying your wife a union was created, not only physical, but also spiritual. Holy Bible expresses this beautifully: 'Man shall leave his father and mother and join his wife, and the two shall become one.'"

"Are you saying Stefan it is normal for me to hold my wife and children as 'number one' in my life."

"It is normal, but this is not what God requires of you."

"What more would Almighty God ask of me a poor, sinful man?"

"I hope you are aware Boro, that God asks men to do things that are not normal."

"That is news to me Stefan. Why would God ask me to do something I cannot do?"

"God commanded man to do things which, on his own, are impossible for man to do."

"I am not aware of any such commands?"

"You read the whole New Testament?"

"I just finished it last week."

"There are many examples in the New Testament where Lord Jesus Christ asked men to do things that man on his own could not do. Could you remember any of these 'impossible to do requests?'"

"The toughest request made by Jesus seemed to me; 'Love your enemies.' That commandment seemed unnatural, and impossible to obey."

"Any more 'impossible to fulfil' commandments?"

"There are quite a few : 'Love your neighbour as yourself. But whoever slaps you on your right cheek, turn the other cheek to him also. Bless those who curse you, do good to them that hate you, and pray for those who spitefully use you and persecute you.' I think I could find more 'impossible to fulfil' commandments."

"This is sufficient Boro. It shows you that God wants men to do the things, which don`t seem normal, and possible for man to do."

"Why would God ask me to do things, He knows I cannot do? What is the purpose of asking me to 'walk on the water'? I would sink like a stone immediately."

"If God said to you 'Come', you would walk on the water, just like Saint Peter did."

"Yes, but he started sinking, after walking on the water to go to Jesus."

"Do you know why, he started to sink. What did Gospel say?"

"I don't know."

"He began sinking because he took his eyes off Jesus, and focused on the storm. He fed his fear and doubts, instead of his faith in Christ."

"Stefan, I believe I would be able to do 'impossible' things with God's help."

"You are convinced now that with God's help, you can do even the 'impossible' things. Based on this couldn't you say that God is your 'number one' in your life?"

"That is a tough question Stefan. My wife and kids would be puzzled and upset, if I told them that."

"Why would they be upset?"

"They would tell me; 'How could anybody in the world be more important to you than us, your family. God is to be respected, prayed to and thanked, but we are part of you. We should be your 'number one' in life."

"And what would be your response Boro?"

"In a way they are right. I should be honouring God, worshiping Him and praying to Him, because He gave us life, and He blesses us with material needs, health and sound mind."

"Let's suppose there are two men. One of them says: "My family is always 'number one', they come even before God. I think and worry all the time about my wife and children, and do everything to make them happy. After I make them happy, I praise God.

Another man says: "God is 'number one' in my life. I honour Him first. I try to live by His commandments, please Him by my life and by practising two commandments of love; To love God first, with all my heart and with all my mind and all my strength, and my neighbour as myself. My family comes after God. Who would be more pleasing to God, first man, or second man?"

"Obviously, the second man."

"Why?"

"Because, He put God in the first place in his life and he lives by God's commandments."

"Do you think is it possible that man who put God in the first place could, because of that, neglect his family?"

"He could neglect it if he completely devotes all his time and energy to please God."

"Are you saying that if he becomes 'fanatical' about God, his family might suffer?"

"Yes, Stefan. I heard of people that all they do is pray and go to church, neglecting their families."

"What are the first two commandments that man having God in the first place obeys?"

"The first one is to love God, and the second one is to love his neighbour as himself."

"Would you agree with me that these two commandments are inseparable?"

"What do you mean 'inseparable?'"

"If you love God, you automatically love your fellow man. Also, if you love your fellow man as yourself, you love God too. If you genuinely obey one commandment, you automatically obey the other one."

"What was the purpose of your questioning about love for God and love for your neighbour?"

"What do you think Boro?"

"I don't know. That is why I am asking you."

"Let me help you to figure this out. Can I?"

"Of course."

"Does it not follow from our conversation, that you please both, God and your family, if God is first in your life?"

"Yes, we concluded that, but I am still not convinced."

"Why not? What is the problem?"

"I am still looking at it with the eyes of my flesh. God is invisible, unknown, hidden, removed from my senses. Only what my senses register is real to me, everything else is imagination."

"I see in your thinking still a lot of doubts, for everything that you cannot see, hear, or touch. The flesh is your safe refuge. Your senses and your reason give you complete picture (you think). Why step into something totally unknown, where your senses and reason are useless. Unfortunately, this is the way majority of people think and behave. As a word sower specialist, you are different from this gang. I know that and I am convinced of that. I understand that you would occasionally retreat and 'hide' in your flesh, as if you needed a 'firm ground' to rest for a while. That is fine. Even the saints had moments when they retreated for period of time in the cocoon' of their bodies. The important thing is not to overstay in that 'cocoon' for too long, but let your soul guide you."

"Are you saying that it is okay to doubt?"

"I am saying it is natural for man to doubt. That stays with man all his life. As man grows spiritually he will be able to overcome more of his doubts, without ever eliminating them completely."

"What is the conclusion of our lengthy friendly discussion on your statement; "If God is not in the first place in your life, you already rebelled against God?"

"Could you answer that question Boro?"

"I think that your statement could be both; right and wrong."

"Do you believe that something can be right and wrong at the same time?"

"I guess it is possible."

"Boro, if something is right, doesn`t it automatically mean that it is not wrong?"

"It is quite acceptable in today`s world that something could be neither absolutely right, nor absolutely wrong, but somewhere in between: little bit right, little bit wrong. Absolute truths are very unpopular, almost extinct, particularly regarding moral and religious issues. This is what prompted me to say that your statement could be right and wrong at the same time."

"Ah, the Enemy is not staying idle," murmured Stefan.

"Wow, the Enemy is all over the place, sowing bad seeds into human minds. He is a dangerous fellow."

"He is dangerous for sure. He is also relentless, sly, intelligent, liar and deceiver. You have to stay on guard against his tricks, at all times. Do you realize now why is important to have God in the first place in your life? Doing this, you don`t neglect your family, on the contrary, you place it under God`s protection?"

"Yes, I do Stefan. One thing bugs me. What could be possibly wrong if I hold my family, or say a friend or a cousin in the first place in my life, instead of God? What`s the harm?"

"What could happen, and does frequently happen is that the family, or cousin, or friend that is in the first place in your life, replaces God, almost becomes a god to you. God becomes distant second. When God is in the first place, everything else will fit in perfectly."

"I understand you, but people would not understand. They would brand me a fanatic, religious nut, uncaring."

"Yes, people might consider you fool, fanatic, religious nut. They might make your life miserable."

"I bet not many men would be brave enough to stand out amongst the crowd and declare: 'God is in the first place in my life. My family and everything else is second."

"You are right again Boro. It is easy to be nominal, Pharisaic Christian, but not easy to be a true Christian, a genuine follower of Lord Jesus Christ."

"But why is it so hard? I thought it would be very smooth and easy."

"It is hard because you have to struggle against your human nature, against your flesh."

"You said it was easy to be a Pharisaic Christian. Who is a Pharisaic Christian?"

"Do you remember reading in one of the Gospels about two men praying in the Church? The first one was a learned Pharisee and the second one was a despised tax collector?"

"Oh yes, yes. I remember. It was a really shocking difference between these two men and their attitudes."

"How did the Pharisee pray?"

"I can`t tell exactly word for word. As I recall, he said something like this: 'Thank you God that I am not like other men; adulterers, thieves, unjust men, nor as this despised tax collector. I do what is required of me; fast twice a week and give a share of my wealth to the Church."

"Do you remember what the attitude of the Pharisee was when he prayed?"

"He prayed to God."

"He prayed to God, but do you remember what was his attitude when he prayed?"

"I am sorry Stefan, I don`t recall that."

"It said in the Gospel that the Pharisee; stood and prayed with himself."

"Isn`t it proper to pray within oneself?"

"He prayed 'with himself' and not to God."

"I understand."

"Do you recall how the tax collector prayed?"

"As I recollect, he prayed something like this: 'God be merciful to me, because I am a sinner."

"What was the attitude of that tax collector while praying?"

"The Gospel said that he was: 'Standing at the back of the church, not daring to raise even his eyes to heaven, and he beat his chest while saying his prayer."

"What was the difference in the attitude during prayer between the learned Pharisee and the despised tax collector?"

"The Pharisee was proud, self-righteous, condemning his fellow man, while the tax collector was humble and meek."

"And what did the Gospel say about these two men?"

"I think it said that God preferred the prayer of the tax collector, rather than the Pharisee`s."

"Do you remember why?"

"It said: 'Whoever tries to put himself up on the pedestal, will be humbled by God. And the one that humbles himself, God will lift him up on the pedestal."

"Good recollection Boro."

"Thank you Stefan. We discussed many issues, but not the one we were supposed to; What do I need to do to perform my calling of the specialist word sower. Do you want to talk about it now, or shall we leave it for next time?"

"Will begin now, and continue next time. Is that good for you?"

"Of course it is. Do I have any choice?"

"You always have a choice simply by exercising your free will."

"I will do as you suggested: Will begin now and follow up the next time."

"Just keep doing what you are doing. Stay active in your parish. Read the Holy Bible and Books of the Church Fathers. Write as much as you can. Pray daily and fast as prescribed by the Church. Live by God`s commandments. Your head is probably overloaded. I am leaving. Bye my friend."

Mighty angel kissed Boro`s wife and children, then gently kissed Boro on the forehead, spread his mighty golden wings and was gone into his world.

Boro murmured something in his sleep, turned to the other side and continued slight snoring.

# Chapter 23

# *The Frustrations*

Boro was heeding Stefan's advice and started seriously reading the Bible and books written by the Fathers of the Church. He started to fast one week before Christmas and one week before Easter, and receiving confession and communion several times a year.

There was no magical conversion, nor exalted feeling after receiving the Body and Blood of Christ, as he expected. He became disappointed and began to think. "What went wrong? Was my confession proper? Did I fail to confess some big sin? How does this bread and wine become; 'Body and Blood of Jesus Christ?' Is this just a priestly ploy? Some Protestants do not believe that the bread and wine become Christ's Body and Blood."

"How do you prove that pieces of bread and wine became the body and blood of the Son of God? The only proof was that Jesus said so. What more authority do I need to believe it? It said that right in the Gospel. But then again, there are many things that Jesus and His Apostles said in the Bible that are hard to grasp. Different people had different interpretations of the same verse, in the Bible. Who is right?"

Boro asked the priest who gave him the communion to explain how this bread and wine became the Body and Blood of Christ? The priest was stunned at such a provocative question, at such unbelief. He said, "How can you ask question like that? Jesus said:

'This is My Body and My Blood.' Holy Church teaches that in this golden chalice is indeed Body and Blood of Jesus Christ. It becomes that after priest's prayer in the liturgy. How it becomes, is a holy mystery."

Frustrated by the slow advancement in his spiritual life and word sowing, Boro started having some serious doubts. "Why am I doing all this; fasting, praying, reading Bible and other religious books. I am trying to behave like a saint. What's the benefit for me? Other men pursue business, earn money, buy properties, drive new cars, have romantic adventures with sexy women, go every year on expensive holidays. They are respectable members of the community. They come to church on Christmas, Easter and Slava, give money to the Church and are commended by the priests and Bishop.

Perhaps, I should do the same and lead a 'normal' life. Maybe I should enjoy life in full while I can. When they bury me, that is the end of me as if I never existed. The other life, the Kingdom of heaven, nobody knows for sure if it even exists. I don't think there would be any sense in having a 'friendly' discussion with Stefan. He would persuade me with my own words that I should, even more diligently: pray, cut the ties with 'the world,' deny myself and follow Christ."

Frustrated and doubting, Boro decided to meet once again with his guardian angel and resolve the issue: either to live the 'normal' pharisaic way as majority of people do, or chose, for the rest of his life; the 'narrow and thorny way'.

Stefan obliged. His presence had a tremendous influence on Boro. He could not resist awe of the majestic beauty and holiness of his heavenly guardian and protector. Immediately he felt much more at ease.

"Glad to see you again Boro. How are you? How is your lovely family?"

"We are all good, and how are you my esteemed heavenly adviser and protector?"

Stefan gave him a very warm smile. "A new title for me. Thank you Boro, I really like it and appreciate it. I am good, always good."

"You know why I wanted to meet you."

"What frustrates you and bugs you?"

"I think one moment I know, but the next moment I am not sure. I am confused."

"We need to go to step, by step, by step, to clear up that doubt and confusion. What do you doubt?"

"Is this life all there is, and with the death of the body, everything else dies? There is nothing beyond a dark grave, absolutely nothing, just the end of me forever, as if I never existed and lived on this earth."

"These are some serious doubts. When did you get infected by these doubts?"

"Recently, after I had some recognition with my poetry writing, and after I attempted practising my calling of specialist word sower."

"When you say: 'practising my trade of specialist word sower,' what exactly do you mean?"

"You know what I am supposed to do as an apprenticing word sower specialist. You told me that yourself."

"Of course, I know I told you that, but I forgot. Could you please remind me what I said?"

"You can`t forget. You just want me to spill out the things a specialist word sower, needs to do?"

"Yes Boro, spill it out?"

"You told me to stay active in the parish. I did, I was in the Executive Board and teaching Sunday school."

"Very good Boro, point for you. What else were you suppose to do?"

"I supposed to form the habit to pray daily and to follow Church prescribed fasting days."

"And how did you do there?"

"Not too good."

"Why not?"

"I prayed one day, missed two days. It was even worse to keep fasting days prescribed by the Church, because nobody else in my family fasted. My wife complained that she would have to cook fasting and non-fasting meals. It was just too much for her, besides, I couldn`t drink coffee without milk."

"You will be prone to the attacks of temptations as long as you are in the body. Fight temptations, by praying to God to help you."

"I asked God for help, but it seemed as if He ignored me."

"God ignored you? What made you to reach that conclusion?"

"I was praying; 'Lord please help me to keep all fasts, to pray every day, to always be relaxed and of clear, quick mind. Help me to become your best word sower specialist. Bless my business to prosper. Give me and my family perfect health. Lord please give me, give me, give me…"

Stefan smiled interrupting Boro: "Sorry for interrupting you, but we can figure out the cause of your doubt and frustration."

Boro was surprised. "How do you figure that out?"

"Did you expect God to grant your prayers, giving you everything you asked for?"

"I didn`t see reason for God to deny my prayers. They were all reasonable, proper, and easy for God to grant."

"You were surprised when you were met by silence from God?"

"Yes I was very much disappointed and surprised by God`s rejection."

"Boro, when you were a little boy, you probably asked your parents for lot of things?"

"Yes, I did."

"Give me few examples of what you asked for."

"I asked my dad, once, to give me the matches. I wanted to make a big, 'beautiful fire' in our haystack in the backyard. Though I asked very politely, seeing nothing wrong in my request, my dad was not amused. He refused to give me the matches. He threatened me if he ever caught me playing with the matches, I would get a nasty spanking."

"How unreasonable of your father? Did he explain why he refused such an innocent, 'reasonable' request to make a nice, big fire?"

"No, he didn`t bother to justify his refusal. I was too little to understand. When I was bit older I understood the consequences of my big, 'beautiful fire.' We would burn our cows food and the fire could spread to our house and burn it."

"Any other requests you made?"

"I loved candy, and chocolate. Never had enough of that stuff. But my 'cruel' parents denied me that pleasure, telling me that these delicious sweet goodies would hurt me. Unbelievable!"

"Do you understand now why they refused to give you 'all you can eat' of these delicacies?"

"I still like good chocolate and occasionally, I pig out on it, but I am aware how bad these sweets can be to my health. I understand why my parents did not allow me to overdo on that stuff."

"Could you say Boro that your parents refused your demands and denied you things, out of love for you and for your well-being."

"I can see that now."

"If your earthly parents, did not grant you every wish and demand, wouldn`t your Heavenly Father also deny some of your prayers, because granting them would not be to your benefit, but to your harm."

"I guess that`s what happened."

"Shall we quit for today?"

"Please stay bit longer. Something else bugs me."

"Sure Boro, it must be something important, since you want me to stay overtime."

"Yes it is Stefan. It has to do with Mr. Eros."

"What`s wrong with him?"

"He is neglecting his job. He is going frequently on long vacations."

"Who is allowing him to take long vacations?"

"It is not me, Jelena did it."

"Well, well, Mr. Eros was very regular 'fire starter' in yours and Jelena`s relationship. What happened?"

"Looks like Jelena convinced him that he was working too much, and should take it easy."

"What did you tell Mr. Eros?"

"I did not want him to work as hard as in the beginning of our marriage. I was willing to give him bit longer time off, but not nearly as long as Jelena."

"Did you and Jelena discuss how often you liked Mr. Eros to perform his 'fire starter' job?"

"No, we were too shy to discuss his job."

"How did you resolve the situation?"

"I would ask Mr. Eros to do his job, but Jelena would find all kinds of excuses to allow Mr. Eros to get 'the time off."

"What kind of excuses did she come up with?"

"I am tired, I have a headache. I have busy day tomorrow. We will do it when we go on vacation. I didn't have a bath today. I just don't feel doing it. We are too old for this stuff. We'll do it next week after we go for nice dinner and have a few drinks. It is full moon, no good to do it tonight. It is a red letter day on the Calendar. I want to watch the late show…"

Stefan was listening to Boro's 'lamentations' smiling: "Poor Boro. You were put on a rationing. Were your feelings hurt?"

"My manhood was slapped in the face. My male pride was wounded. Me, former 'conqueror' was forced to 'eat a humble pie."

"You were unhappy about your love life restrictions Boro?"

"I was, but looks like nothing I can do about. What do you think of my predicament Stefan?"

"I sympathize with you Boro. You always had a strong sexual drive."

"Thank you for your sympathy Stefan. Can you help? Could you convince Mr. Eros to be bit more active and do more frequent fire starting?"

Stefan smiled shaking his beautiful angelic head: "Sorry Boro, this is way out of my instructions. I can give you just some friendly advice."

"Anything that might help."

"Before I give you my advice I want to ask you few questions regarding involvement of Mr. Eros in your marriage. Did you expect Mr. Eros to be as busy later on in your marriage as in the beginning?"

"I realized that my desire for Mr. Eros involvement might decrease as I was getting older, but I expected that he would be available any time I wanted."

"Evidently, that didn`t happen, because both of you have to want Mr. Eros to do his job."

"Do most women like Jelena, loose interest in Mr. Eros as they get older?"

"Many of them do."

"Why is that?"

"God`s will Boro. He built in humans sexual desire, made sexual act pleasurable, so that mankind would fulfill Gods order; 'Go forth and multiply."

"Are you saying Stefan that the purpose of man and woman having sex, is primarily to have children?"

"Yes Boro, that is the way God ordained. The desire for intimacy decreases as people get older, since they did their share of 'go forth and multiply.' The pleasurable component for lot of women diminishes quicker than for men. Eventually, Mr. Eros will be fired. It could be you that fire him, because you might not be willing or unable to do your part in the intimacy. It could be Jelena."

"Wow, that is very bleak picture of the future. I am especially disturbed that eventually I might be unable to do my part in the relationship. That would be the death of my manhood. I just refuse even to imagine that horrible day."

"God will take care of that. You just won`t care, nor will you have any desire for the intimacy anymore. Your body, soul and mind will undergo big changes by that time."

"Just one more question Stefan: Is it a sin to participate in the intimacy, if only pleasurable, recreational component of it is wanted?"

"God blessed intimacy between man and women in the marriage. Pleasurable component was created by God; therefore God blesses it within a marriage."

"Are you saying that any other sexual relationship outside of the marriage is sinful?"

"That is how our Almighty Father sees it."

"Stefan, I got a huge headache. The mankind is at the point beyond return. What God sees as sexual sin became a norm. Lot of humanity ignores and disregards God`s laws and commandments. They decided that God was: 'Unfair, conservative, patriarchal, too narrow minded, did not do very good job with the creation.' God`s creation (mankind) ignored Him and chased Him out of their homes, relationships, families, school, government, even the churches. They 'corrected God`s failures and unfair commandments,' showing God who is the boss; His majesty the man."

With noticeable sadness in his angelic voice, Stefan replied. "I understand Boro why you got a 'huge headache.' Humanity has gone way overboard in corrupting God`s commandments."

"I am amazed that God is so patiently allowing men to break, ignore and ridicule His moral laws. How long is Almighty God going to tolerate this corruption?"

"Neither angel, nor man knows that. Lord is waiting patiently, giving to mankind opportunity to repent and abandon the road leading it to the torments of hell."

"Lord is waiting patiently?"

"God waits patiently, but He is also giving a message to mankind: 'You went astray, repent and come back to the road of your salvation."

"How is God conveying this message to the mankind?"

"One of the ways is using 'the sticks' on the mankind. Another way is through people still brave enough to spread God`s Word, God`s word sowers."

"Lord used lot of unpleasant 'sticks' on me to bring me back to the road of salvation. What kind of 'the sticks' is God using on the humanity?"

"God`s sticks are bad and unpleasant things God allows to happen to humanity: Wars, famines, pestilences, drought, flood, earthquakes, tornadoes, hail, rebellions, crime, epidemics."

"Wow, almighty has a terrible arsenal at his disposal. Is humanity aware of that?"

"Only very small minority is. Most of mankind does not believe that these 'sticks,' have anything to do with God. Men removed God from their lives to some far away cloud, up high in the Heaven. The nature is left to itself to terrorize the mankind."

"Sorry Stefan, I kept you too much on 'the overtime.' This discussion was an eye opener for me."

"Glad to help Boro. I think you better understand now the importance of sowing God`s Word. Bye for now."

Mighty angel kissed Boro, Jelena and children and vanished.

## Chapter 24

## *The Future Has Arrived*

It was a beautiful crisp, early autumn day. Boro and Jelena relaxed at the verandah of their Dalmatia farm. Boro had for a long time dreamt of getting property outside of the city. Jelena preferred the conveniences of the city; nearness of the church, doctor, shopping, their families. Jelena`s sister convinced her to move to the 'wilderness,' forty minutes drive from the city.

The happiest time for Boro and Jelena was when their children came with their families. Their six grandchildren had lots of fun playing soccer, hiking, and fishing in the creek meandering through the farm.

Boro was seventy three years old when they bought the farm. He was almost bald and slightly stooped. His health was still pretty good. He followed a strict regimen observing the Calendar of the Orthodox Church, fasting every Wednesday and Friday and all other Church prescribed fasts.

He completed a book of poetry, written in his mother tongue, lamenting suffering and exoduses of his people. At that time Boro had already achieved some literally success. His first book went into the third edition, selling over half a million copies. He was particularly happy for the translation of his book into; Mandarin, Swahili and Urdu. The words had been sown all over the world. God`s specialist word sower was doing his job, sowing the words.

He was surprised of the commercial success of his first book. There were no plots, no dramatic events. He realized that the book would be heavily criticized, mostly by the secularized Christians. That was exactly what happened. Liberal media in America were fuming about this "Poorly written, boring, dull and hateful booklet, written in broken English."

There was sharp criticism even by a few "enlightened "Orthodox clergyman and theologians. Boro did not go into any lengthy discussion, or rebuttals. He replied politely that the book expressed his view of life and faith, from the viewpoint of a practising Orthodox Christian.

Besides being a book by a totally unknown author, an amateur theologian, an amateur writer, it had, as some critics wrote "The air of enchanting originality, simplicity and genuine and strong Christian beliefs." That is what attracted people to read it."

Boro kept his book publishing very simple and basic. His helpers, agents and advisers were his family and few friends. He was invited to appear on several American talk shows. He felt very uncomfortable appearing there, fearing that he would be easy prey to talk show hosts, who could trick him and take his words out of the context. At the insistence of his publisher, he agreed to appear on two of these TV shows.

At the beginning of the first show, he felt intimidated and nervous. After repeating Jesus prayer mentally several times he settled down a bit. To his surprise, the show host was very polite and considerate. Boro answered his questions calmly and to the point, without going deeply into the theological issues. His basic stand was: "This is my belief as an Orthodox Christian, based on the Holy Scripture and holy Tradition. It is my mission in life to share these beliefs with anybody willing to read the book. I would be very gratified if this book prompts any reader to go a step further and learn more of life as an Orthodox Christian."

He got several invitations to speak to the parishioners of local Orthodox churches. He went to speak, knowing that this was true word sowing. He was returning to his Creator the talent invested in him.

Writing the sequel to his first book, took lot of time and effort. This book was more difficult to write. It had to be; exciting, interesting to read, and based on the Bible and dogmas of the Orthodox Church.

After a lot of soul searching, persistent praying and rewriting, Boro completed this book in twelve months. This book sold more copies than his first book. Their financial situation was great. Money was no problem anymore. That is what enabled them to purchase Dalmatia farm.

They decided to keep chicken, turkeys, ducks, several goats, and Boro's favourite pet, young donkey Mica, who became favourite pet of his grandchildren. They decided also to have a big organic garden to be self-sufficient in fruit and vegetables.

There was a problem in the execution of so ambitious plans. Boro was too busy writing books. He never was an eager farmer. He liked to watch the plants grow and pick up a ripe tomato, or an apple. Jelena loved to work in the garden, but she was unable on her own to handle all those ambitious projects.

While on one of their Caribbean vacation they met young couple. They told him, they would like to move to America. Boro got the idea: "Why not ask Fidel and his family to come to America and help them out with the land and livestock." He called Fidel and explained the idea. He was excited to come to America. Boro immediately began doing the paperwork to bring Fidel and his family to America. In six months Fidel, Carmelita and their two children arrived to America.

To accommodate Fidel and his family, Boro bought a neighbouring property, twenty five acres farm, with an older brick house, double garage and a huge wooden barn. He made an agreement with Fidel and Carmelita to help Jelena with the livestock and garden. The arrangement worked very well. Fidel was diligent and smart farmer and handyman. Carmelita and Jelena made their "garden of Eden" envy of local farmers.

Boro had a set life. He was at peace, but he still wanted to return to his Creator few more talents. He went full speed preparing to write his next book. Due to sensitive material, he had to be careful, to avoid the possibility of a costly litigation. This book was intended to depict the downfall of the Orthodox Christianity and its collusion with the spirit of the world. It was an alarm ringing loudly to the Orthodox Christians and other people of the dangers of the secularized Christianity, no matter how genuine it appeared to be.

Boro was beginning frequently to think of his death. Within the last few year he was preparing to face it by, reading Church Fathers, praying, fasting. At some moments, he felt at peace and unafraid of death, but often fear would grip his heart: "What if all I had done was not sufficient, and at my death instead of holy angels, fallen angels grab my soul after it separates from the body."

Like many times before a thought flashed in his mind: "Perhaps Stefan could help me out on this."

One night Stefan appeared. Boro greeted him excitedly: "Stefan, Stefan my dear friend, I missed you, didn`t talk to you for a long time. How are you?"

Stefan greeted elderly man with a smile; "Hello Boro, I am good as always .How are you?"

"Not bad for an old man. Pretty good on the days when my prostate is behaving, my knees and hips are not inflamed and my back does not hurt."

"Quite a big list of exceptions," smiled Stefan. "It looks like your body is getting bit worn out from long use. How is your soul?"

"I hope my soul is fine. I am worried Stefan."

"What are you worried about?"

"I did lot of sinful things in my life. Will I qualify for Kingdom of Heaven, or will the dark angels grab my soul?"

"As usually, you ask tough questions Boro. You have strengthened your faith considerably by reading holy Bible and Fathers of the Church, fasting, praying and discussing issues with me. On the other hand, no mortal was ever sure that he would move into the presence of God after his death."

"That is scary. Doesn`t that mean that it is impossible to insure our salvation? Why bother then?"

"No Boro, this does not mean that it is impossible to obtain the salvation. The most devoted saints, who spent their life praying, fasting, glorifying God and living according to God`s commandments, were not sure if they had done enough to deserve the Kingdom of Heaven."

"But, why Stefan, why?"

"Salvation is gift of God. It is by God`s grace that men are saved."

"Why not then just live as I like and leave it to God, hoping that He would be merciful and grant me salvation?"

"You need to have some qualifications before you get into the Kingdom of heaven."

"Qualifications? You are talking almost as if there is some kind of competition for a valuable job."

"It is quite like that. I told you about the qualifications the saints were trying to obtain. That`s what every man should strive, to get a better chance of God granting him the salvation."

"I got it Stefan: The harder you try to please God, the better is your chance of salvation."

"I am glad you understand it Boro. No more doubts?"

"No, no more doubts. I have a question."

"What do you still question?"

"I read in some 'Christian' books that Our Lord is so merciful, that everybody will be saved. 'No questions asked.' What about that?"

"Our Lord is merciful, but He is also holy and just. Soul stained by un repented and un forgiven sins cannot be in His presence."

"Are you saying this idea that everybody gets saved is false, is not from God?"

"That is exactly what I am saying. No easy way, no free ticket to the Kingdom of heaven. Everybody is eligible to get saved, but everybody does not get saved."

"You said that everybody is eligible to be saved. Who is 'everybody'? Does that include; atheists, Muslims Buddhists, or any other faith or sect?"

"In reading The New Testament, do you recall any verses saying who gets saved?"

"To my recollection there were some verses on this topic in the Gospels as well in the Epistles. Let me see if I can remember."

"Take your time Boro."

"I remember now. I am not sure in which Gospel Jesus said; He was 'The only way to the Father.' Meaning that those who do not believe in Him as The Son of God will not be saved."

"That tells it all."

"Some people told me: 'That is not fair, it excludes lot of good people, who don't believe Jesus was the Son of God?'"

"What was your answer to them?"

"God gave everybody opportunity to be saved. The terms are clear."

"What about all people that profess belief in Jesus Christ, are they automatically saved?"

"They are eligible to obtain salvation, Why wouldn't they get it?"

"Simple answer is; they don't want to pay the price to qualify for it?"

"Again these qualifications, just like for Olympic games."

Stefan changed the theme "Do you watch television?"

"I don't watch it very much, just occasional news and sports."

"Would you like you to watch a show on the angelic heaven vision?"

"What is angelic heaven vision?"

"It is much, much more advanced than earthly television. Would you like some snacks with the show?"

Boro smiled. "Angelic snack? What is it; popcorn, chips, beer?"

"It is anything you want Boro, better than earthly stuff; healthy, non-filling, non-intoxicating. Here hop in," saying this Stefan showed Boro a gondola under his wing. It was furnished with a soft comfortable chair and a small round table. At the table were snacks Boro liked; beer, chips and popcorn.

Boro sat in the chair. "I am ready Stefan. Where is the screen?"

"Why don't you make yourself comfortable, try heavenly snacks, and the show will begin."

He tried first some heavenly chips, and took a sip of green coloured heavenly beer.

"I am ready Stefan. What kind of show is on the program?"

"Boro, this is the angelic production of; 'This is your life.' Look."

Boro looked. He was right in that heavenly show. He saw himself being born. He felt horrified and shocked getting out of the comfort of the "world" he spent first nine months of his life in. He was very comfortable in his mother's womb. It was nice and warm. Everything he needed was provided. He could even play a bit, moving his limbs.

But now, he was forced to leave his cozy, comfortable home. He was pulled, through some tight tunnel. It hurt terribly. As he left his 'nine months home,' he was blinded by a shining light, and shocked by coldness and endless space he came into. Why? Why? What forced him on this horrible, painful trip? He would love to return to the safety, security and comfort of his old home. He sensed that would not be possible. There was no way back. The force that placed him in his old home planned this expulsion. In his desperation he started the only kind of rebellion he could; he began crying, after he was hit on the bum by a huge, scary looking giant.

He had to breathe now on his own. He was wrapped up in some coarse rags. It hurt his sensitive skin. It was much, much nicer in his 'nine months home.'

Next thing He saw was the whole world. His regular mind knew that it was impossible to see the whole world, but right at that moment, it seemed that in heavenly, angelic show, anything was possible. He was seeing people all over the world ---innumerable masses.

To his horror, he saw millions of little beings, which were living in 'the nine months home,' as he did, were mutilated, killed and thrown into some boxes, like rotten meat.

They called these little 'humans to be' -fetuses. It was clear to Boro that these little 'nine months home' inhabitants were not wanted by somebody to see the light of the day alive.

"What is happening with these little tenants of 'nine months homes' Stefan? Who is killing them, why?" asked Boro horrified.

"Their landlords, that is their mothers, decided to kill them, because they did not want them to come out of the 'nine months home' alive and just like you, join new world, new existence."

"Mothers killed them? the fruit of their wombs, the blood of their blood. Why?"

"The Enemy was very successful in seducing and deceiving humanity and showing them how to justify any sin, any crime, any violation of God's commandments."

"But how could the landlords of those fetuses, their mothers, justify killing part of themselves, their own children?"

"The landlords treated little tenants as undesirable intruders into their lives, and wombs. The Enemy whispered to them: 'You are the owner of your womb. It is your body. You created this intruding tenant with a bit of help from an outsider. You can do with it whatever you want. Remove it without any remorse, just as you would remove a malignant growth from your body. If this fetus comes out of you alive, it will cause lot of problems in your life. It will make your life miserable. Your career will suffer. It would cost you money; spoil your love life, your career. You would not be able to go on exotic vacations, and enjoy unlimited freedom. The laws allow removal of your unwanted tenants and disposal of it as 'biological material.' Nine months homes owners all over the earth do it. Professionals, called the abortionists will do it quickly, freeing you from an unwanted responsibility."

Boro got sick to his stomach watching carnage of millions of poor, helpless, little "humans to be" all over the world.

"Please Stefan, remove this screen, it is absolutely sickening. Why God allows mutilation of these innocent, helpless 'humans to be?' Why does He not stop it? Can He stop it?"

Stefan looked at Boro with a serious, sad face: "Boro, Our Lord created everything, sustains everything. He can do anything. He could stop killing of these helpless little 'humans to be.'"

"Why doesn't He stop this carnage?"

"God gave men the commandment; 'Do not kill,' but He does not stop many killings, including little, powerless 'humans to be.' Mothers use their free will to do with their bodies as they want.

They may not be punished in this life, but will surely be away from God in the life to come, unless they repent for their horrible sin. As for the innocent, little 'humans to be,' whose lives were violently cut short; they were victims of murder and ugly passions in this life. In the life to come, they will be without stain and in God's presence. Here, I will remove this from the screen."

In a second, Boro was unable to see ugly mutilations any more. He sighed a sigh of relief.

Next, he saw innumerable masses of people climbing a huge endless hill. It looked like as if climbers were on some kind of a journey. The summit of the hill did not seem to be very high, but it was hard to see, since it was hidden in a light bluish fog.

On the way up some travellers disappeared falling into the pits and crevices dotting the hill amongst green, lush vegetation covering its side.

As they reached the top of the hill, many climbers got disappointed. There was hardly any plateau at the summit, it was just a ridge. No place to stop, relax and enjoy the view. One had to move immediately back or forward. The other side of the hill was less hospitable then the ascending side. Vegetation was much sparser. There were more deep holes, crevices and sharp stones.

The descending side seemed to be steeper than the ascending side. Climbers looked back on the pleasant side of the hill. They were unable to see clearly the point where they began their journey. It was enveloped in a bluish haze. Lot of climbers wanted to go back to descend on the pleasant side, but they were unable to make even a step backward. Strange force within them was pulling them only forward.

They all started descending pulled by that mysterious force. The travellers were curious to see the final destination of their descent. Golden orangey mist and fog enveloped the bottom of the descending side of the hill. Only some travellers with very sharp eyes claimed that they got the glimpse of the final destination point, but none of them were really sure. Their eyes were fooling them.

## A Kingdom to Buy

The descending side was more dangerous to the travellers. Many deep crevices, gullies, pits and sharp stones suddenly appeared before the travellers. Many of them got tired, slipped, fell in and disappeared. Sometimes, travellers thought that they saw a valley at the bottom of the descending side. That vision would quickly disappear. Nobody was sure; nobody knew what awaited them at the end of their journey.

As they were descending, the summit was less and less visible. It was getting enveloped by thicker and thicker bluish fog. The ascending side of the hill was no more visible. It became just a nostalgic memory in the minds of the travellers, remembering green grassy hill, flowering meadows, birds singing in lush, green forests. Lot of climbers did not bother contemplating of the destination of their journey. All they cared was to have the descent as pleasant as possible and the least painful.

There were two kinds of roads on the descending side: The narrow roads were covered in many places by thorns and sharp rocks. The wide roads were much more pleasant to walk on, with lot of soft grass covering the road, and with very few thorns and sharp stones.

A mysterious tiny voice was whispering right into the heart of the travellers: "Be wise, take the narrow, rocky, thorny path to travel on. Suffer some pain and discomfort now on this short trip down and you will enjoy beautiful, flowery, lush meadows after the end of your journey, for very, very long time."

"However," tiny mysterious voice continued:" If you choose to walk on the wide, comfortable, grassy road, you won't get hurt much on your descent, but the wide road will bring you at the end of your journey to the very ugly terrain strewn by very sharp rocks and thorns, which will hurt you badly for very, very long time. Choose wisely."

The travellers got confused. If they only knew what was really awaiting them down at the end of their journey. They tried to see through that orangey golden haze covering the destination of their journey. To no avail. Most travellers used the wide, grassy, comfortably road on the descent, reasoning: "How do I know if this mysterious, tiny voice is a friend, or a foe, true, or false. I have no clue what awaits me at the end of my journey, perhaps nothing. If only that stupid haze would lift off from the valley I could see what is down there, then I could make my choice. Why should I suffer pain and discomfort? My reason tells me that it is natural to go the easiest way. Enjoy now. Don`t worry about hazy, fog shrouded future. Perhaps, closer to the end of the journey, if I see that tiny voice was right; I could switch to the narrow road. The end of the journey is still far away. There is lots of time to make that decision. I will take it easy now, handle the problems later."

Only few brave travellers chose thorny narrow roads, while huge waves of humanity crowd the wide roads, making fun of; "stupid, self-hurting fanatics" travelling on the uncomfortable narrow roads.

Even some of the travellers from the narrow roads, not being able to withstand pain, discomfort, laugh and sneering from the wide roads crowds, switch over to the wide roads.

Closer to the end of the journey, very few travellers switch over from wide to narrow roads. They just could not stand leaving their comfortable wide, grassy roads, for the rocks and thorns of the narrow roads. Though they were getting much close to their final destination, weary travellers were unable to penetrate with their eyes through the thin curtain of the orangey golden fog, hiding the mysterious journey`s end valley. Some travellers claim that they saw through that golden orangey fog and knew what was there. Most travellers reject their claims as "fantasy and hallucinations of gullible, worn out fools."

Close to the end of the journey, traveller's bodies undergo tremendous changes. They have no more energy. It seemed as if the life force was leaking from their bodies, just like air from a punctured car tire. Bodies became crumbled, disfigured, like old wrinkled, worn out, stained coats. It seemed that some mysterious programmer was turning down traveller's life energy as they were getting to the end of their journey and did not require any more energy, nor vitality.

## A Kingdom to Buy

The whole journey seemed like a dream to the worn out and exhausted travellers: "Did I really start my journey just a while ago, seems yesterday, in that beautiful pleasant valley, which still hazily lives in my memory? Am I the same person that started the journey? Why cannot I see anymore, the summit, the pleasant valley? Fog is everywhere around me."

The more weary travellers near to the end of the Journey, the more fear, anxiety and confusion seize their minds and hearts. The memory of their climb on the pleasant side of the hill flashes in their memory, remembering joy, passion and excitement on the way up the hill. Merciless 'one way only' force is pulling them steadily down towards the end of their journey.

The travellers wonder: "Where does this force come from. I cannot see it, hear it touch it, but it rules my life?" Barely stumbling down, the travellers looks like ripe fruit in the fall. Any moment, their life connection could dry up and snap. They will be seized by the unseen force of gravity and fall on the ground.

Boro watched in awe seeing travellers taking off their bodies like old coats. They called that 'the undressing.' Old bodies were usually deposited into the ground while, the airy body tenants continued the new phase of their Journey.

The airy body tenants, from the wide roads, landed on very rough and unfriendly terrain. It was like a jungle strewn by hot sharp rocks and ugly thorns.

There was pain, suffering, sighing and crying without ceasing from the innumerable masses of the airy body tenants. The torturous road seemed to have no end. There was no way to escape this horrible torture and punishment.

Much smaller number of the airy body tenants from the narrow roads, landed on the lush, soft green meadows, greeted by beautiful young men like Stefan. Hand in hand, they moved towards a bright shining light.

"How did you like the show Boro," asked Stefan.

"It is amazing. It looked so real. I saw myself in the show. That is impossible! Your technology in heaven is amazing, much more advanced than ours."

"Remember Boro, I told you that the show was: 'It is your life.' That is exactly what it was; The journey of your life, from your birth to the undressing, which you call the death."

"But, Stefan, that is impossible. I saw myself being born, living my life and dying. How is that possible?"

"We do not play tricks in heaven. You were given the ability to see your life in its entirety. Remember: no past or future in heaven, only present."

"I saw myself dying. My body was buried in the ground, but 'real me' was not there. Where did I disappear?"

"Did you see what happened to your fellow travellers at the end of their journey?"

"I did. At the end of the journey, they took off their bodies, which were buried in the ground, and they continued their new phase of the journey."

"Did you recognize anybody?"

"I recognised anybody I wanted. All I had to do was just to think about that person, and I saw them instantly. How is that possible Stefan? Am I going crazy?"

"You are not going crazy. Your mind is confused, because natural laws were violated. Your mind is trying to solve that mystery. It cannot, because this is outside of its power."

"One more thing surprised me Stefan. After the undressing,; the transformed travellers looked like themselves when they were young."

"Boro, what do you think were these beings, who began new phase of their journey, after the undressing?"

"How could I know Stefan?"

"You said that you saw your body buried into the ground."

"Yes, but I thought it was some kind of trick. It is impossible for me to be alive and dead at the same time."

"What happened after you undressed'?"

"I took off my very heavy old coat of my body, which became very uncomfortable, hurting me and dragging me down to the ground."

"Was your undressing easy and quick?"

"Oh no! It was anything but easy and quick. Way before the undressing my body coat started gradually to squeak, creak, and ache. It felt sometimes as if that old body coat was full of sharp thorns pressing me and causing me awful pain. When that happened I could not think about anything but how to relieve that awful pain. I thought myself to be a 'good man.' Why was God punishing me so cruelly? Why wouldn't God arrange for me to have a quick, painless, easy undressing?"

"Were you mad at God because of that?"

"I tried not to be mad at God, but I was upset and disappointed. I thought that I did not 'deserve' to be treated so harshly by God. Why did God allow this awful pain to humiliate, torture and degrade me?"

"Any possible explanation why you suffered such painful and humiliating undressing?"

"I can't think of any."

"Did you witness the undressing of any of your friends, or family?"

"Yes, I did."

"Did some of them undergo, long suffering before the undressing, like you did?"

"Some of them did it easily, painlessly and quickly, as gently as falling asleep, while the others went through pain suffering and humiliation like me."

"Were these all 'good people,' honest, moral, living by God's commandments?"

"Some of them were good people; others were sinners, unbelievers, just ordinary people."

"Are you saying that some bad people were having it easy, while some real good, God fearing people had it extremely tough?"

"Yes Stefan, to my great surprise, that is what happened."

"Why were you surprised to see that?"

"I believed that if you were in God's 'good book,' God would be nice to you, shield you from the misfortunes, pain and suffering, while the guys from the 'bad book,' would be subjected to pain and suffering. It just did not work out that way."

"I told you God has no 'good book,' or 'bad book.'"

"Please help me to understand this."

"Do you believe that God loves you and that whatever He allows to happen to you; good things, bad things, painful humiliating things, are in order to place you in His heavenly Kingdom in the life to come?"

"I believe that God is always in control, and works for my best interest in this world, and in the life after the undressing. Pain could be awful Stefan. When my body was ravaged by pain it was very hard for me to accept: 'It is Okay, God allowed this for my own good.' I was moaning and groaning in pain wondering why God was punishing me so harshly without reason."

"Are you saying Boro that you didn't see how that pain and suffering would help you in your new phase of the journey, after the undressing?"

"That is exactly what I was complaining about."

"When you were little kid and you got very sick, how did your parents help you to get better?"

"My mom told me that I got seriously ill when I was just four years old. I got huge boil on my neck. I was crying in pain, could not eat, could not sleep. To save my life, my parents took me to hospital. Doctor examined me and said that this was a bad, life threatening boil, and it had to be removed right away. My parents agreed. The ugly thing was removed from my neck. This life saving operation was very uncomfortable and painful. Medication they gave me after the surgery was bitter and awfully tasting, but my parents gave it to me forcefully, because, without it, I may not be able to survive."

"Very good example Boro. You suffered pain for a short time so that your life could be prolonged for a long time."

"Are you comparing my sickness and cure when I was small boy with pain and the depravity I was suffering before the undressing? I am not sure what the connection between these is?"

"I think you are aware of the similarities between these two situations, but you just want me to confirm it. Am I right?"

"Of course Stefan you are always right. Are angels ever wrong?"
Stefan smiled." What do you think?"
"I think angels are never wrong."
"Why do you think so?"
"Because, you are God`s servants, with direct communication to Almighty. You have the instructions which you follow. They are set for you by God. Therefore, you cannot go wrong."
"Wonderful explanation Boro!"
"We went bit astray Stefan. We did not finalize that issue of painful and degrading pre undressing time. Are you going to confirm my conclusion?"
"Be glad to Boro. Just as that short pain, surgery and bitter medicine were necessary to save your life, pain and sickness play similar role in the pre undressing time, with a big difference, they are used to save your life for God`s Kingdom."
"Hold on Stefan. How does my torturing, humiliating and degrading pain help in my salvation?"
"You may never be able to understand this with your mind, because it is unable to comprehend God`s plan for your salvation.

Just as your earthly parents did, God also uses 'carrots and sticks' to keep you on the right path to the heavenly Kingdom. God used in your life many unpleasant sticks, which at that time were painful and humiliating. Later in your life you realized that these were necessary to bring you back on the road of salvation. Remember Boro: stomach ulcer, failure in the school, pain, loss of job and business, suffering, humiliation. All that had a purpose in God`s plan of your salvation. That is why God allows pain, suffering, degradation and humiliation in your life prior to the undressing.

As you said, some bad people had easy time before undressing. You thought that was 'unfair,' because you, holding yourself to be; 'a good man,' were 'discriminated' and dealt 'unfairly,' by God. You can speculate what was God`s reason for allowing on one man pain and suffering, while giving the other comfort and pleasures. The best is: Do not question God`s ways. As you had trusted your parents when you were a small boy, trust God that whatever He does is with the purpose to bring you to join Him in His heavenly Kingdom."

"Great sermon Stefan. That was some heavy stuff. I am disappointed that my mind is quite useless in trying to figure out these things. It seems to me that I have to accept anything that happens to me with gratitude to God. Does that mean Stefan that I should thank God for allowing terrible cancer to eat away my poor body, causing me an awful pain and agony?"

"I understand Boro that you are frustrated for not getting precise answer to your question. You don`t need to thank God for allowing that terrible cancer to destroy your body. You accept it as a bitter medicine to cure your soul for heavenly Kingdom. You express gratitude to God; in everything, not for everything."

"Let me make sure that I understood you Stefan. When that ravaging cancer hits my body, should I not pray to God to take it away from me, to cure me?"

"You should pray to God to cure you of that terrible invader of your body. As in any prayer, God may grant your prayer and allow healing of your body, or He may allow that monster to degrade and destroy your body. In either case, you should thank God, and pray to Him to give you the strength to withstand pain and suffering, without blaspheming against God and blaming Him for your sickness and the misfortune."

"It is hard for my mind to accept all this, but I understand now how I suppose to behave in sickness."

"Did that pain and suffering last right to the time of your undressing?"

"Pretty well. The pain would subside when I took heavy painkilling medication. As my body grew weaker and immobile, the desire for living started decreasing. I had enough of the torture. I just wanted it to end, be what it may."

"Did you find comfort in your family and friends visiting you?"

"I did. Often, my visitors and I did not know what to talk about. What do you say to a dying man who is in awful pain? I disliked particularly false comforters who were trying to raise my hope, convincing me that I will get up again and be old myself, strong, of sharp mind and healthy. I knew they were lying with the best intentions, which is why I was not too upset with them."

"Were you able to pray?"

"In my own way I did. I was not able to say longer prayers, but I repeated 'Jesus prayer' silently every day, more when pain subsided. Also, I had icon of God Mother and baby Jesus beside my bed. I kissed this Icon many times daily and touched with it my head and the most painful spots on my body. That was my way of praying. I believed this helped me not to go insane and blaspheming?"

"Did you have a confession and communion before the undressing?"

"When my family saw that I was getting near the end, they called our priest. I told him I was aware that I have sinned a lot in my life, and that I felt genuinely sorry for causing harm to anybody, and for all the sins I committed. Finally, I told the priest that I forgave all those that sinned against me. After I received the Body and Blood of Jesus, I felt more at ease. Half-jokingly, I said to my family: 'Well, I am now ready for my Journey.' They cried."

"Did you undress soon after getting holy communion?"

"You know that already. Why...?"

Stefan interrupted Boro. "Why do I still ask? It is only for your sake, for you to become aware of the meaning of the events in your life. We went through this discussion many times before. Remember?"

"Oh I'm very sorry Stefan, I forgot."

"No problem Boro. You might be getting tired. We covered lot of things this time. Perhaps we'll end this now." Saying this, Stefan kissed the old man and his wife and instantly vanished. Two old people kept snoring like a poorly tuned orchestra.

# Chapter 25

## *The Golden Years*

Though he was four years older than Jelena, Boro was in much better shape than her. What helped him maintain his relatively good health was a strict regimen of fasting and moderation in food and drinking. He was also active, spending every day at least an hour walking outside on their farm. Jelena was having problems with her hips, knees, shoulders. She was getting easily out of breath.

They still liked spending two weeks of every year in the hot Caribbean sun, going most of time with their children and grandchildren.

Boro acquired steady praying practice. He read every day Old and New Testament and books of Church Fathers. It was as if he was stepping out of the earthly life into that promised Kingdom of heaven, which was becoming to him more and more real. Aging, and loss of the vitality, coupled with occasional, pains and aches, were weakening his ties to the world.

The chains tying him to "the world," were gradually being loosened. More and more of their family and friends were dying. They felt lonelier after every funeral. Their children and grandchildren had their own lives and circles of friends, while their generation was being thinned out.

Slowly, a thought crept in Boro's mind: "My brothers and sister are gone, so are most of Jelena's brothers and sisters. Most of my generation is gone. What is the sense of me being here any longer?

I am getting useless and a nuisance to my children. I wonder what my guardian angel would tell me."

As many times before, beautiful, ever young angel appeared. He greeted the old man cordially and respectfully: "Boro, my dear friend and true Lord`s word sower specialist, how are you?"

Smiling within his heart Boro replied; "Stefan, my dear guardian and protector, I am good as an old man inching to the end of his life journey could be, ambushed occasionally by pains and aches."

"How old are you now Boro?"

Boro could not resist. "You forgot how old I was?"

Stefan shook his head smiling: "Again, eh? I am not upset at you remark Boro. You know that I know, but I love to hear it from you. Remember why?"

"Sure I know. Please don`t mind my silly question."

"No problem. How old are you now?"

"I am eighty four."

"I see that you are still in a good shape. Congratulations."

Boro sighed, "Thank God, I don`t too have many reason to complain."

"Did you want to discuss with me something that you thought about lately?"

"Yes Stefan. I am feeling more lonely and almost a stranger in this world. All my brothers and sisters died, as did lot of my friends and relatives. It seems to me that my generation is pretty well gone. I am wondering Stefan, when my departure time will come."

"Our Creator has wisely hidden from men the time of their departure from this world. Only select people are given hints of the time of their death."

"But why God keeps it a secret?"

"Boro, you can speculate and guess, but this will remain secret for good reason. Your Creator decided that it is better for you and for your salvation not to know your time of the undressing, just as it is not given to you to know your future. Your Creator knows what is best for you and you should accept that. Do not strain your mind with these thoughts. It will lead you nowhere. Have faith."

"I understand all you said Stefan, but I cannot figure out why would it be harmful to my salvation if I was told of my time of death. Couldn't you whisper this to me?"

"You are tempting me to violate my instructions. You know that I cannot do that. I tell you only what Lord allows me to. Please accept that."

Boro felt a bit embarrassed, seeing that he pushed too far with his curiosity. "Sorry Stefan. Please accept apology for my annoying curiosity."

"It's fine Boro."

"Is God wanting me to stay here a while longer and continue the word sowing?"

"You did great job as Lord's word sower specialist. Lord wants you to do more."

"What does God want me still to do while I am in this old body?"

"Simply continue doing what you were doing since you became aware of your gift. Witness with your life that you truly are God's soldier and true word sower specialist, living by God's commandments, and by prayerful communication with God. Receiving Holy Communion frequently, and by helping anybody you can to grow in faith. Do all this, plus your writing and lecturing."

"I will continue doing all this to the best of my abilities."

"I am sure Boro you will. I am leaving now, but will meet soon again. Bye my friend."

Mighty angel kissed old man and women on their foreheads and was gone. While early dawn was breaking over the hills on the east of Dalmatia farm, Boro and Jelena continued sleeping.

# Chapter 26

# *Buying Time*

The next year the whole family celebrated Jelena`s eightieth birthday. It was happy and noisy celebration. Boro hired a small orchestra. They opened Jelena`s birthday celebration with her favourite song; "O Jelo, Jelo, Jeleno…"

Jelena and Boro cried hugging and kissing each other. It was happy and sad occasion at the same time. He remembered how erect, proud and beautiful Jelena was when they met fifty six years ago. "Is that old, stooped, overweight, grey haired woman, limping heavily--the same beautiful, lively, vivacious girl I married?"

After her eightieth birthday, Jelena started complaining of getting easily out of breath. She was unable to help Carmelita in the garden. Even simple house chores exhausted her. She hated to see the doctor, fearing that at one of these visits; he would hit her with bad news. Boro and their children finally persuaded her to see their family doctor. After examining her, Doctor Kumar told them that she needed to go to the hospital right away.

Boro took her the same day to hospital. Detailed tests revealed that she had problems with circulation. Several serious blockages were diagnosed. Operation was seemingly successful. After several days in hospital, she came home to the Dalmatia farm. Her recovery was very slow. The best thing was that she did not have much pain. Boro spent most of time taking care of her. Sometimes, he even missed going to the church, when she felt bad.

After about six months, there was sudden improvement. She felt invigorated, started doing household chores, even helping Carmelita. Boro was happy with her improvement, but a worm of doubt crept in his mind: "Could this be a short improvement before the end?"

Unfortunately, he was right. The recovery lasted only a week. On the weekend, they celebrated the birthday of their son. Everybody was happy and excited, particularly Jelena. She couldn't stop crying and kissing her son. Boro had a feeling that all this crying and kissing was a sign of Jelena's beginning to say 'good bye' to her family and this world. His fear was justified because on Monday, She was unable to get up from bed. She was pale and very tired.

"What's the problem honey? What hurts?" asked Boro.

"Nothing hurts. I have barely enough energy to breathe."

"I am going to call an ambulance to take you to the hospital. I am sure they will fix you there. They have pills for everything."

Dismissing his idea with a movement of her hand, Jelena said in a very weak voice. "I don't think there is a pill that will return my energy. I feel that my body is beyond help. Taking me to hospital won't help anything."

Boro was upset at her talk. "Don't be silly, they will help you and in a few days you will be on your feet. Let me help you to dress. Ambulance is on the way."

Jelena's only comment was a sad, tired smile, while shaking her head left and right.

Tests revealed serious problems with Jelena's heart. The only remedy was huge open heart surgery, which was extremely risky. If nothing was done, her heart could collapse any time. Family was in huge dilemma, what to do? Boro asked doctor Kumar to visit them at Dalmatia farm. They respected his judgement and advice.

"Doctor Kumar if your wife was in situation as Jelena what would you do?" asked Boro.

Hesitating with his answer Doctor Kumar replied: "As a doctor, my initial thought would be: Have the surgery, though it is very risky, because it is the only way to save her life. That would be a doctor speaking, the professional who made an oath at the beginning of his career, to do everything possible to cure his patients and prolong their life. On the other hand, speaking as a husband I would strictly respect the decision of my wife. After all it is her life."

"What do you think would your wife decide?"

"Hard to guess Boro, but I would think that after she would be explained the risks of the surgery, she would refuse it."

"What do you believe her reasons for refusing surgery would be?"

"I am pretty sure her thinking would go something like this: "Clearly, benefit of the surgery is buying a bit more time, but at what cost? I would like to live longer to enjoy my family and simple joys of life. But, I am an old and sick woman. I have no energy even to smile at my grandchildren. I am becoming a burden to my family, particularly to my husband. At the best, I would be buying few extra months of staying in this old and sick body. Let God handle my demise. He knows best."

Boro sighed, "Thank you Doctor for your precious advice."

Sitting on their verandah overlooking the creek winding through the Dalmatia farm, and sipping coffee, Boro and Jelena enjoyed beautiful, sunny, crisp Indian summer day.

"I almost wish this was not so nice, so pleasing," sighed Jelena.

"What do you mean?"

Jelena's eyes swelled with tears. "I think you know very well what I mean. The Life has been so good to us lately. God blessed us in everything; good healthy family, friends and this paradise on earth. I would like to enjoy this at least a hundred more years, but I know I won`t. Honey it is so, so hard to leave such beauty and blessings."

Boro hugged Jelena and kissed her on the cheek. "I understand what you mean. When we leave this world, I believe that in God`s Kingdom will be indescribably nicer, lovelier than here."

Jelena sighed with a tired smile. "We may believe it, but we don`t know for sure. Do we?"

"Most of things in life, we don`t know for sure."

"What do you mean?"

"Do we know for sure that the sun will rise up tomorrow?"

"What a stupid question? Of course sun will rise tomorrow as it always did from the creation of the world."

"So, honey, you are a prophet, you can see into the future?"

"Forget it. I am tired, going to bed."

Boro stayed on the verandah by himself. He got up and poured himself good portion of his favourite brandy. He sat there sipping golden liquid warming and relaxing him. He felt that the life was about to change significantly. He needed his trusted friend and protector to talk to.

That night, as many times before Stefan appeared in all his angelic glory in the old couple's room.

Boro greeted him enthusiastically, like dear old friend: "Stefan, Stefan my dear friend. How are you?"

Stefan smiled at old man. "Boro, I am very pleased you ask me how I am. How are you and Jelena?"

"For my age, I am still pretty good. I can take care of myself and Jelena, walk, read, write. My appetite is good. Few things remind me of my age, but I try to silence, or ignore them."

"You are brave man Boro, a non-complainer. God loves such people. And how is Jelena?"

"Not good. I am worried for her. She is very sick."

"Are you afraid that she will leave you soon?"

"You mean die?"

"That is what I meant."

"She already had a very risky surgery, and now in order to buy some more time, she would need even riskier one. Doctors said there was very small chance of full recovery, because her body is in poor shape. I prayed many times to God to give her back health and allow her few more years to enjoy with me and our children, and grandchildren. It seems that God is ignoring our prayers. We cannot figure out why. Why wouldn't God grant her a few more years. This would not harm anybody. On the contrary, it would make us all happy and thankful to God?"

Stefan put his arm around Boro`s shoulder. Boro felt such quiet "happy" energy filling his heart. His guardian and protector was never so close to him."We discussed this a few times before about possible replies God gives to man`s prayer?"

"Granted as prayed for, rejected, granted different than prayed for, wait."

"Do you recall what we concluded of why God answers prayers as He does?"

"We concluded that man can endlessly speculate about God`s reason to grant or not to grant a prayer, but he will never know God`s way. For man`s own benefit God has hidden it from him."

"Does God give man the reason his prayer was granted or rejected?"

"I don't know how to answer that Stefan. I asked you before: What is the point to praying, if we have no clue if our prayer will be heard, and will not know why our prayer was rejected."

"That is a loaded question Boro, the trademark of a word sowing specialist. I could answer this question, but it would be much better if you answer it."

"Sure."

"Now, please try to answer your question: What use is praying if we don't know if our prayer will be accepted, or rejected?"

"That is a tough one Stefan. Can you help?"

"I am glad to help. When you were a kid, you asked your parents for toys, food, chocolate, bike, money to go to movies. Were you ever sure that your request would be granted?"

"I was never sure. Sometimes I had better chance to get what I asked for."

"Even if you were refused, you kept asking your parents again and again for this and for that. Why?"

"They were my parents. Whom else could I ask? Though there was no certainty that I would get what I asked for, I believed that sometimes my request would be considered 'right and proper' and I would be given what I asked for."

"Are you drawing similarity between you asking your parents for things and asking your Heavenly Father for things?"

"Certainly, there is similarity, though it is not the same thing."

"Using your talent and experience of an outstanding word sower specialist, could you please try to make your own conclusion regarding praying to God, based on our discussion here?"

"I am not sure how good conclusion I will give, but I will try my best."

"That is all I am asking."

"We need to keep praying to our Heavenly Father, because this is our way of staying in touch, communicating with Him. God instructed us and expects us to pray to Him, not only giving Him our requests for 'health, wealth and happiness,' but also praying for others, and thanking God for everything; Life, mind, health, material things, family. The fact that we do not know if our prayer will be granted, is not the reason to stop asking. When I ask for; 'good and proper' thing, which is in God`s will for my life and to the benefit of my salvation, my Heavenly Father will bless me and grant my prayerful asking."

"Excellent summary Boro. Do you now have a better understanding of why God did not 'hear and grant' your prayer to restore Jelena`s health?"

"I do not know which 'request' is good for me and my salvation, but God knows, and does not grant me all prayers. I can only speculate that giving back health to Jelena would not be beneficial to her salvation. I do not know exactly, but this is just my thought."

"Perhaps you might want to hear my 'speculation' explaining Lord`s refusal to restore Jelena`s health and give her longer stay on earth?"

"Stefan, did I hear you right? You said 'my speculation.' I thought you speak only certain truth. Isn`t the word 'speculation' forbidden by your instructions?"

"You are quick. If I could, I would blush now. I am glad you 'caught' me in this as you surely think is a 'controversial' saying of mine."

"Sorry Stefan, but it does seem to me to be quite a controversial statement you made. I am anxious to hear your explanation."

Stefan laughed. "Wow, I am in trouble now, me and my big angelic mouth. In one of our previous get together we discussed why God has hidden men`s future from them. I said as well that not even us angels know everything about God`s Providence. That is why I said 'my speculation,' meaning that I do not know details of God`s Providence, but within the framework of my instructions, I expressed my opinion."

"Thank you Stefan. I believe that your 'speculation' would be much closer to the truth than mine."

"Without being falsely modest I agree with you. Do you know why?"

"You are an angel, super intelligent being, in close communication with God. You are incomparably superior to me. That is why your speculation is much closer to the truth, than mine. I would like to hear your speculation Stefan."

"I think God decided that restoring health to Jelena and giving her few more years of life, would not be beneficial to her salvation, nor to the salvation of people closest to her, yourself, your children and grandchildren."

"I see clearly now. Jelena will leave me soon. How much time does she have Stefan."

"No use asking Boro. Not allowed to tell."

"Fine Stefan, but could you please arrange that her undressing is not preceded by a long time of suffering and pain?"

"Our Loving Creator has granted your prayer to allow Jelena the departure from this life with just mild pain and suffering for very short time before her undressing."

"I thank Almighty God for this mercy and I thank you my dear guardian angel and protector for conveying my prayer to God."

"Glad to help Boro. I sense that you are getting bit tired, so I am going to leave you now. I will see you soon."Saying this mighty angel of Lord kissed the old man and his wife and disappeared.

# Chapter 27

# *The Undressing*

Within a few days Jelena`s health turned for worse. She had no energy at all. She was hardly able to get up and go to the bathroom with Boro`s help. Amazingly, she said she hardly had any pain.

Family consulted Doctor Kumar, who came to their house and checked up Jelena. He said to the family that there would be no sense torturing her by taking her to the hospital for another risky surgery.

"You just make her as comfortable as possible. She loves her house and be surrounded by her family. She told me that her wish is to die in her home, her beloved Dalmatia farm," said Doctor Kumar with the family gathered in their large, posh living room.

Family agreed with Doctor Kumar. Everybody was super nice and loving to Jelena. Boro called their priest. Father Mirko came, and after hearing Jelena`s confession, gave her holy communion. She gave him a weak smile "I guess I am ready now for my journey."

She and Boro spent a lot of time together. He read her from the Bible, and her favourite: chapters from his books. She was unable to hold her attention for longer than few minutes. It tired her out. People came to see Jelena. She knew that they were saying "good bye." Every visit ended in tears, Jelena cried and the visitor cried.

Stefan kept his promise. Jelena did not have much pain. She was withering, losing energy and vitality and eating and drinking less and less. It just took too much effort to do that. She was rapidly losing weight starting to look like those emaciated saintly women who spent their lives in the desert, subjecting their bodies to meagre food. Sign of close end was Jelena`s loss of voice. Her only communication was weak, sad, but peaceful smile. Boro communicated with her by squeezing her hand for "yes" or "no" answers. Eventually, she was unable to do even that.

One beautiful Sunday morning, Jelena fell into a coma. She was not responding to any voice or touching. Their son suggested calling an ambulance to take her to the hospital.

Through tears, Boro said: "There is no use son. Nobody can help her now. She would not want to be taken to the hospital to die among strangers. She wanted to die at our home, and we are going to honour her wish."

Boro, his children and their families, together with Jelena`s family gathered in Boro and Jelena`s bedroom to say good bye to her.

Boro invited their priest to say prayers for dying Jelena. Everybody kissed Jelena and said their good bye with teary eyes. Boro was holding Jelena`s hand and in low voice saying prayers.

Jelena undressed late afternoon that Sunday. Everybody was sobbing and crying. Boro lit a wax candle prepared for this occasion and placed it besides Jelena`s head. In few hours, people from the funeral home came to take Jelena`s body.

Tearful Boro waived to Jelena`s body as it was being taken through their front door. "Bye my love. Thank you for wonderful love and togetherness. You are leaving me alone. How am I to live without you?"

That evening, their house was full of neighbours, friends and family coming to express their sympathy. People left after midnight.

Boro was very tired, actually exhausted. He went to bed. As every night he kissed the icon of Godmother and baby Jesus after crossing himself three times. He laid on his back, crossed his hands on his chest and prayed for his beloved Jelena. Then, he realized he had a visitor standing beside his bed.

"Oh Stefan, thanks for coming."

Stefan put his hand right on the heart of old man. This acted on him like a huge dosage of the tranquilizer. He stopped crying and became very calm and serene.

"I know you are going through a tough time Boro. I came to console you and assure you that your beloved Jelena has stepped on the lush green meadow after her undressing."

'Could I see her?"

"This very moment if you like. Look:"

Boro looked and his heart stuck to his throat. There was Jelena undressing, getting out of her old, ravaged, and worn out body. An angel, like Stefan assisted her in getting out of her old 'body coat.' The angel acted like a doctor delivering babies. Boro saw that Jelena had a tough time undressing, because many strong ties held her within her body.

Mighty angel used something like golden scissors to cut the ties holding Jelena to her body. One, by one ties were cut and finally Jelena flew out of her old vestment, which, lay on the bed. The angel assisting Jelena in her heavenly birth, washed her in a heavenly shower.

Jelena emerged out of the heavenly bath, the way Boro met her the very first time; tall, shapely girl with honey golden hair falling down her shoulders. Boro looked with awe. The same beautiful smile, brilliant white teeth, soft, chocolate brown eyes."

"She is beautiful again Boro, isn`t she?" smiled Stefan.

Boro sighed. "Oh, yes she is beautiful, angelic beauty. I wish I could be with her now. Could you arrange that Stefan please?"

"No Boro. I am sorry you cannot join your beloved wife yet. It is not yet your time to undress."

"But why not Stefan? I am a very old man. My life is losing its purpose since Jelena left me. I did my share of the word sowing as God wanted me."

"Lord still needs you in the body to complete the mission He gave you."

"But, what else could I do Stefan. I am just an old, sick, lonely man. I am afraid I won't be much of use in the word sowing."

*A Kingdom to Buy*

"Boro, Lord knows the best."

"I am not sure Stefan that I am going to have the energy to do more word sowing."

"You do your share Boro. Lord will take care of your energy, as He always did. Isn`t that right?"

"Yes Stefan, it is right. I am grateful that Lord always kept his bargain, thou I did not often keep mine."

"Do not forget Boro, I am near you always, just a thought away."

"I will need you more often now. With Jelena gone, you are my best listener and adviser."

"You have your children, family and friends to talk with. I am sure they would all be glad to talk to you and help you out."

"They have their own families, responsibilities. Old person in poor health, is not a desirable company."

"Your children and grandchildren love you very much and enjoy talking with you and helping you."

"Thank God, you are right. My children and grandchildren were great to me and Jelena."

"You need to get some sleep Boro. It is busy day for you tomorrow and the day after tomorrow handling Jelena`s funeral. I am leaving you now, but we will meet soon. Bye my dear friend."

With these words, mighty angel put his hand on Boro`s heart and kissed old man on the cheek. Next minute, he was gone. Old man turned to the other side, and loudly snoring continued sleeping.

## Chapter 28

## *The Second Wind*

The next two days were hectic for Boro and his family. Many people came to the funeral to express their sympathy. After "magic" touch of his guardian angel, Boro did not shed a tear. He was in perfect peace.

After Jelena`s burial Boro felt lost in the huge house. "Perhaps, I should sell this house and move into the city into a one bedroom apartment. This is a waste, living alone in such a big house. I cannot take care of it. I have to cook, wash clean. I am too old for that."

One night he dreamt an unusual dream. He was walking on his farm beside the creek. It was overcast, chilly spring day. He was well dressed, but still felt chilling wind getting through his clothing. He felt lonely and sad. He was just rounding the curve in the pathway, when he saw a tall slender figure of a young girl coming towards him. He thought: "Who could that be. Perhaps a girl lost her way?"

The girl was approaching him slowly. It seemed that she did not touch the ground, as if she was walking on the air. Boro recognised Jelena, just the way she was after her undressing. She smiled seductively at Boro.

"Look at me honey, just like when I was your bride. Come join me. What are you still doing in that old decrepit body. Nobody needs you on earth any more. You are just burden to our children.

I am eagerly awaiting you. Come," she invited him outstretching her hands. Boro hesitated for a second.

"Honey, you are beautiful and I would love to be with you, but Stefan said…"

The apparition interrupted him angrily. "That winged flying boy? You believe him more than me, wife you spent fifty five years with? I am deeply upset with you."

Boro felt awful for that scolding from "Jelena". "Honey, you know that I am forever in love with you, but God."

All of a sudden, the apparition angrily stomped on the ground, so violently that Boro bounced off the ground. With a shrill, hissing, angry sound, it disappeared in the trees besides the creek.

Boro woke up in cold sweat. "What was that? Pleasant meeting with my 'beloved wife' turned into something scary. I don't get it. Stefan will help me to explain this unusual dream."

Indeed Stefan appeared the next night. He was very cheerful.

"I got your message Boro. What bugs you?"

"I had a very strange dream. Initially, it was very pleasant, but it turned out into a frightful nightmare. Do I need to tell you the whole dream?"

"Yes."

Stefan was listening carefully, while Boro was telling him last night's dream.

"What's the meaning of this dream Stefan?"

"What do you think Boro?"

"I don't know, that is why I am asking you for an explanation."

"Did the apparition really look like Jelena after the undressing?"

"No doubt Stefan, one hundred percent."

"You were very happy and excited to meet your beautiful young wife."

"Oh yes, she looked gorgeous."

"Why didn't you give her your hands when she outstretched her hands and invited you to join her?"

"I felt something intriguing and suspicious in her invitation. This was just a hunch, a vague feeling of discomfort, that is why I did not outstretch my hands right away. I wanted to explain what you told me about my continuation of word sowing."

"She did not like that, especially when you mentioned my name?"

"To my surprise, she got angry, belittled you and scolded me for not trusting her."

"How did you react to that?"

"Well, I was surprised of her reaction. I still wanted to remain on good terms with my 'beautiful wife of fifty five years,' but my hunch, my vague feeling, prompted me to explain what God still wanted me to do."

"What happened then?"

"She got real angry, stomped her foot on the ground so hard that I bounced off the ground. Then she gave some shrill hissing, angry sound and disappeared."

"And what happened after that?"

"I woke up."

"Boro, do you think that apparition was Jelena?"

"I thought it was her. She looked exactly as her after the undressing, but after she spoke to me I got suspicious."

"What did you think that apparition was, after her reaction to my name and Lord`s Name?"

"I knew that my Jelena would not react like that. She was with good angel after her undressing. This apparition could not be from God`s side, but from Lucifer`s side, because it could not stand mentioning of your name and Lord`s name. It hated that."

"Why do you think this apparition came to you?"

"I believe its purpose was to spoil my word sowing mission, as Lord wants me to continue it. It could have been an evil angel assuming appearance of my beloved Jelena to trick me, but thanks God it did not succeed in that."

"Why do you think you were able to defeat the evil one?"

"I don`t know."

"Long time ago I disclosed to you that God gifted you with a wonderful gift: The discernment of good and evil. You used it in this case. Your spirit sensed evil one, and led you to do what was necessary to defeat it. Men should be very suspicious of any apparitions, because Lucifer can masquerade even as a bright angel of God, or even as Lord Jesus Christ. It is the best to ignore these apparitions, cross yourself, say prayer and don't pay any attention to them."

"Thank you Stefan for your help and explanation."

"My pleasure Boro, I will see you soon. I will let you get some more sleep. Bye my friend."

Saying this, mighty angel put his hand on Boro's head, blessed him and in the next moment was gone.

# Chapter 29

## *More Word Sowing*

Boro`s energy level and overall health improved amazingly in the following weeks. No pain, able to walk hours around Dalmatia farm. His mind and spirit were sharp and alert.

"Just as Stefan told me,' thought Boro." Lord is keeping His end of the bargain, providing me with lot of energy and good health. I must keep my end of the bargain. Vast field of human hearts is eagerly awaiting the seed of God`s word."

"What should I do to complete my word sowing mission? I need to work without delay before old age and sickness prevent me. Perhaps, I should talk with my heavenly protector and adviser."

Sure enough, Stefan appeared that night.

"Boro you look good, invigorated and full of energy. How do you feel?"

"I feel great. No pain, no worries, lot of energy. Just as you told me a while ago, God kept His end of the bargain and restored my health, energy, mind and spirit. Thank you for your contribution in this."

"My part was minor. I asked, God blessed you with all these wonderful gifts. Enjoy."

"I realize that I have to keep my end of the bargain. I am willing, but I don't know what Lord wants me to do. Could you please help me to figure that out?"

"Sure Boro. Are you satisfied with your word sowing mission?"

"I put my heart, my mind and my soul to perform my word sowing mission the best I could. I am not sure if my word sowing made a worthy contribution to the Lords plan of men salvation. Was my message helpful to people to change their lives and to begin to follow Our Lord Jesus Chris? That is what bugs me Stefan."

"It is important that you did your best. That is all God expects from you. You can compare it to the farmer sowing the seeds. He sows good seed, he does it properly. That is his part of the bargain. The other part of the bargain; good soil, sunshine, heat, moisture, is God`s to provide. So it is with the word sowing.

Your words were good, to God`s liking. You sowed words properly. That was your job; the rest is up to God. Any man upon hearing good word can accept it or reject it. A good story applying to this is the Parable of the Sower, told by Jesus in one of His sermons. Do you remember that parable?"

"I think I do."

"Would you mind telling it briefly in your own words?"

"I will try. The sower went to sow the seeds. The first seeds fell aside and the birds came and ate them. Some seeds fell on the rocky ground without much soil. They sprang up quickly, but because of lack of the soil, they withered as soon as sun`s rays hit them. Other seeds fell amongst the thorns, it grew, but thorns grew and choked them. Finally, some seeds fell on a good ground and yielded good crop."

"Very good Boro, do you remember how Jesus explained the meaning of this Parable?"

"The seeds that fell aside were people who heard the word, but did not understand it. The Enemy came and took away what was sown in their hearts. The seeds falling on the rocky, shallow ground that sprung up quickly, but were quickly scorched by the sun, were people that heard the word with joy, but not having the faith, endured only shortly. Minor tribulation or persecution caused them to stumble and lose the words. The seeds falling among the thorns are people who heard the Word, but worries and cares of this world, choked the word and it did not get fruitful. The seeds sown into a good ground are people who heard the word, understood it and it produced good benefit to them."

"What is your conclusion from this Parable about your mission of the word sowing?"

"Only small fraction of the words sown will be heard, understood, acted upon and bring benefit to the people hearing them."

"What kind of the benefits are you talking about?"

"The benefit of being directed towards their salvation. To help them return their talent given them by God, to God with an interest, just as I am trying."

"You should never get discouraged by the visible lack of success in your word sowing. You just keep sowing. Lord will do His share. Some people will hear, understand and benefit from your word sowing. Jesus had only eleven Apostles, but they sowed His Words very well, and many of their successors continued sowing the words. That changed the world."

"I am an old man Stefan. I know that my time in this body is limited; three, two, five years? God blessed me with an abundant energy and good health for the time only He knows. I am not sure, what part of the word sowing God wants me to handle in my final years in the body."

"Is there group in your word sowing that was the toughest to sow the words?"

"I think the most reluctant to hear the word, understand it and benefit from it, are younger people."

"How young?"

"From teenage years up to about age thirty five."

"What's special about that age?"

"The body. Usually strong, healthy and being enchanted by the passions and the joys of the world and senses. People think that they will live forever, know everything. They pamper and spoil their bodies."

"In your experience, they are the hardest to reach?"

"Yes, I think so. They could be compared to the seed sown into the thorns. The cares, and even more, joys of the world, choke the seed of the words, so it cannot grow."

"Boro you answered your question."

"I did?"

"Yes, you identified the toughest area for you as a specialist word sower. Why don't you make it the crown of your word sowing mission to address that age group."

"I am afraid of failing. It is a tough nut to crack Stefan."

"Borooooo, you do your part. You sow the words the best you can. Leave the rest to Lord. Do not worry about the outcome. It is in God`s hands."

"I am going to do it Stefan. I hope that God will bless me with good health and energy to complete my task."

"Boro, God always keeps His promise. You make sure you keep yours."

"I will. This is now my most important goal in life. I will begin tomorrow."

"God`s blessing is on you and your mission. I am just a thought away. I will help." The mighty angel touched Boro`s heart and his forehead, saying: "Be healthy in your body and mind," he vanished.

## Chapter 30

# *The Word Sowing Finale*

The next morning Boro got up feeling great, with clear sharp mind, and energized body. He had to narrow down the topic for his last book. He decided to spend three days in a friend's cottage alone. He notified his family, loaded stuff into his car and drove three hours up North. His friend's cottage was in the middle of pine forest at a small crystal clear lake. The closest cottage was about half a kilometre away. The next three days he spent in prayer and relaxation, preparing himself for his capital work. When he came back to Dalmatia farm, he knew what he wanted to write.

He had to take a snap shot of the age group he was addressing his book to. He had to have a clear idea about life of young people in the paganised "Christian" America. There was huge amount of information to be obtained. He just did not have time to do this time consuming job.

At the recommendation of his publisher, he hired a professional research assistant. The lady was a middle aged widow with two grown up children and several grandchildren. Boro liked Daisy from the time he met her. He sensed that she liked him too. It was amazing how quickly they understood each other, almost as if they read each other's thoughts. Daisy was a computer wizard, a skill Boro never mastered. Boro explained what information he needed. She supplied him the research information as he progressed in writing his book.

This book was much harder to write than the other books he wrote. After twelve months of working on the book Boro was about half way in its rough version. He was doing lot of rewriting, and changing.

Then, the doubt struck him. He started to panic. He tried to remember Stefan's encouraging words, the Parable of the Sower, which supposed to erase his doubts. Nothing helped. His mind argued with him; "Yes but, what if this colossally flops? Who is going to read a book with today's computer technology. People need just to touch a few buttons, and will get any information they want. People are too busy now days, too sophisticated to read a book written in broken English by some old man with a fundamentalist, Orthodox agenda."

Boro was ashamed to share his doubts with Daisy. She sensed that her boss had serious doubts about his life project, but did not say anything.

He turned again to his guardian angel. To his surprise Stefan did not appear the first night, not even on the second, nor on the third night. Boro was dumbfounded. "This never happened in eighty years we were meeting. What could have happened to Stefan? Is he upset with me? Is Lord angry at me for poor quality of my work?"

The fourth night Stefan appeared. He was his usual, beautiful, mighty, majestic angel of God. As soon as he saw him, all of Boro's doubts and anger evaporated.

"Finally Stefan, I was afraid something happened to you; space travel collision, or busy with the other protégés?"

"Neither one. Keep guessing Boro."

"Were you upset with me?"

"I won't keep you in suspense any more. The reason I did not appear immediately was Daisy. She was capable of giving you a good, honest advice. What is the reason you did not wish to discuss with her the problems you had in writing?"

"I cannot hide anything from you. I guess it was my professional pride that kept me from discussing my project with Daisy, thinking: 'I am a well-known writer, a seasoned word sower. I am thirty years older than this woman. How could I lower myself and ask her for advice. I am her boss."

"The Enemy got to you Boro. I was giving you the opportunity to overcome your pride and have a good chat with Daisy. When I saw that you were unable to shake the Enemy off, I came."

"That was the Enemy playing with me?"

"Yes Boro he did a skilful tackle on you. He instigated all these doubts about the success of your book."

"That scares me Stefan. I thought I was immune to the Enemy`s attacks."

"The Enemy can attack you, trick you and deceive you until your last breath."

"But why would the Enemy attack me now?"

"When you became aware of your word sowing specialist mission, you were troubled by the Enemy."

"Yes."

"What was the Enemy`s goal in attacking you?"

"He was trying to spoil my word sowing mission, because it was working against him."

"What did you conclude was the way to chase the Enemy away."

"The first thing I had to realize on my own I was no match for the Enemy."

"You needed help to fight against him?"

"Yes, I asked Lord Jesus Christ for help."

"Did you ask God for help this time?"

"I kept praying to God regularly, but I did not ask God for help in this invasion of the Enemy."

"Why not?"

"I did not think that my problem had anything to do with the Enemy playing his tricks on me. I believed this was just a temporary snag, which I could handle by myself, without 'bothering' God."

"Do you think this was right and good reasoning?"

"I see now that it was not."

"And what do you think how you should have handled this Enemy attack, this snag?"

"I should have admitted to God that I had difficulties, which I was unable handle on my own and needed God to help me."

"What do you think Boro was a sign that the Enemy invaded your territory?"

"When I thought; 'I am smart, experienced, wise, I can do it on my own, I don`t need any help.' Red light, the Enemy has invaded."

"You are now much better equipped to fight the Enemy. As a reward Lord will not allow the Enemy to tempt you, until you finish your book. This is very rare gift God grants. Thank God Boro."

"Thank you Lord for this wonderful gift. Please give me health, energy and clear mind that I may finish this book to Your glory and for the salvation of my fellow men."

"Go do it Boro. You have now Lord`s shield guarding you. Watch your pride. Humility is a great virtue. Make it part of your life, like breathing. I am leaving you now. I will be on watch and on guard. Bye my friend."

Stefan put both of his hands on Boro`s head and then on Boro`s chest. "Blessing of God; health, vitality and humility," whispered Stefan over sleeping Boro, and vanished.

## Chapter 31

## *Closing the Curtain*

The next morning Boro woke up fresh and light, like a thirty year old man. He knew in his heart despite feeling so great-- the time was running out. He had to focus on his capital work. As usually, before starting to write, he read the Bible and spent half an hour praying. He continued praying almost without ceasing repeating mentally Jesus Prayer: "Lord Jesus Christ Son of God be merciful to me a sinner."

After prayers he met Daisy for the breakfast she prepared. He greeted her cordially. She was very pleased and flattered. During breakfast, they talked about writing and research that had to be done.

With sound of guilt in his voice Boro said: "I owe you an apology Daisy. I think you sensed lately that I was troubled by some things and was not able to accomplish much writing. I got an attack of doubts and despair. Fear seized me that I would not be able to write a good book and that it would actually be a disaster of the book. My foolish pride prevented me from discussing this with you. I believe that with your sharp mind and experience you would be able to help me to overcome these doubts and fears. Please do me a favour: If you see that I am stuck, or that something bothers me, do not hesitate; talk to me, help me."

With tears in her eyes Daisy said; "It will be my pleasure to help whatever I can."

The next twelve months passed unbelievably fast. Boro kept a strict regimen of writing and praying. The only day when no writing was done was Sunday. It was time devoted to the church and family. Lord kept his bargain. Boro was in excellent health, vital and of sharp mind. The anti-Enemy shield was working wonderfully; No fear, no doubts, no despair. Spending time with Daisy during meals was very relaxing, enjoyable time for both of them.

Exactly two years after he began writing, Boro`s most valuable book was done and ready to be sent to publishers. All his books were published by the same company, a medium size publisher doing mostly, religious fiction books. Daisy convinced Boro to send the manuscript to five other major publishers, as she said; "To see their reaction."

Four publishers thanked Boro for sending them the manuscript, but "with regret" declined to publish it, since it did not fit into the scope of their business. The fifth company, one of the biggest in America expressed interest, under the condition that the author would be willing to make some changes in the book. They proposed to send one of their vice president to come and meet Boro and his associates.

Boro and Daisy were very excited about this great news. The meeting was scheduled in a hotel in town. Boro came to the meeting with Daisy and his trusted friend and lawyer Sava. Big publisher was represented by their vice president Mr. Govorsky and his assistant, a beautiful young attorney.

After exchanging courtesy greetings and small talk, Mr. Govorsky took the podium.

"Mr. Boro, we love your book. It is original, exciting, interesting. It has a worthy message. We think it could be a great success. In order to achieve that, we believe that some changes would have to be made in the book, to appeal to a large segment of American public."

Boro was getting suspicious of the motives of this silver tongued sweet talking executive. He interrupted him: "Mr Govorsky; let me express my gratitude to you and your company for willingness to consider publishing my book. Before we go any further I want to know what are the changes your company insists to be made in order to publish my book. And second question, what happens if I am unwilling to make these changes?"

With a polished smile Mr. Govorsky replied. "We would not be willing to publish your book if the changes we are asking for were not implemented in its entirety. In answering your first questions, here is our list of the changes to be made, as well the explanation why we wanted these changes. As an experienced writer, I hope you will agree that all these changes are very reasonable, sensible and in the spirit of the twenty first century. To induce you to accept our proposal, we are willing to give you right now an advance cheque for a hundred thousand dollars and later a generous contract for the royalties."

"How much time do we have to reply to your offer? asked Boro.

"A week, two weeks if you wish. We are willing to wait."

Boro looked at Sava and Daisy. They understood each other immediately."We don`t need two weeks, not even one week, we just need couple of hours to give you our answer. I am going with my associates for lunch. We will look at your proposal, and in two hours when we meet again in this room we are going to give you our answer."

Bit taken aback, Mr. Govorsky handed Boro the file."Here you are. We will meet here in two hours."

After lunch, Boro took out of the file publishing company`s proposed changes. To his surprise everything was on one page. He gave it to Sava; "You got the best voice, please read it slowly and loud for me to understand."

Sava started reading:

Proposed changes to book written by Mr. Boro: Dear Mr. Boro; In order for us to assume considerable risk of money and reputation as one of the best American Publishing companies, we are asking you to make the following changes, which would make this book appealing, enjoyable and instructive to most American people regardless of their race, sexual orientation, religion, or lack of the religion.

We believe that the message of your book would remain very much as you intended it to be, even after all proposed changes are implemented. This is what we are asking you to change: As written, the book has a very narrow viewpoint of a Fundamentalist Orthodox Christian. Statements that only practising Orthodox Christians will be saved is highly unfair and insulting to lot of people.

We propose that you treat all religions as different routes to the same goal, and that everybody would reach that goal, whatever each reader individually believes. If this book was religiously neutral and non-offensive to any religion, even atheists, we believe that it would achieve a phenomenal success in the American and worldwide market. We are enclosing the following agreement whereby you take obligation to implement these changes. Yours truly, Roman Govorsky, Vice President of Sales.

"Well what do you think ladies?" asked Boro.

"Knowing you for so many years, I am sure that you already had made up your mind," said Sava.

"Perhaps I did, but I still would like to get your opinion. What do you think Sava, as a lawyer?"

"This is not a legal issue. This is a moral and conscience issue. I am sure that you already decided on that."

"Thank you Sava. Daisy, what do you think?"

"Very much the same as Sava, this is a moral and conscience issue, and I am also sure that you already made your decision. I agree with it, as I am sure Sava does. Just stick to it."

Boro's eyes filled with tears: "Than you my dear friends for your support. Let us go and meet Mr. Govorsky."

Back from the lunch, Boro addressed Mr. Govorsky: "I am honored Mr. Govorsky that such a reputable publishing company as yours, has shown interest to publish my book. I am very pleased and tempted by a very generous offer of the financial reward your company offered. During lunch I and my friends read your proposed changes. I agree with you that in the twenty first century they look, and indeed are very reasonable.

In your reasoning justifying the requested changes you wrote that the book was written from a narrow viewpoint of a Fundamentalist Orthodox Christian. I consider this statement a great compliment, because that is exactly the viewpoint that I live by, represent and promote a genuine Orthodox Christianity. I have omitted the word 'fundamentalist,' because it can be construed in people's mind that I am some Orthodox militant 'jihadist,' calling for 'holy war' to spread Orthodox Christianity by any means.

I never believed in that kind of Christianity, and I never promoted it in any of my books, including this one. If the changes your company requested were implemented in my book, it would make my book just another commercial enterprise to make a pile of money and bring me worldwide fame. It would also take out the heart and the spirit of my book. It would be just like a good looking cadaver. Respectably looking, but dead. Our position is: The changes you wanted are not acceptable to me. I thank you for your offer, but I am declining it."

Boro saw that Mr Govorsky was getting quite uptight and nervous.

"Thank you Mr. Boro. I am very disappointed, that we won't have the opportunity to publish your book. Would you mind give me half an hour to call my headquarters and report about the outcome of this meeting."

"Of course, take your time. We will wait for you here."

Govorsky and his attractive attorney left the meeting room. They came back in about forty five minutes.

Mr. Govorsky looked like a changed man; smiling, confident and excited."Sorry, we are bit late. I reported to our top executives the result of our meeting. They were disappointed by your refusal to make the changes we requested. The fact is Mr. Boro that our top guys like your book very much. They hate to lose the opportunity to publish it.

Our legal department finally came up with a smart solution: We will not insist that you make any changes to your book, but we will put a disclaimer statement at the beginning of the book, something like this: 'Dear reader: religious views, statements and ideas in this book are the ones promulgated only by the author of this book, not by the publisher of this book, ABC Publishing Inc. We hope that you will read it, enjoy it and benefit from it. For ABC Publishing Company, President Maxim Hernandez."

"Do you need more time to discuss this proposal with your advisors Mr. Boro?"

"No, we will consult and make the decision right away. What do you think Daisy?"

"It sounds good. Let`s do it."

"What do you think Sava?"

"I am also for it. I would insist, that final wording of publisher's disclaimer, has to be approved by us, before putting it in the book."

"You heard my advisors Mr. Govorsky. I am in agreement with them. We are gladly accepting your offer with the provision of the final wording to be approved by my legal counsel. If you agree with that, we can shake hands."

Beaming, Mr. Govorsky got up and shook hand with Boro. Everybody was happy and excited.

"Now, just a few more details," said excitedly Mr. Govorsky.

"More details? Are you offering us to drink a toast to our agreement?"

"I will take care of that. We need to sign paperwork to formalize our agreement. Our attorney already prepared everything. Please read it and sign.

Sava and Daisy read the pre agreement letter. They both said it was fine. Boro read it carefully, took out his fountain pen and signed. Mr. Govorsky took out of his briefcase cheque and gave it to Boro.

"Now, let`s go and celebrate our deal. I have taken the liberty to order a limo for five of us and a place for dinner in the best restaurant in town."

Celebration was something to remember. First the brandy they toasted their deal was 'out of this world.' The food was extraordinary, the service great. The crown of everything was a small orchestra, and singer performing Boro`s favourite songs.

Boro cried thinking of his beloved wife. He got up and wiping off his tears said: To my dear wife of fifty five years. Jelena, I devote this book to your memory."

Boro came back to Dalmatia farm, happy and a bit tired. The writing business was over. He asked Daisy to stay with him a bit longer to help with the inquiries and readers' letters.

They started getting readers' letters just after Christmas. It was initially just few weekly, and after January hundreds weekly. Daisy asked Boro to hire one part time student to help with answering questions.

There were all kinds of letters and comments from nasty and ugly ones to very complimentary. Boro used most of his time during the day to reply to the letters selected by Daisy. He realized that this was part of his word sowing mission. He gave readers simple, short, to the point advices and recommendations on how to get back on the path of salvation.

Several letters from readers of 'The Narrow and Thorny Road,' made Boro happy that some of the words sown fell on good soil and were bringing abundant fruit.

Bryan from New York City wrote:

"Dear Mr. Boro;

I am one of those young people (35 years old), who had the hardest ears to hear Jesus's message calling for the repentance and dedication of life to His glory. I am a very successful stock broker. The epitome of fulfilled American dream: big, well-furnished house in the suburb, a beautiful, successful wife, and two precious children, one Porsche, Audi and Rolls are in my triple car garage.

Besides all this wealth and achievement I felt a hunger for something lasting. I guess my soul was hungry. Quick fix American way wore out for me. I remember that my grandmother told us: 'Watch out for those quick fixes. Even good meal takes time and loving care to prepare.

'When I saw your book in the book store I passed by it thinking: 'another quick fix religious fantasy.' I cannot explain why, but I came back and bought your book. I am very glad I did. With help of a cousin of my wife who is Orthodox, I have stepped on the narrow and thorny road toward my salvation.

Thank you for sowing the word in my heart."

Boro noticed that he was getting tired, and some of his pains started visiting him. Still, he was in a pretty good shape for a ninety years old man.

'The Narrow and Thorny Road' book was doing phenomenally millions sold, money just kept pouring in.

Boro felt that he finished everything he supposed to. He kept his bargain by finishing the book and doing great finale in his word sowing mission.

"What am I supposed to do now? Just keep existing, eating, and breathing. No goals, no plans, no dreams? My siblings have died, all but one of my in-laws died, most of my friends are gone. What am I still doing here?"

Six months after his book was published, Boro paid Daisy a very generous bonus, thanked her for her friendship, help and advice. He arraigned for her to come every week to pick up and answer reader's mail.

One beautiful August morning, Boro was sitting on his porch overlooking the stream, running through Dalmatia farm. He had his coffee and newspapers. He was content but he had vague feeling of getting bored with all this. "Should I go on the trip around the world, visit exotic places, try new foods? No, I have done it. It would not please me anymore. Wonder if I did good job in my word sowing mission? Need to talk with my friend Stefan. He will give me the best advice."

Stefan obliged coming that night.

"Boro, my dear friend, how are you," he greeted old man enthusiastically.

"Well, for a ninety year old guy, pretty good. Bit tired, pains and aches paying me regular visits, but otherwise good. I can take care of myself, go for walk. My brain is still good, but seems to be getting dimmer. How are you my heavenly visitor, protector and guardian?"

"Thank you for asking Boro. I am always good."

"When you appeared to me the very first time, I was just a skinny seven year old village boy. You were young, beautiful, mighty angel of God. Eighty three years later I am wrinkled, stooped, sickly old man, but you are young, mighty, beautiful angel of God. Interesting, isn't it Stefan?"

"God's creation is beautiful and interesting. I am like this since our Lord created me."

"I have completed my word sowing mission Stefan. What now?"

"Since you finished your last word sowing mission, Lord removed from you "the anti-Enemy" shield. The Enemy is again allowed to tempt you. God blessed you with excellent health, vitality and sharp mind for the time you were writing your book. You have completed your work. You are again subjected to aging and sickness, as all men are."

Boro sighed, "So, it is bye, bye good health, vitality and clear mind. I noticed last month that I was getting easily tired, my pains and aches were more and more frequent guests. Is my allotted time running out Stefan?"

"Boro, a while ago you were shown heavenly show 'It is your life.' In that show you saw yourself undressing. Remember?"

"Yes I remember. I think I was sick and in lot of pain before I undressed. I complained to you why God allowed so much pain and suffering, since I tried to live by God`s commandments."

"We had an interesting discussion about that. We did not figure out why some good people suffer terrible pain before their death, while some bad people have it easy way. God has hidden this even from us angels. I am curious Boro what is your explanation?"

"When God afflicts good, righteous people with sickness, pain and poverty, He is actually working on their character, because, the only way the character could be built is by overcoming the temptations and trials. Just as the army will not get its battle experience, unless it fights a tough enemy. Sometimes it seems to me that this short earthly life is God`s training camp. God`s athletes train, toughen themselves, by overcoming all kinds of obstacles and opponents. The more obstacles and competitions they win, they get better and become God`s Champions."

"Very well said, any other reason in your opinion why God allows sickness and tribulation on men?"

"I feel that sickness, tribulations and misfortunes are in a way tools in God`s hand, the sticks God uses to bring us back onto the road for our salvation. I had quite a few of these 'sticks' applied on me. At the time they were applied I hated them. But, years later I saw that these were very much necessary to correct my behaviour. I thank God for these sticks."

"Do you think sticks always work?"

"Because man has free will, they don't always work. If God allows sickness, pain and degradation on man, to correct his ways, man might construe these as vicious and unfair, and become bitter, accusing God of unfairness."

"Are you saying that God is taking a risk by allowing sticks to be applied on men to induce them to correct their wrong ways."

"I think He does. One man will accept 'sticks' as corrective measures by His loving Creator, and will straighten his ways. The other man will see these sticks as unreasonable, unfair attacks on him, 'a good man' and will curse and bitch becoming an apostate."

"God will allow sickness, pain and degradation to befall you for a certain time before your undressing. How do you understand these very unpleasant 'sticks' hitting you?"

"I am a sinful man. I tried to live according to God's commandments, but I have sinned lot. I did try to repent. God only knows if I am worthy of the Kingdom of heaven. The sticks applied on me were tools of corrections, and also I believe served to weaken my love for 'the world,' turning my hope to the life after the undressing."

"Boro, this is the last time of my appearance to you in your world. The road is clear for you all the way to the journey's end valley. If God allows, I will meet you during your undressing. Be brave on this last, short, section of the narrow and thorny road you travelled on the hill of life. Fight temptations from the Enemy and from your own body. Your mightiest weapon is your prayer.

Some days, pain will overcome you, so that you won't be able to pray. Ask me and I will pray for you. Do not forget prayers to Holy God Mother and to your Patron saint, Holy Martyr and Victory Bearer Georgije. Suffer you pains and afflictions bravely, without blaming God for them. Remember God allows them to afflict you with a purpose, to your ultimate benefit; salvation of your soul."

Listening to Stefan, Boro cried. His life was going to end soon. No more enjoying his children, grandchildren, friends, his beloved Dalmatia farm. No more meetings with his friend and guardian angel. What a huge change? Another painful birth.

"Stefan, my dear friend and guardian, you materialized in my life. You became real to me. Many time in my life when I avoided near misses, or unpleasant situations, I sensed that you protected me. I smiled and said: 'Thank you Stefan.' You are my real and the best friend and advisor. Thank you and our Almighty Father for straightening my wrong ways. I sincerely pray to God that you accept me when I dispose of this coat of my old body. Bye my friend."

Angel and old man hugged each other. Stefan said to Boro: "If I had body, eyes and tears I would be crying now. I feel just like you Boro."

Stefan put both of his hands on Boro`s head and said solemnly: "Blessing on you Boro: strength, courage and grace on the last section of your life journey, strewn by rocks and thorns of pains and afflictions. Bye my friend."

The next second, mighty angel was gone. It was just old, sickly man murmuring in his sleep: "Bye, bye, bye."

The next morning, Boro had difficulty getting up from bed. His back hurt, his legs were shaky. He just felt spent and exhausted. His family insisted in taking him to the hospital for tests.

Boro refused. "I am not going to the hospital, but I would like to have a visit by Dr. Kumar."

Dr. Kumar came the next day. Boro asked Dr. Kumar to check him first, and after that his family to join them. Dr. Kumar examined Boro and concluded: "I cannot set up exact diagnosis of your sickness. Extensive test in the hospital would be required for that. I established few facts. Your heart is getting weaker, with an irregular beat. Your lungs are getting clogged up. I think you might have something more serious in your bones, but again without more tests, I cannot be sure."

"Are you suggesting that I go to hospital and have all these tests, to find out what is going to finish me?"

"Not necessarily. It is a personal decision. If you decide to go to hospital for all these tests, you might get diagnosis of your main health problem. We might be able to apply some medication, or therapy to improve your condition. Your body is just winding down, your immune system too. You might be unable to survive more radical treatments."

Boro interrupted Dr. Kumar. "By going to hospital and getting all of these torturous tests, I might find out my main sickness; you might find a temporary cure. I know I would be buying just a bit of time to breath, eat, sleep and suffer few months longer. How much time could I buy?"

Dr. Kumar shrugged his shoulders: "Hard to say. Could be years, could be only months."

"Thank you for your extraordinary and compassionate service Doctor Kumar. May God bless you and your family. I am an old and worn out man. I have done in this life what my Creator chose me to do. There is no more work for me here. I am at peace. I had long life, and it is time now to let my old body whither, so that my soul is free to leave it."

Boro called his children to join them. Dr. Kumar explained Boro`s situation and added that he is sympathetic with his decision to stay at home and die at the Dalmatia Farm. There was lot of crying and sobbing from his family. His son insisted to take Boro to hospital.

"Thank you my children for caring to see my old face little longer. I decided, just like your mother to die here. As my late baba said; "I have eaten my allocated portion of the bread."

For the next three months Boro suffered terrible pains, but never complained. Little icon of God Mother with baby Jesus was within his reach all the time. Often, he would cross, kiss it and press it to his chest. When he felt his life end nearing, he asked the priest to come. Father Mirko came, and after lengthy confession gave Boro Holy Communion.

Boro gave him weak, but happy smile: "My travel on the thorny and narrow road is ending. Hopefully Stefan will meet me at the end of my journey. I am ready for the last trip."

The next day Boro died.

Did Stefan meet him at his undressing?

God only knows!

CPSIA information can be obtained at www.ICGtesting.com
Printed in the USA
LVOW07*0255160814

399380LV00001B/2/P